I0549586

Hedgerow Lies!
By
F. Del Meath

Copyright© 2011 Franklin Delano Meath

ISBN-13: 978-0615479279 (F. Del Meath)

ISBN-10: 0615479278

Cover Artist: Derek Sitz and Brett Sharp

All rights reserved. No part of this book may be used or reproduced electronically or in print without written permission, except in the case of brief quotations embodied in reviews. Due to copyright laws you cannot trade, sell or give any eBooks away.

This is a work of fiction. All references to real places, people, or events are coincidental, and if not coincidental, are used fictitiously. All trademarks, service marks, registered trademarks, and registered service marks are the property of their respective owners and are used herein for identification purposes only.

Franklin Delano Meath
1528 Payne Avenue
Saint Paul, Minnesota, 55130

Phone :
651.774.7120

E-mail :
fdelmeath@ieihome.us

Web:
www.ieihome.us
Or
www.neatleash.com

Thank you for purchasing the book

I dedicate this book to my lovely wife Wendy,
My son Del and all of my friends and family.
Thank you all for your spirited opinions and
Encouragement over the years...

Acknowledgements:
I wish to acknowledge the contribution of Brett
Sharp to the success of publishing this novel.
Without his expertise, encouragement, and
knowledge of the internet, none of this would have
been possible.

Introduction

For obvious reasons I have to declare that this book is a
work of fiction...
But that is today... What happens when people pull their
heads out of the sand? Will they recognize what is
happening in their own backyard?
Misdirection is the key to a magician's success.
The same can be said for politicians.

The reader will have to decide if this book will still be a
work of fiction tomorrow...

"Fallen, fallen is Babylon the great!
It has become the dwelling place of demons,
a haunt of every foul spirit
a haunt of every foul and hateful bird;
for all nations have drunk the wine of her impure
passion,
and the kings of the earth have committed fornication
with her, and the merchants of the earth have
Grown rich with the wealth of her wantonness."
                                                    Revelation 18

Chapter One

He was just starting to shave when the telephone rang. His first impulse was to ignore it, but on the fourth ring he dropped the razor on the sink, snatched a towel from the wall-rack, and walked to the living room.

"Yeah?" His voice revealed his irritation as he snatched up the phone.

"Is this Ron Mattson?"

It had been two weeks since he had heard the voice, but recognition was instant. He felt a surge of excitement. "This is Mattson," he said, "who's this?"

"I told you before", said the voice, "no names". Mattson heard a muffled cough, and then the voice continued. I have some of the papers I promised. Do you still want them?"

"Hell yes, I want them. I just don't understand why you won't give me your name. What are you afraid of?"

"You'll understand that when you read the papers. I don't have the complete file yet, but I have enough to back up everything that I've already told you."

"How will you get them to me?"

"You aren't going to like what you read." said the voice, ignoring Mattson's question.

"So?" Mattson felt his irritation growing.

"I'm just telling you because if you have any doubts, now is the time to back away. If anyone finds out that you have these papers it could be very dangerous for you."

"Do you want my help or not?" snapped Mattson. "You sound like you're trying to talk me out of it?"

"I need your help," said the voice. "I just want you to understand what you're getting yourself into."

"I do understand." said Mattson. "Now I want to see something to back it up. When do I get the papers?"

"You'll find them under the front seat of your car on the driver's side. Protect those papers, Ron. They'll be your only protection if anyone discovers that I've talked to you."

"Don't worry," said Mattson. "I'll take care of them, but if they're so damned important, why give them to me? Why not go public yourself, or give them to someone in the government?"

"I'm not sure who I should give them to," said the voice. "I'm taking a risk even talking to you. Remember, this thing has been in the making for more than thirty years. I have no way of knowing how far down the line people have been included. Until these papers are made public, I don't feel safe talking to anyone.

"What about the big newspapers? You can trust them, can't you?" asked Mattson. "I could put you in touch with some people that …"

"I know enough people." snapped the voice, cutting him off. "Are you familiar with the 'Pentagon Papers and the trial of Daniel Ellsberg?"

"Only vaguely," conceded Mattson. He remembered the case, but the details were fuzzy. It was during the Viet Nam war.

"Let me refresh your memory." said the voice. "In 1971 Dr. Ellsworth was working for the Rand Corporation. He had access to one of fifteen copies of the Pentagon Papers, and he gave it to Neil Sheehan of the New York Times. That file totaled about seven thousand pages dealing with our involvement in Vietnam dating back to Harry Truman in 1945. It conclusively established that the American people had been consistently lied to, not only by our government, but also by five consecutive presidents about that involvement. Ellsberg believed the war was morally wrong and he wanted the bombing and killing of the Vietnamese to stop. He believed the only way to make that happen would be to make the truth available to the public. Sheehan and a few others at the Times agreed, and they came up with a ten-day installment series supported by the documents they had received from Ellsberg.

"The first installment appeared on June 13, 1971, and the next day all hell broke loose! The Attorney General told the Times that they were in violation of the Espionage Law and ordered them to stop the story immediately and return the papers to the Department of Defense. An injunction was obtained preventing the Times from further publication. Luckily, Ellsberg had anticipated the injunction and had also given much of the material to the Washington Post. They immediately began running articles based on that material and the Justice department filed suit against them.

"The courts eventually rejected prior restraint of publication, and the story was printed. Everyone in the government was pissed. The court told them to protect their secrets by using criminal prosecution as a deterrent. The Times and the Post were sweating their balls off, but finally, a deal was struck. No criminal prosecution was ever brought against those newspapers. Ellsberg wasn't so lucky. He was indicted for conspiracy, theft of government property, and violation of the Espionage Act.

In 1973 a federal judge finally dismissed the case against Ellsberg. There was such a clear and obvious pattern of government intimidation and misconduct that even the judge was appalled. A secret group called the 'White House Plumbers,' even broke into the office of Ellsberg's psychiatrist".

"So," shrugged Mattson, "the story still got out. The system worked," "what's the problem?"

"I think you're missing the point," said the voice on the phone. "The full impact of the Pentagon Papers was diluted. Even newspapers the size of the Times and the Post were no match for the power of the government. There may be bigger newspapers than yours, Ron, but in this case, size really doesn't matter. "

Mattson thought he detected a slight chuckle following the statement, but a second later the voice continued and there was no mistaking the determined tone.

"What I want you to understand is that the people behind this won't make the same mistakes that were made back in 1973. After the Ellsberg fiasco no one is going to be the first to stick out his neck. Big newspapers have too many people involved. Before this even hit the press they would know about it and find a way to stop it." There was a brief pause and Mattson could hear labored breathing on the other end of the line. He waited. After nearly a minute, the voice continued.

"Your paper is small, but if you pick it up, I guarantee, the rest of the media will be forced to follow your lead. They won't dare ignore it, and by that time it will be too late for anyone to stop."

"Bullshit," snorted Mattson "If a story can be squashed that easy, we never would have heard about Monica and Clinton. We wouldn't have heard about Watergate, for that matter."

"Don't be stupid," said the voice in a sudden burst of anger. "Those were cases where you had the Republicans and the Democrats fighting each other. Two equally powerful opposing forces. They were each out to get the other regardless of the cost. But, there are a lot of stories out there that are stopped before they ever get to the public. I don't want this to be one of them. Let me make this very clear. Until this breaks, we don't have any allies. 'Remember, Ron, the 'Hedgerow Project' is a pilot project that began right here in the Twin Cities. The first stage was the walls. They have been working on them for nearly thirty years. The foundation began here and it has now been extended throughout the United States. The second stage is about to begin and it must be stopped."

"I don't know what the hell you're talking about," said Mattson, "but if it's as big as you say, how the hell do you expect me to stop it?"

"Public awareness is the only way. And that's going to be your problem. You'll have to convince your boss that this story has to be made public. You'll have to find people you can trust. But I'm warning you now, the worst possible course at this time will be to contact anyone connected with the government. And that includes state, as well as federal"

"You say the papers are in my car now?"

"Under the front seat drivers side." said the voice. "I have to go now, but I'll be

6

in touch as often as possible. There was another pause, and once again Mattson could hear the heavy breathing.

"I'll be back to Washington tomorrow. If I can get more of the report, I'll contact you immediately. If not, I'll be back in a few days and I'll talk to you then." The phone clicked off before Mattson had a chance to answer. He stood staring at it, frowning, as he wiped at the soap drying on his face. "Damn it," he growled, "who the hell is that guy?"

Flinging the towel into a corner, he grabbed his shirt from the back of a chair and raced down the stairs to his car. The envelope was pushed far back under the seat. He grabbed it, then hesitated before straightening up, and glanced suspiciously around at the other parked cars up and down the street. There was no one to be seen and he suddenly felt like a fool. With the feeling of foolishness also came anger. Straightening up, he slammed the car's door and carried the manila envelope back to his apartment where he ripped it open and pulled out a small packet of papers that he flung immediately on the table, almost as though they had burned him. Pulling out a chair, he sat down, silently staring. He had never seen such a document. It looked almost too official to be real. Even the texture of the paper was like nothing he had ever felt.

Mattson was not a slow reader, but it took him nearly an hour to absorb the twelve, single spaced, typewritten pages. By the time he was finished his face was pale and he was barely breathing. He dropped the papers back on the table and went into the kitchen to pour a cup of coffee.

Walking back to the small living room his hand began to tremble slightly as he sipped at the cup. A strange sense of excitement, mixed with anger and confusion, was bubbling up in him. He stood staring at the brilliant white papers that seemed to leap out amidst the clutter of ashtrays, unopened mail, empty beer cans, and other papers laying on the table.

Twenty minutes later Mattson swung his car into the Radisson parking ramp, drove to the second level and found a space near the door. Clutching the brown manuscript envelope tightly under his arm he walked downstairs and out to the street.

As he walked the three blocks to the office he forced himself to look straight ahead, desperately fighting the urge to look over his shoulder. Breaking his morning ritual of stopping for coffee in the lobby restaurant, he went directly to the elevators and pushed the button for the tenth floor. As the doors were closing he saw two men dressed identically in expensive looking dark, almost black, suits, come in from the street. His breath caught in his throat for an instant as they glanced in his direction, their eyes skimming him from top to bottom, and then dismissed him as they turned and went directly to the restaurant. He chided himself silently for his paranoia all the way to the tenth floor. He hadn't seen them in the building before. So what if they had looked at him? What the hell were they supposed to look at? He was the only damned person in the lobby. Still, when the elevator doors opened he almost leaped off and hurried down the long hall to a door marked, 'Capitol City News'

8

Inside, at a long wooden table pushed tightly against a gray wall marked by yellowish water stains, a stocky white haired man in a wrinkled blue shirt and a pair of jeans sat under a bare light bulb hanging from a ten- foot ceiling. He was busy clipping sections of newspaper articles and placing them in small cardboard folders. Directly in front of him, a woman, with tired eyes and a narrow, angry looking mouth, talked quietly on the telephone while she jotted notes in a book on her desk. She looked up as he entered.

"Hi, Marge," Mattson smiled at her, gesturing toward the door leading to an inner office. "Is Harry in?" Marge gave a quick nod of her head and waved him to the door without breaking her conversation.

He walked past her and opened the door. "Okay to come in?" he asked.

"Come on in, Ron."

Harry Bower, a bald man of sixty, with a huge bulbous whiskey nose and perpetually red watering eyes, put down the paper he was reading and motioned Mattson to a chair. Rolling his own chair back from a steel desk with an oak veneer top, he revealed a pot-bellied, almost pear-shaped body, and smiled at Mattson "I've been sitting here since you called. What's the problem?"

Mattson ignored the chair, crossed the room to an old worn leather sofa, and flopped down, dropping the manuscript envelope on the cushion next to him. "I don't really know where to start, Harry. This could turn out to be one hell of a problem. '

Harry chuckled. Pushing himself still further back from the desk, he rubbed

9

his hand over his bare scalp and stood up. "I can handle anything this morning except a lawsuit. Come on, Ron, let's hear it." Harry's face suddenly expressed mock fear. "It's not a lawsuit, is it?"

Mattson was silent. Unconsciously he began toying with the envelope at his side.

"Well?" asked Harry, impatiently.

"Harry, let me ask you something," Mattson opened the envelope and took out the papers. "If you had absolute proof of a conspiracy, how would you handle it?

"That depends." Harry frowned. "What kind of conspiracy? For what purpose?"

"Not for" said Mattson, nervously, "Against. Against this whole damned country."

The unexpected seriousness in Mattson's voice surprised Harry and he sat down again. Leaning forward with his elbows resting on the desk, he cradled his chin on his clasped hands.

"Russia and China have been doing that for years," He chuckled, then seeing that his humor drew a sudden glare from Mattson, he grew serious.

"Maybe you'd better give me a little more information, Ron. I haven't heard a good conspiracy plot in months."

"You're going to hear one now," said Mattson. He pushed himself off the sofa, crossed the room, and dropped the papers on Harry's desk. "These were given to me this morning."

"What are they?" Harry eyed the papers suspiciously, not touching them.

"They're part of a government study the military has put together for isolating sections of major cities in this country with a sophisticated network of walls."

"I don't understand," Harry looked skeptical. "Why would they want to do that?" Mattson shrugged, "From what I know so far, I'd say plans are being put together for a military takeover under the guise of nationalized public service," He dropped the papers on the desk, walked back to the sofa and flopped down.

"What?" Harry snatched up the papers. "You're joking!" His eyes widened suddenly and a look of alarm crossed his face as he studied the papers. "Good Lord! Ron, these are classified!"

"You're damned right, they're classified," said Mattson. "The fucken things almost burn your hands."

Harry sat staring at the pages laying on his desk as though half expecting them to burst into flame. "A military takeover? Are you serious?"

"That's what it looks like to me," said Mattson. "Go ahead, Harry, read the damned thing and tell me what you think.'

Harry scanned the first page, letting his eyes rove over it without really reading." Before I do," he said, "Why don't you give me some background? Tell me what the hell this is all about."

Mattson scrunched down on the sofa, flopping one leg over the other. "Harry, except for a couple of phone calls, everything I know about this is right there in front of you. Basically, it's about some people in very high places that intend to turn this country on its head. They've been planning it for years."

Harry was still hesitant " If these really are classified," He gestured to the papers, "We can get into a lot of trouble just by having them in our possession you know that, don't you? "

"Of course, I know it," said Mattson. "What the hell am I supposed to do? I can't just throw them away. Besides, if what they contain is true, we're already in a lot of trouble." He waved his arm in exasperation. "Harry, why don't you just read them and then we can talk."

Harry looked at him for a moment, undecided. "Maybe I should get someone from the legal department in here?" He glanced at the closed door.

. "We can't," said Mattson, "we can't say anything about this yet. You'll understand when you read them"

Harry stared at him for nearly a minute and then dropped his eyes to the papers, and finally brought them back to Mattson. The struggle between curiosity and better judgment was obvious. Finally he shrugged, giving into curiosity. "What the hell," "I'm damned if I do and damned if I don't. Okay, get yourself a cup of coffee and I'll look them over." He skimmed over the first three pages and then stopped. The horizontal lines in his forehead had deepened as he read. Shifting irritably in his seat, he flipped back to the first page and began reading again.

Mattson watched and saw his consternation grow as the full impact of what he was reading began to penetrate. He figured it would take Harry at least an hour to read the twelve pages and watching him, he suddenly felt tired. Scrunching even lower into the sofa, he closed his eyes, forcing himself to be patient. He tried to put the papers out of his mind, but with his eyes closed, pictures of the high wooden barriers being constructed around the city kept creeping into his thoughts.

When they first began to appear they had been called, 'Noise Abatement Barriers' and they just didn't make any sense. He had done a series of articles on them, suggesting that they were just another rip-off of the tax-payer's money. Shortly after they began to appear, lumber prices had shot through the roof. Highways in the state were crumbling; there were more potholes than there was pavement. Why the hell were they building those walls when they couldn't even maintain the highways? He noticed that shortly after his article came out, the wooden barriers were being replaced by concrete. Fool that he was, he thought that his articles might have caused the change. Mattson's thoughts continued to drift and he began to doze, still trying to console himself with the fact that there was no way he could have known their real purpose.

He underestimated Harry's reading ability by nearly twenty minutes. When Harry finished the last page he dropped the papers on his desk, spun slowly in his chair and gazed thoughtfully out the window of his tenth floor office. His eyes went automatically to the east, toward Mounds Park, where he could see sections of the walls that he had just read about. From this position he could see two sections of the walls clearly, although they were now nearly obscured by trees and shrubbery that had been planted to make the walls less offensive. Each section was at least a mile long, over two feet thick and standing fifteen feet high. Beyond his sight, he knew, the sections stretched for miles around the city following the freeway system. He swung his chair back to the desk and looked at the bushy-haired reporter sitting across the room.

"Have you shown these papers to anyone else?"

Mattson, startled, shook himself awake and sat up. Fumbling in his jacket pocket he dug out a crumpled pack of cigarettes and lit one. He took a long deep drag. "I haven't said a word to anyone except you, Harry." He took another long drag and tapped the cigarette on the edge of the ashtray sitting at his side. "Scary, isn't it?"

"Scary?" Harry snorted. "If these papers are authentic, it's terrifying!"

"They look pretty damned authentic to me," said Mattson.

"I don't know, Ron," Harry sat shaking his head, "After nearly forty years in this business, this is the first time I've even seen anything from the government stamped like this. I hate to admit it, but they look real as hell to me, too. How did you get your hands on them?"

"The guy just called me." Mattson shrugged. "Apparently he read the series I did a few years ago when I called the walls another government rip-off. He wouldn't give me his name, but he said if I believed the only purpose for those walls was noise control, I was an idiot."

Harry grunted. "That's right. You did a series on the sound barriers, didn't you?"

"Yeah," Mattson crushed out his cigarette and stood up. He paced back and forth for a minute, frowning, then walked to the window and stood looking at the traffic on the street below. "I figured they were just another rip-off to drive up the price of lumber. They were throwing up walls in places that didn't make any sense. They were putting them in places where there weren't even people to complain about the noise. Then I started seeing them where they don't even have freeways completed. I wanted to know why they were spending millions of dollars for sound barriers, when there wasn't anyone to even hear the fucking sound!"

"Like the tree falling in the forest?" asked Harry.

"Exactly." Mattson nodded.

"It was a good story," said Harry. "I remember it caused one hell of a stir in the transportation department."

"That's all it did," said Mattson. "They finally laid it all on the Metro Council planning department. Some guy down there told me it was justified because the population in those areas was expected to rise in the next ten years. Anyway, two weeks ago I got the first phone call. The guy told me noise pollution was only a cover for the walls. The real purpose was to control civil disobedience." Mattson turned from the window and picked up page two of the report. "Listen to this,"

15

' A two year study, conducted between July, 1972 and July 1974 to determine the feasibility of incorporating noise abatement barriers into contingency planning for civil disorder indicates cost factor to be negligible. It is suggested that this be absorbed through existing, highway projects, funded jointly by federal and state agencies... It is further suggested that dilution of anticipated adverse public reaction to permanent barriers can be accomplished through employment of psychological techniques, placing special emphasis on the necessity of lowering noise pollution. Any reference to the primary purpose for the barriers would receive universal rejection and must be avoided." Mattson dropped the paper on the desk.

"Wow, talk about understatements," Harry shook his head in amazement, "This is insanity! Where else do they have the walls?" he asked.

"I think they're in all the major cities," said Mattson, "This was supposed to be the place where they would perfect their ability to overcome public opposition. And, believe me, when people saw those ugly bastards going up right in their own back yards, there was plenty of opposition. But hell, there was just no stopping it. The walls went up, and they stayed up. After fighting it for awhile, the public just took them for granted."

"I know," Harry nodded in agreement. "Today we don't even notice them. In fact, I read a couple of weeks ago about someone in Washington suggesting the possibility of running a fence along the entire length of our border with Mexico. They say it's the only way to stop the increasing flow of narcotics and aliens. Is that a part of it, too?"

"I don't know," Mattson shook his head. "They talked about that twenty or thirty years ago, too. In those days they called it 'McNamara's wall' because it was the same plan he wanted to use in Vietnam to separate the north and south."

"Sure, I remember that," said Harry. "At the time it seemed almost laughable. Now I'm not so sure." He seemed lost in thought for a moment. "It never got off the ground, but isn't that about the same time that they started building the walls around here?"

Mattson shrugged, "I think they went up around here in the early eighties. The first time they talked about a fence along the Mexican border was before that. I think Nixon was still in office."

"Doesn't matter", said Harry. "These are the walls we have to worry about. Do you have any idea who the guy is? How he found out about this?"

"Not the slightest," admitted Mattson, going back to the sofa. "The first time I talked to him I thought he was a nut. Really hyper, you know what I mean? Then, damn it, the more he talked, the more sense he seemed to make. I'm sure he's connected with the government in some way. He gave a lot of verbal background on the development of this operation, but this is the first time he actually gave me any proof."

"Is there any chance that he is just a nut? Maybe he's some clever computer kid that threw these papers together himself?"

asked Harry. "They can make magic on those damned computers these days."

"There's always that chance," admitted Mattson, "but I've got a feeling about this guy. Some of the things he told me during our first conversation had to come from the Military. Hell, he was talking about things that covered the whole spectrum of living, and how Hedgerow is being put into place to change it. It wasn't just the walls, either," continued Mattson. "He was covering everything from farming to health care... shit, you name it and this project covers it."

"You think he was in it from the start?" asked Harry

"Not from the start." Mattson shook his head. "He's too young. I'm not even sure if he's in on it now. I think he probably found out about this thing fairly recently. But he sure as hell did a lot of research. In order to do that, he had to have access to the files, wherever they are."

"What, exactly did he tell you?" asked Harry. "Just start at the beginning and try not to leave anything out."

"Okay," Mattson leaned forward, elbows resting on his knees. "He said this idea of walls first came up during the Watts riot in 1965. It was just one of a number of options at the time. They kicked it around for a while, but after things began to settle down they dropped it. A couple of years later, in 1967, there was a flare-up that set off over a hundred and fifty major riots in this country. The worst was in Detroit, but they all had one thing in common, the inability of police to contain the riot to one area. That's when the idea of the walls was given top priority.

"My sister lived in L.A. just outside of Watts", said Harry. "She damned near had a heart attack thinking it would spread into her neighborhood."

"Threats were made to take it into the white areas," said Mattson, "but it was more of a promise for the future if things didn't improve. The more militant of the rioters would like to have taken it right into Beverly Hills, but it lost momentum. Anyway, two years later, in Detroit, it did spread everywhere. Roving gangs spread out over the city. It began with a police raid on an after-hour bottle club in the black ghetto and within twenty-four hours there wasn't a neighborhood in Detroit that was safe. The police were helpless and even the National Guard couldn't put it down. The Governor finally called in the regular army. That's when this thing went into high gear." Mattson gestured to the papers on the desk. "They knew if they had those barriers in Detroit the cops could have confined the whole thing to one neighborhood."

"Son—of-a-bitch!" Harry smacked his palm on the edge of his desk, "I can't believe we're sitting here talking like this." His look at Mattson was almost a glare. As though, he wanted to kill the messenger. After a moment his anger subsided. "I'm sorry, Ron. It's just that I can't believe anyone would want to do something like this. Shit, I can't believe anyone, not even the government, would have the balls to try something like this."

"It's not the government, Harry. It's just a few powerful bastards in the government that want to run the world. And it doesn't surprise me a bit. Guys like that have always been around. What pisses me off is that even if we manage to get this story out there; those same bastards will come out with a fucking spin that will pacify half the idiots in this country."

"You think so?" Harry looked doubtful.

"Hell yes, said Mattson, bitterly, "It was only a few years ago that they finally admitted dropping nerve gas over San Francisco. They even did testing here in the Twin Cities, and claimed it was only smoke". Mattson's brief laugh was more like a snort, "Remember their original cover story on that one? They said it was a study to determine if Minneapolis could be camouflaged in case of a missile attack. What a bunch of crap! When in hell was a computer driven missile ever confused by smoke?"

"As I recall, said Harry, the public bought the story."

"I don't think they ever really bought it," said Mattson. "But what the hell could they do? People don't want to believe their government lies to them and uses them for guinea pigs."

Harry didn't answer. He had the papers in his hands again, nervously fingering the pages. "You say you got these this morning?" he asked.

"They were put under the front seat of my car. The guy called a few minutes later and told me they were there."

Harry scowled and dropped the papers on the desk. "Okay, what do you want to do?"

Mattson shrugged, "I'd really like to get going on this, Harry. This is something I can get my teeth into."

"I've got a feeling that this is something that's going to bite back," said Harry. "I don't want you going off half cocked on this thing. At least, let's make sure these papers are authentic." Mattson was about to protest, but Harry stopped him with a wave of his hand. "We need more information. If we tried to run this story without verification, they'd crucify us. You know that!" Harry's concern was growing. The more he thought about possible consequences the more agitated he became. Pulling a handkerchief from his pocket, he wiped perspiration from his forehead, and then rubbed the palm of his hand over his bald head. "Damn it," he growled, "If this is real, it's dynamite. This is a top-secret government document. It has the highest possible classification. It's not a witch-hunt on the city council. I'm not even sure what the legal ramifications might be. My God, look at this," he picked up page four and waved it angrily, "This is signed by a Major General!"

Mattson nodded, his own anger rising. "That's the problem, Harry. This thing is too damned big. We can't just sit around and wait for something to happen. We've got to get on it now."

Harry had no immediate response. The two men sat there, each lost in his own thoughts, neither man speaking. Finally Harry let out a long sigh, almost as though he was in pain, and pushed himself away from the desk. After a moment he stood up and stalked across the room to a small table holding a coffee pot and mugs. Selecting one of the thick mugs, he filled it with coffee and turned.

"You want some of this?" he asked

. Mattson nodded and came over to the table. Accepting the coffee he stood sipping it while Harry poured himself a cup, added sugar and cream and walked back to his desk. He stood there stirring it with the erasure end of a wooden pencil.

"Ron, I know you want to jump into this thing and say to hell with the consequences. Believe it or not, that was my first impulse."

"That sounds like a No." Mattson carried his mug back to the sofa and sat down, his face sullen.

"We won't, because we can't," said Harry. "Why the hell can't we?" demanded Mattson. "Once this story is on the street, they won't dare do anything. Other papers will pick it up. The public will come down so hard that..." he stopped, suddenly, unable to find the word that he was searching for.

"Don't be stupid," snapped Harry, his anger suddenly breaking loose. "If we print this and we're not able to back it up, we're screwed! It might cause a stir for a while, but that would be the end of it. We'd lose any chance we might have to stop this thing. And it's anybody's guess what they would do to us."

"Well, we can't just sit on it." Mattson shook his head stubbornly. "Something has to be done."

"We will do something," promised Harry. "We just have to do it right. Otherwise the people behind this are still going to be there when everything's over."

He stopped stirring his coffee and dropped the pencil on the table. "Do you remember General Westmoreland?" he asked.

"Sure," Mattson nodded. "He was the General in charge for a while in Vietnam. Why?"

"I saw him interviewed on television a long time ago," said Harry. "He made a statement that night that has stuck with me for years. He said that 'future conflicts would have to be of reasonable duration because the staying power of American public opinion is extremely limited."

"He sure as hell had that right, said Mattson. "But he was talking about a war. We're talking about something that's happening right here in this country."

"It still applies," said Harry. "You said it yourself. They'll come up with a cover story." He threw his right hand in the air in a gesture of disgust. "I can't imagine what the hell could be said to justify this, but believe me, they'll have a story, and they'll totally discredit us. They'll hammer it home until the public uproar dies down, and then they'll have our ass. We're talking about something that a group of maniacs have apparently been preparing for the past twenty or thirty years, maybe longer. Do you think for one minute they're going to let a single story in an off-beat newspaper wash their careers down the drain?"

"Fuck their careers," growled Mattson.

Harry shrugged. He sipped from the hot mug of coffee and held it between his two cupped hands, watching his reflection in the black steamy liquid. He gave Mattson time to cool down.

"Ron," he said, finally. "I know how these things work. We can't just print this story and depend on public opinion to do the work for us. Unless we have some help, whoever is behind this will have it white-washed, explained away, apologized for, and forgotten within three months. In four months they'll be back in business." He set his cup on the desk and turned to the window. "I hate to admit it, but we're nothing more than a piece of toilet paper in the real world of publishing. We barely meet the monthly expenses. How the hell would we defend ourselves? Think about it. If they damned near stopped the New York Times and the Washington Post ... what do you think they'd do to us?"

"All right," conceded Mattson," we can't print the story and we can't talk to anyone in the government. What the hell can we do?"

"I didn't say we can't print the story," said Harry. "We just have to wait until we have all the facts. The first thing we have to do is find out if these papers are the real thing." He waved the packet Mattson had given him. "Then we have to find out how many people are involved. Something of this magnitude would need a hell of a lot of support. Minnesota is a test site so let's find out who's involved from around here."

"The guy on the phone thinks we could blow it just by asking questions," said Mattson.

"We'll have to risk that," said Harry. He waved the packet again. "Something else bothers me," he said. "This, for the most part, is about eleven years old. We have to get our hands on something more recent. We

24

have to know how far things have gone since this thing was authorized."

"With a little luck I should have more of it in a few days," Mattson stood up and walked to the window next to Harry. "The first time I noticed those damned walls was about fifteen or eighteen years ago. I remember they started popping up in areas where nobody paid much attention. Nobody had any idea what the hell they were for, anyway. Then suddenly they started building them all along the freeway and bringing them closer together. I took a drive around the entire beltway a few years ago and it seemed like the whole damned city was walled in."

"I know." Harry nodded. "I never gave them much thought, either. Lately, though, they really do seem to be everywhere. I see that some of them are made out of concrete. Why is that?"

"They probably ran out of trees," laughed Mattson. "When was the last time you looked at the price of lumber?"

Harry laughed, lightly. It was the first time he had lost his frown since Mattson had come into the office. He shuffled the papers together and put them back in the envelope. "All right," he said, handing the envelope to Mattson. "I want you to re-type these on plain paper. Leave out anything that refers to this as classified material. We're going to need something to work from, but I'll feel a lot better if we don't have the originals lying around. You'll have to find some place to hide them."

"What about a safety deposit box?"

"No good," Harry shook his head. "That's one of the first places somebody will look for them. The government could get a court order in five minutes. That's why I don't want to chance keeping them here. With the new Supreme Court rulings nothing is safe, especially a newspaper office."

"Don't worry," assured Mattson, "I'll find a safe place."

"How well do you get along with Benny Morris?" asked Harry

"Great. Why?"

"I'm going to put him on this with you. He's a good digger and he knows how to keep his mouth shut. Right now he's covering the liquor probe and he's been working pretty close with a couple of guys from the State Crime Bureau. That might be a good place to start."

"Not a bad idea," agreed Mattson. "We can use my series on the walls as a cover story. If anyone gets curious we can say there was a strong reader's response, and we're doing a follow-up. We can say the readers want to know more about the tax money involved."

"That's reasonable," agreed Harry. "Benny's at the courthouse this morning covering the liquor hearings. As soon as he gets back I'll brief him and tell him to get in touch with you."

Mattson gave a quick nod, picked up the brown envelope and walked to the door. "I'll take these papers home and type them." His hand touched the knob on the door, and then stopped. "Harry," he asked, "have we got an old typewriter around here? I don't want to put this on my own computer."

"Good thinking," said Harry. "The first thing they'll do is grab your computer. Too bad we haven't got an old one laying around that you could donate to them. See if Marge can find one for you. I'm sure she's got one someplace. If she asks questions, just tell her your computer crashed."

Chapter Two

Benny Morris pulled off the freeway at the Marion street exit, drove around the new vocational building and continued up the hill toward the massive Cathedral sitting majestically at the top. As he passed the church, Selby Avenue branched off from Summit Avenue at a right angle.

For nearly a hundred years Selby had been the home of hard working, hard drinking, middle-class, Irish Catholics. An average Sunday morning found streets around the Cathedral Church lined with devout hard working Catholics, mostly women, pushing reluctant kids in front of them, on their way to kneel and pray and make excuses, to the Priest standing next to the door, for the less devout, hard drinking Catholic men who were still at home nursing hangovers from the night before. Many of them knew each other, and the Priest knew them all, including those still at home. Selby Avenue had been a solid middle class neighborhood in its heyday, but that day was long gone.

During the early fifties city planners, pressured by the threat of an increasing population were in a frantic rush to begin building its freeway system. The site they selected was a strip of land six blocks north of Selby known as Rondo Avenue. Because this was the heart of the black population, most people at the time believed there was a lot more involved than just building a freeway. The most obvious location for a freeway running to Minneapolis, and beyond, was University Avenue, a street that had traditionally connected the two cities, first by electric streetcars and later by city buses. University Avenue sat only a few blocks further north and was comprised mostly of restaurants, bars and assorted small business enterprises. Even though its location was the ideal connection between St. Paul and Minneapolis, University Avenue was never even in serious contention during the planning. Had University Avenue been selected there would have been no major displacement of families, but Rondo Avenue ran directly through the residential and business section of the black population and that was the street selected. Most of the people living on Rondo were unwilling to leave the area of their birth and they were unwanted in other sections of the city. But eventually they were forced out of their homes and because most of them were poor, they were forced into the only direction left open to them, south, toward Selby Avenue. Resentment rose quickly between blacks and whites.

Life long residents of both colors who were able to afford it, and unable to cope with the change, sold their homes and moved to the suburbs. The old, the helpless, and the poor who could not afford to move became targets for a new breed of youth roaming the streets. Born of broken dirt-poor families and filled with anger and frustration they lashed out with violence. Police, acting on orders to avoid confrontations, half-heartedly patrolled the streets with dogs. Iron grates began appearing on windows and doors, and Firemen, unsure of police protection, chatted over coffee in their firehouses dreading, and at times, even ignoring calls to the area. Fires in buildings that could have been extinguished in an hour burned through the night.

Politics had cleared the Rondo area and greed paved it. The earthmovers came in like an invading army. In their haste to cash in on the federal money and benefits the politicians of St. Paul destroyed two thriving business communities, one black and one white, and transformed them into vacant lots and burned out boarded up buildings as the only reminder of what had been. When it was over, burned out shells and empty gutted hulks lined the streets between Selby and the new freeway. It remained that way, ignored by the rest of the city, until a new promise of federal money made restoration not only worthwhile, but also highly profitable for the movers and the shakers. The earth-movers came in again. The burned out hulks came down and the entire area became a vast vacant lot. In time a few street names were changed and shiny, brightly painted new buildings began to appear, but only a small number of the original residents survived the change. Selby Avenue was on its way back again, but Benny remembered it as it had been, and he knew it would never be the same

Benny drove past Selby, following. Summit Avenue, a wide, tree shaded street, lined on both sides with huge ornate mansions and carriage houses where decisions had once been made that had shaped the nation. Railroad and banking empires had been created in the drawing rooms on one side of the street while the likes of Sinclair Lewis and F. Scott Fitzgerald toiled at their typewriters on the other. Summit Avenue had been spared the turmoil that demolished Selby Avenue, but the empire-shaping era was gone. Today even the buffalo- skin wall papered home of James J. Hill stood empty and lifeless. A metal plaque nailed to a brownstone was the only reminder of Fitzgerald. The mansions remained, but many of them had been converted to rooming houses and had lost the aura of mystery and dignity that had surrounded them for over a century. Even the giant Elm tree sentinels that had shaded the magnificent street were beginning to die.

A few blocks beyond the church Benny saw the address he was looking for and pulled to the curb. He sat for a moment staring at the three-story wood and brick mansion that had been divided into rented rooms and small apartments, and slowly brought his mind back to the present and the reason he was here. Two hours earlier he had returned from the courthouse feeling bored and restless. The daily hearing on the liquor probe had been totally lifeless. Sitting for hours listening to the repetitious rhetoric of the equally lifeless council members could only be viewed as a punishment, and he was sick of it. The liquor investigation had been a farce from the beginning, but the only group in the city that still seemed to be unaware of it sat on the City Council. Still, he supposed, if it were not for the liquor probe, they would find something equally inane with which to waste their time. They would continue to sit, each piously pompous, each trying to out-do the other, hoping to stumble over something that would ingratiate them with the voters. When he was summoned to Harry Bower's office he had been prepared to ask for another assignment, never suspecting that Harry's call was for precisely that purpose. He listened with astonishment to the incredible story that Harry told him.

"You're kidding, aren't you?" he had asked. "You're telling me that those walls are being built to turn this country into some kind of concentration camp?" He shook his head incredulously. "C'mon, Harry, you can't really believe that?"

"What I believe has nothing to do with it," growled. Harry. "I've seen those papers and for my money they're authentic. I want you and Mattson to check them out."

"Okay," Benny shrugged, "It's your money. We'll check it out. It's just a little tough to swallow, that's all."

"Why is it?" demanded Harry. "Someone put those papers together, didn't they? That means that someone is thinking along those lines. If 'Big Brother' is ever going to take over, I can't think of a better way to do it."

"Yeah, but hell, Harry, This isn't some third world country. This is the United States." Benny shook his head. "I just don't see it happening. Not here. "

"I'm having the same problem," admitted Harry, but until we get to the bottom of this I want you to keep an open mind. No, I want you to do better than that. I want you to treat this as an established fact and dig like hell to prove to me that it's not. If there is something to this, I'm not going to get caught with my head in the sand like some damned Ostrich!"

Forcing his thoughts back to the present, Benny switched off the ignition, climbed out of the car and started up the long sidewalk leading to the house. In the vestibule he found the number to Mattson's apartment on the mailbox. Apartment eight was on the second floor. He took the steps two at a time, hearing the clacking of the typewriter even before he reached the door.

At his knock the typing stopped and he heard Mattson's voice.

"Who is it?"

"Benny Morris. Harry sent me over."

"Come on in, Benny. The door's open."

Benny opened the door and stepped in. Mattson was across the room seated at a small wooden desk. He waved Benny to an over- stuffed arm-chair in the corner and turned back to the typewriter.

"I'll be with you in a minute. I've got one page left to type. Did Harry fill you in?" he asked.

"He scared the shit out of me, if that's what you mean." said Benny, dropping into the chair.

Mattson chuckled and continued typing.

From where he sat, Benny could see a small kitchen and a door leading to what he assumed must be a bathroom. The living room was small, but well lighted from two large windows in the Southwest corner of the room. Books, magazines, and old newspapers were stacked on a dust-covered television set near the desk. Five minutes passed before Mattson pulled the paper from the typewriter and turned around.

"That does it," he said with a touch of triumph. "Can I get you something? Coffee, Beer?"

"No thanks." Benny shook his head and pointed to the papers on Mattson's desk. "Is that some of the stuff Harry told me about?"

"These are the original copies the guy gave me." Mattson grabbed a stack of papers from the desk. "Harry wanted me to make a copy."

"Why not zerox them?"

"I had to take out a few things," said Mattson. "I didn't want them to look as official as the original. No big deal. There's only a dozen pages."

"From what I hear, they're pretty powerful pages. I can't remember seeing Harry that shook up since I've known him."

"Take a look for yourself." Mattson gave Benny the packet of original papers and stood up. "Sure you don't want a beer or something?"

"Maybe a beer," relented Benny, looking at the first page. Mattson went to the kitchen and took two cold cans from the refrigerator. Snapping off the tabs he came back to the living room and set one on the floor next to Benny.

Benny hadn't seemed to notice the beer, but by the time he turned the third page his hand moved unconsciously to the floor and picked it up. "Damn," he muttered, "I don't believe this." He looked up, opened his mouth to speak, then changed his mind and continued reading. After two more pages he was unable to contain himself.

"Ron, this is insane. The son-of-a-bitch that put this together has to be absolutely out of his mind."

"It's more than just one, son-of-a-bitch," said Mattson, gulping the last of his own beer and tossing the empty can into a wastebasket. "This is a bunch of sons-a-bitches."

Benny's eyes turned back to the papers. Much of the terminology was technical and unfamiliar to Benny and he had to constantly refer to previous pages in order to get a complete picture. After nearly an hour he set them aside and took a long drink from his warm beer. He was only on page seven but he needed time to sort out the thoughts and emotions that were rushing through him.

Mattson waited patiently, remembering his own first reaction.

"Ron, where in the hell did you get these?"

"Some guy put them under the front seat of my car this morning." Mattson told him about the phone calls.

"You don't have any idea who the guy is?"

"That's one of the things we have to find out," said Mattson

"Well, I'll tell you one thing," said Benny. "Harry sure as hell didn't overstate it. When he first told me about this I thought he was on some kind of trip. Now I think, maybe I'm tripping, myself." He shook his head in disbelief. "Can you imagine what it would be like if something like this actually happened?"

"I think it's already happening." said Mattson, cynically. " Hell, I remember during the Watergate hearings when some judge said, 'if the American people really knew the truth they'd be shocked to find out how close we came to becoming Nazi Germany.' He leaned over and pulled one of the pages from the stack. "Listen to this,"

He said. "At the present time the Army is preparing and coordinating contingency plans with appropriate city and state agencies for deployment of federal forces... Thirty-two active Army and Marine, brigade size forces have been assigned civil disorder areas. In our opinion, these forces, working in conjunction with local law enforcement agencies will be more than adequate.' "Christ," said Mattson, throwing down the paper, "That's about sixty thousand men."

What the hell do they mean by adequate?" asked Benny. "Adequate for what? I thought they were talking about a civil disorder. This sounds more like a war."

"When the government intentionally sets out to create the disorder," growled Mattson," you can bet your ass it's a war. Hell, here's another part." He snatched up another page and began reading. "The effectiveness of psychological techniques to create confusion and heighten hostility and tension in selected urban areas against specific groups should not be underestimated."

"I hate to believe it," said Benny, "but they don't leave room for a hell of a lot of doubt, do they?" He leaned forward, grabbed the report and started reading again. After a moment a thought struck him and he looked up. "You remember that riot we had out in San Francisco awhile back? Do you think these guys had anything to do with that?"

"Who knows?" Mattson shrugged. "But you can bet your ass that someone from Hedgerow was there observing it. Why do you ask?"

"Well," Benny frowned. "Somehow the guy that did the killing, an ex-cop or a firemen or something, got off with a lousy five year sentence. When the public heard the verdict they went crazy. When the riot started someone spread it around that they were all homosexuals. They really went nuts then. "

"I remember that," nodded Mattson. "In fact, we even reprinted some of the articles that came out in the Frisco papers. Some of the public officials made statements that were so stupid and provocative everyone wanted to riot."

"That's what I mean," said Benny. "What you just read about using psychology to heighten hostility and tension against specific groups seemed to fit right in.

Mattson slapped his open palm against his forehead in a gesture of frustration "Damn it, I never made the connection. You're absolutely right. They were protesting what they considered a double standard of justice, and someone turned the issue completely around. Instead of attacking the courts for an injustice, they had to defend themselves against being labeled homo's and freaks."

Benny smiled, "I don't know if this plan was in operation then," he said, "but someone sure as hell confused the issue." He turned back to the report and continued reading.

Mattson watched him for a minute, then stood up and went into the kitchen. To kill time he began rinsing off dirty dishes, his mind still racing, knowing that somehow he had to get this story to the public. He had to get it into print, but at the same time, not

37

having the slightest idea of how he would get Harry to let him do it.

It was almost another hour before Benny set down the report and stood up. "This is absolute lunacy," he said. "It's like something out of science fiction."

"You think it might be phoney?" asked Mattson.

"No way," said Benny, flatly. "Whoever put this together had to have access to the Pentagon for some of this information."

"That's the way I figure it, but Harry wants to go slow. He thinks we need more information before we do anything."

"I think he's right about that, Ron. This is the sort of thing where we get only one shot. If we blow it by moving too fast," he shrugged," that's the end of the ballgame.

I think we should sit tight, ask a few questions, and wait to see if your contact can come up with something more."

"That's something that bothers me, Benny. Even if we do get more, what do we do with it? Where do we go from there? If someone pulls an armed robbery you just pick up the phone and call the cops. Who the hell do you call in a case like this?"

"We'll have to wait." said Benny. "We wait till we have all we can get. When the time comes, when we have all the facts, we print the story and hope that the public can handle it."

"That's the point," grumbled Mattson. "Will they handle it? Ellsberg had a hell of a time getting the public to believe him. When they finally did, they looked at

38

him like he was a traitor. How do you tell people that their own government is planning to enslave them... how the hell do they accept that? I don't think there's any way to get them to believe us even if we do print it. Shit! The public won't do anything except give it back to the government to investigate. It's like asking Hitler to save the Jews."

"Hey, slow down, Ron." Benny was pacing slowly back and forth, "In the first place, we're not necessarily talking about the government. We're talking about some people in the military and maybe some politicians and a few rich bastards that ought to be in a mental ward." He stopped pacing and turned to Mattson. "In reality, we don't know who the hell we're talking about. That's why we need more information. Anyway, this isn't the first country to have a few crazy Generals."

Mattson said nothing. He sat slumped forward in the straight-backed chair, contemplating his hands. Benny was right, he knew that. The information they had now was not enough. They had to have more.

Benny dropped back into his chair, sighing. "I'm like you, Ron. I'd love to jump into this thing with both feet. I just don't think we should do it until we have more documentation. If we can get enough I know damned well there are people that will listen."

"Okay," agreed Mattson, "I'll try to dig up the rest of the report. But what if we don't get it? What then?"

"We could always put it in a novel and call it fiction," laughed Benny. "At least it would get people thinking."

Mattson didn't appreciate the joke. "Harry thought maybe you could feel out some of the guys at the state crime bureau. Maybe somebody heard something?"

Benny nodded. "He mentioned it to me. I'll check it out, but I doubt if they'll know anything more than we do. Something this big isn't likely to be passed down to the grunts." He motioned to the papers on the desk. "How about that General and the other two guys mentioned? You want me to see if I can find something on them?"

Mattson nodded. "The General shouldn't be much of a problem, but I don't know where you'll start with the other two."

"Leave that to me." Benny picked up the stack of papers and sorted through them until he found the names he wanted. Scratching them on a scrap of paper he walked to the door. "How will I get in touch with you?"

"I'll probably be here or at the office. If something comes up, I'll leave word with Harry." Mattson crossed the room and laid a hand on Benny's shoulder. "I guess I don't have to tell you that this thing could blow up in our face?"

"It's going to blow one way or the other," shrugged Benny. "Let's just hope that something is still standing when it's all over." He turned and walked out the door, pulling it quietly shut behind him.

Chapter Three

When Benny was gone, Mattson placed the original report in the manuscript envelope and laid it on top of the desk. Then, picking up the copy, he stapled it together and stood slapping it in the palm of his hand as he looked around the room. After a full minute he walked to the window and pulled down the shade. He looked at it for a moment, undecided, then pulled out the staple he had just put in the paper and inserted the pages one at a time as he let the shade re-wind.

Grabbing his jacket, he picked up the envelope and went down the stairs to his car. He had briefly considered hiding the original papers in the apartment also, but almost immediately discarded the idea. If anyone was seriously looking for them it would be one of the first places they would look. The same held true for his car. He considered the office, but Harry was right. They would simply come in and tear the place to pieces. They probably will anyway, he thought, once the story hits the press. Still, undecided, Mattson got into his four- year old Toyota and turned on the ignition. The afternoon rush had not yet started when he reached the ramp leading to the freeway. Gradually easing the car to the left he got into the lane taking him north on 35-E. Within three minutes he began to see the sound barriers. At Roselawn Avenue he slowed the car and pulled to the side of the road. Sliding across the seat he took a Polaroid camera from the glove compartment and got out on the passenger side. Concentrating on the West side, he snapped two pictures of the walls and got back into the car. The huge walls had gone up everywhere. Another few miles and 35-E curved to the right, heading for Duluth, but

Mattson kept to the left, now following 1-694. Most of this area had been covered in his article, and his interest began to grow as he crossed over 35-W. New sound barriers had been erected here, also, but these were different. The new walls, extending from the old wooden barriers, were made of a material resembling stone. The construction and the design were modern, but the effect was the same. It was not much different than driving alongside the walls surrounding the Stillwater state prison. Mattson pulled to the side of the road at the next off ramp, snapped three more pictures and then crossed over the bridge and took the ramp back down to the freeway heading back to 35W where he turned in the direction of Minneapolis and Bloomington. Every few miles he pulled to the side of the road and took pictures.

Just before reaching the crosstown freeway he pulled over again. This time the walls had been constructed in areas that had absolutely nothing behind them but barren fields. Looking in both directions he wondered how he could have been stupid enough to believe these barriers were intended to block noise. What the hell were they blocking the noise from, the wild geese flying across the empty fields?

Mattson could see that newer walls had been put up to connect with the older walls already in place. Son-of-a-bitch," he growled, "when they finish this they'll have three major sections of the city divided. He began taking pictures of the walls on the opposite side of the freeway, when he suddenly became aware of a patrol car that had pulled to the side of the road directly across from him. Two men sat in the car quietly watching him and he felt his blood suddenly surge. From their present position on the other side of the freeway they could not reach him and they made no gestures. They just sat there and watched him. In a couple of minutes he saw another car pull up behind them and a tall man in a dark business suit got out and walked up to the patrol car. After a moment the man in the suit went back to his own vehicle and both cars drove off.

Mattson breathed a sigh of relief, but then a thought struck him. Maybe they were just going up the road to turn and come back on his side of the freeway? Remembering the papers in his car he decided to get the rest of the pictures another time. Walking casually back to the car, pretending to check his camera on the way, he climbed in and started it. Across the road another patrol car suddenly shot through the traffic with its siren screaming. Mattson's heart skipped as he eased his own car onto the freeway. He had no way of knowing if they were going after a speeder or coming after him. Those damned papers, he thought. If they were found now everything would be over before it even got started. The ride back to St. Paul took longer than expected and by the time he reached his apartment it was already growing dark. He pulled the Toyota into a parking space near his apartment and cut the engine. Sitting in the semi-darkness he let his mind wander over a few of his friends, trying to think of someone that he could trust with the papers. In fifteen minutes, for one reason or another, he had eliminated all of them, not because he could not trust them,

43

but because he suddenly realized that he could be placing them in serious danger. He finally gave up, got out of the car and slammed the door after him. Damn, he thought, who the hell would have thought it would be so hard to find a place to hide a few lousy papers?

Going up the walk to his house, another idea struck him and he stopped. Why not, he thought? If anyone came looking for the papers they would go through his apartment, but it was unlikely that they would go through every apartment in the building. He turned and hurried back to his car for a flashlight. Back in his apartment, Mattson went directly to the kitchen and picked up a chair. He carried it back through the living room and into the hall. He stood for a moment, listening. Finally, satisfied that he was alone, he carried the chair to the far end of the hall. Above him, barely visible in the dim light, was a trap door that he remembered from the summer before when the building was being rewired. Standing on the chair he pushed the trapdoor out of the way, grabbed the edge of the opening with both hands and pulled himself up. There was barely enough room for him in the tiny crawl space, but he managed to pull the flashlight from his back pocket and flick it on. Wires criss-crossed in every direction, and the spaces between the joists were filled with a powdery dirty white insulation. He crawled forward about ten feet, cautiously, kneeling on the joists, being careful to avoid putting pressure on the floor between them. All he needed at this point was to crack the plaster in the apartment below. Sweat began forming on his forehead and dripping down into his eyes. Deciding he had gone far enough he stopped and pulled aside some of the insulation.

Taking the envelope from inside his shirt he placed it carefully between the joists and covered it with insulation. As he started to turn around, he felt wires brushing against his heels and he stopped. Realizing he had no other choice he raised his foot over the wires and backed slowly to the opening. Gripping the edges of the opening, he eased himself down on the chair. He quickly discovered that replacing the trap door was considerably more difficult than removing it had been. He was sweating and nervous and the fiberglass from the insulation was beginning to itch. It took five minutes of silent struggle and cursing before the door fell into place. Picking up the chair, he carried it back to his apartment feeling totally exhausted. On his way through the kitchen he suddenly remembered that he hadn't eaten since breakfast, but the itching had become intolerable and he pushed the thought of food from his mind. He went directly to the bathroom, stuck the plug in the drain, turned on the water and began peeling off his clothes. When the tub was full he climbed in and began scrubbing the fiberglass fibers from his body, convinced that it was everywhere. Within five minutes he was fighting to keep his eyes open. Forcing himself from the tub he grabbed a towel from the rack and walked into the bedroom where he flopped on the bed, not even bothering to pull back the sheets.

The morning light was just creeping into the room as Mattson rolled over on the bed trying to shut out the screeching in his ear. After a moment he realized it was not going to go away and he turned over and picked up the telephone on the third ring. "Hello?" He had forgotten to open a window and the room was stuffy. He shook his head, trying to wake up.

"That you, Ron?"

Yeah, Benny," Mattson rubbed the sleep from his eyes. "I just woke up. Any luck yesterday?"

"I've got a line on one of those guys:" Benny was unable to keep the excitement out of his voice.

"You did it that fast? You're joking!" Mattson was suddenly wide-awake, sitting on the edge of the bed

"Like hell I am," laughed Benny. "Look, I don't want to go into this over the phone. Can you meet me at Harry's office?"

"I'll be there in twenty minutes," promised Mattson.

"Okay, I'll see you there," said Benny.

The telephone clicked off. Mattson set it back on the hook and threw on his clothes. On the way to the bathroom he took time to plug in his coffeemaker. It was ready by the time he came out and he poured himself a cup. Too hot to drink, he could only sip it as he collected the best pictures from the batch he had taken the day before. Glancing at his watch he saw that fifteen minutes had   passed since the telephone call. He set the cup on the desk, grabbed a sweater from the closet and went down to the car. The sky was overcast and the weather was cool, but far to the East he could see traces of sunshine.

Chapter Four

They were waiting for him when he walked in. Harry Bower and Benny Morris sat together on the sofa pouring over newspaper clippings spread on the floor in front of them.

"You guys working overtime?" asked Mattson.

"I think Benny is," said Harry, obviously pleased. "He got me up at six-thirty this morning." Harry motioned to the table across the room. "Get some coffee and sit down. I think we've got some good news."

"I can use a little of both," said Mattson, walking to the table and pouring himself a cup. "What's up?"

Benny stretched, yawned and leaned back against the sofa. He reminded Mattson of a cat that had just spied a bird and knew that he was going to get it. "After I left you yesterday," said Benny, "I spent the next couple of hours in the library checking reference books. From there I went to the Dispatch and Tribune and got a look at their files." He waved a hand indicating the pile of clippings on the floor. "Our General was quite a guy. He even made 'Who's who' about twenty five years ago."

"Did you say, he was?" asked Mattson.

Benny nodded. "He died in 1973 from a cerebral hemorrhage."

"Oh, great!" Mattson flopped in the leather chair near the window. "I thought this was supposed to be good news?"

"It is," insisted Benny. "General Sleighton was a real gung-ho 'Patton' type that made news wherever he went. I found articles on him going back to the Second World War when he was only a Colonel."

"So?" asked Mattson.

"So," said Benny, "they buried him with full military honors and every major magazine in the country did a complete lay-out on him. One of the pictures I found was taken in Germany in 1958." Benny leaned over and picked a clipping from the floor. "Here, take a look." He gave it to Mattson.

Mattson looked at a clipping of two Army officers talking to a group of civilians.

"The Captain standing with Sleighton is the General's aide," said Benny. "According to the article the aide's name is Clifton and his home town is right here in Minneapolis."

Benny waited, but after a moment he realized that Mattson still didn't understand. He laughed. "Ron, that guy, Clifton, is one of the guys named in that report."

"No shit?" Mattson peered closely at the clipping. "I'll be damned," he whispered. The tired, drawn look was suddenly gone from his face and his eyes were bright as he began to read the clipping.

"We're trying to get a lead on him now," said Harry, "I've got a friend at the Credit Bureau checking him out."

"The Credit Bureau?" Mattson looked up.

Harry nodded, " I know what you're thinking, Ron, but don't underestimate those people. They have access to files in offices all over the world, and they're better computerized than the Pentagon. Believe me, if they don't have the information, it probably doesn't exist. They'll come up with everything on this guy Clifton from his birth to his last enema."

"It will also create less suspicion if it looks like some one is just running a credit check." said Benny. "In the meantime, I'm working on the other angle."

"What's that?" Mattson turned to him.

"With the State Crime Bureau," said Benny. "I grew up with a guy named Chuck Sauerly. He's with one of the special units that check up on all the other units. I don't expect much, but if anyone over there knows anything, it will be Chuck."

"According to the report," said Harry, "the Army is coordinating the whole operation with city and state officials. If they really intend to utilize local police, the State Crime Bureau has to know about it."

"That makes sense," agreed Mattson. "But, if he does know something, how do you get him to talk about it?"

"I'll have to wing it," said Benny. "I'll use your idea about a follow-up on government funded rip-offs."

"I pulled Ron's series from the file yesterday," said Harry, walking to the desk and pulling a newspaper from one of the drawers. "There are some great winter pictures of those walls. Suppose you take this with you?" he said to Benny.

"Good idea," said Mattson. "You can take these along, too." He pulled the photographs from his pocket and gave them to Benny. "I took these yesterday. The location of each wall is marked on the back."

"There's just one thing," said Harry, turning to Benny. "If your friend does know something, he could be in on it. If he is and he figures out what we're really after, we could be knee deep in shit before we even get started."

"I trust him," said Benny. "But you're right. Cops are funny creatures. He spends a hell of a lot more time with his friends on the force than he does with me." Benny turned to Mattson. "It's up to you, Ron. If you want me to talk to him, I will. There's a risk, but I might learn a hell of a lot by what he doesn't say. He's a baseball fan so I'll start off with something about the new stadium they're trying to push. If he talks about that and clams up when I mention the barriers I'll know damned well he knows something."

Suddenly the sharp ring of the telephone interrupted them. Harry snatched it up. "Yes?" he said, impatiently. His face brightened. Recognizing the voice on the other end and he reached for a pencil. "You didn't waste any time, John."

"That's probably the guy from the credit bureau," whispered Benny. He looked at the folder Harry had given him. "These are really great pictures, Ron. You must have frozen your butt off, taking these?"

Mattson smiled, remembering. "I think it was about ten below, that day."

"I'll take them with me," said Benny, standing up and putting them back in the folder. "You want me to talk to Chuck?"

Mattson nodded. "Yeah, check it out. We have to start somewhere."

"Okay, I'll check with you guys later." Benny crossed the room and opened the door. "Will you be around if I need you?" He asked Mattson.

"I'll be here for awhile," said Mattson. "If I leave, Harry will know where to find me."

Benny nodded and left the office, pulling the door quietly shut behind him. Harry, still talking on the telephone was busy scratching on a pad of paper. Mattson crossed the room, knelt down and began flipping through the clippings on the floor. He concentrated on the most recent, looking for something more about Clifton.

"All right, John," said Harry into the telephone. "I think I have it all. If anything more comes in you'll be able to reach me here. And thanks a million, we really appreciate this." He hung up and waved the pad of paper, triumphantly. "We've got it:"

"Was that about Clifton?" asked Mattson dropping the clippings.

"It sure was." Harry was elated. "I told you not to underestimate those people."

"What did they say?"

"To begin with, there are thousands of people named Clifton in the world, but only a half dozen living here in the Twin Cities," said Harry. "Of those, there is only one Norman G. Clifton with a service record. He lives in Edina and owns a real estate office in Minneapolis. His military record states that he retired from the service in 1974 with the rank of Major."

"Hot damn:" Mattson clapped his hands together. "That has to be him. Everything fits. His retirement is only a year after the death of General Sleighton."

"It looks that way," agreed Harry. "He might even be the one that's feeding you the information."

"That's a little too much to hope for," said Mattson. "Do you have his address?"

Harry wrote it on a piece of paper and gave it to him. "Here's his home address. It's in Edina. And here's the address for his office in Minneapolis. I didn't bother with the phone numbers, but you can get them out of the phone book if you need them."

"Mattson glanced at the address and shoved the paper into his pocket."If anyone calls for me I'll be back this afternoon.

"Hold on a minute," said Harry. "Where are you going?"

"To Edina," said Mattson. "I want to have a talk with this guy. If he's the one that I talked to on the phone I'll be able to tell."

"Didn't he say he was going to be in Washington today?"

"That could have been bullshit," said Mattson. "He might have said that just to stall me."

"You'd better be careful," cautioned Harry. "If Clifton isn't the one that called you, and he does know something, you can bet your ass he's on the other side."

"His name was in those papers," said Mattson, "so he must know something. "And if he's the one who called me, he has tc be on our side. Anyway, I won't know until I talk to him and hear his voice.

"Just be careful," cautioned Harry.

Mattson nodded and left the room, closing the door behind him.

Chapter Five

In an effort to save time and avoid traffic, Mattson took Jackson Street down to the river and turned right on Sheppard Road. The weather bureau had just announced that the last winter had been the longest and coldest in Minnesota history Now, nearing the end of August, the weather was warm, but in his mind's eye he still remembered last May when he could see floating chunks of ice making their way down river as empty barges fought the current on their way up to the grain terminals. Each year he swore to himself that he would never spend another winter here, but by the end of June he had stopped thinking about the cold winter mornings, the freezing snow, and the booster cables. By mid- August the blazing sun had blotted out any plans that he might have had for a warmer climate. He knew if he didn't make a move soon he would be trapped again. This time, he promised himself, he'd stick to his plans come hell or high water. With any luck at all, when the snow starts flying again, he'd have this story wrapped up and he'd be lying in the warm Florida sun.

In ten minutes he came to the old Univac plant. Barely reducing his speed, he curved around it, swung down the ramp onto Old Fort Road heading west. Traffic increased slightly as he approached the turn-off for International Airport, but thinned again as he began passing the rows of motels lining the Bloomington strip. Another ten minutes took him to France Avenue and directly into Edina. This was unfamiliar territory and it took nearly as long to find the address as it had taken to get there. The house was a small A-frame type, with a false red-brick front, standing forty feet off the street and almost totally concealed by the well-kept shrubbery. Parking the car, he followed the narrow winding flagstone walk to the front door and pushed the button. A couple of minutes passed. There was no answer. He pushed it again.

This time the door opened, revealing a slender, chisel faced, man wearing a light sweater and tan slacks, who peered at him over wire-rimmed glasses. He appeared to be somewhere in his late sixties, and even in casual dress he held himself with a military rigidness that had a distinct air of authority.

"Yes?"

"Good morning," said Mattson, smiling, "I'm looking for Norman Clifton."

"I'm Clifton," said the man. "What can I do for you?"

"Hi," Mattson said cheerfully, forcing a wide smile. "I really glad I caught you in, Mr. Clifton. I work for the Capitol City News, and if you have a few minutes, I'd like to interview you?"

"And why would that be?" The voice was brisk, the eyes, reptilian cold.

"Our paper is putting together a series dealing with the feelings of former service men regarding the possibility of a new draft. I understand that you were a Major and that you recently retired."

"Not so recent," said Clifton. "I retired in 1974."

"Well, sir, there's been a lot of talk recently about bringing back the draft. Apparently the Military is having a lot of trouble filling the ranks with qualified people. Enlistments are down, and many highly trained personnel are leaving the service for the private sector. Even the huge re-enlistment bonus doesn't seem to be working. Some people feel that enactment of the draft can make up in quantity what they lose in quality."

Clifton eyed him narrowly, and Mattson wondered if he found his words as weak and hollow as they sounded to his own ears.

"Quality can't be replaced with quantity." said Clifton, "but, I suppose the greater the selection, the greater the opportunity to fill the need. The military today is highly specialized, but the basic soldier has always been the backbone of the military. That will never change."

"Well, that's exactly why I'm here, Major. To get the perspective of men like you. Men that have been a success, in both Military and private life. I believe you also served on the staff of General Sleighton?"

"That's correct." Clifton seemed to expand slightly at the mention of General Sleighton. His eyes swept quickly over the street and came back to Mattson. "I don't really have a lot of time, but I suppose I can give you a few minutes. Is that your car at the curb?"

Mattson glanced at the Toyota, suddenly aware of how bad it really looked, especially in this neighborhood. "Yes sir." An apology was evident in his voice.

Clifton studied it for a moment, nibbling at the inside of his lip, then, nodding to himself, he turned away. "All right, come in and we'll get started. I do wish you had called first. You were lucky to find me in. I'm usually at the office this time of the morning." He motioned Mattson to a chair while he took a seat by the window.

"I really should have called," agreed Mattson, "but I was in this area taking some pictures and I thought I'd take a chance."

"You're a photographer, too?" asked Clifton.

"Not a very good one," admitted Mattson. "My editor is thinking of doing a story on government waste and he sent me out to get some ideas. You know, on things like a new Stadium, or maybe those so-called 'noise abatement walls'. I did a story on them a long time ago and the public seemed to like it. I was getting a few pictures, just in case."

"I don't think I read it," said Clifton. "What did you say?"

"Oh, just general complaints about the way politicians waste our tax money. Actually I was just blowing off steam. I had been thinking about building a house, but when those walls started going up, so did the price of lumber…I guess I got carried away, but the public seemed to like it."

"Yes," said Clifton, looking out the window. "Too damned much money being spent on that foolishness." He turned back to Mattson. "Now then, where shall we start?"

Mattson frowned in spite of himself. He was hoping it was Clifton, who had called him, but the voice was not the same and his momentary interest appeared to be nothing more than polite chatter. "I suppose we should start with some background, sir. Could you tell me a few things about yourself?"

"Very well." Clifton's manner made it obvious that this was not his first interview. "I enlisted in the army in 1943, immediately after graduating from the University. That same year I received a commission as a Lieutenant and was assigned to duty in Europe. In 1946 I returned to the states. When the Korean conflict broke out I requested duty overseas and was reassigned to Seoul. It was there that I met General Sleighton and joined his staff. I remained with him until his death in 1973.

"Wow," Mattson laughed, as he jotted in his notebook. "You just covered thirty years in a couple of seconds."

"There was a lot more involved, of course," said Clifton. "I was merely giving you the highlights."

"Were you with General Sleighton in Viet Nam?" asked Mattson.

"We were in that area, off and on, for about three years," said Clifton.

"Off and on?" asked Mattson.

"General Sleghton's field," explained Clifton, "was essentially logistics and planning. Naturally this necessitated extensive travel between Washington and Viet Nam."

"Excuse me," said Mattson, looking up from his notebook. "I recall seeing a clipping of you and the General in Germany in about 1958."

Clifton nodded. "You must be referring to the General's inspection of 'Allied Defense Mobility Capabilities," Clifton smiled. "It seems that you already have a lot of background, Mr. Mattson."

"Not really, sir. It's pretty sketchy. Actually I don't know anything at all about your personal life. For example, is there a Mrs. Clifton? Are there any children?"

"I'm afraid the Second World War, followed by Korea and Viet Nam were not conducive to marriage and children for career officers. At least, not in my case."

"I think I know what you mean," said Mattson. "It's just that when I saw this house and the neighborhood, I thought..."

"This house belonged to my sister," said Clifton, curtly. "She died shortly after I retired."

"I'm sorry." Mattson flipped the page. "Well, I guess that takes us to the big question, sir. What is your feeling about a draft?"

"Mr. Mattson, I've been a military man all of my adult life. I have absolutely no reservations concerning the draft. I think every young man should be required to experience military service. It's a tremendous experience and it's an obligation young people owe to their country.

"Owe to the country, sir? You mean, from a patriotic sense?"

"Certainly," Clifton's mouth tightened. "Young people today have lost sight of what this country is all about. They have no idea of the sacrifices that have been made to keep this country great. If you went into a classroom today and asked someone to tell you about Stalin, they wouldn't have a clue as to whom you were talking about. To the generation today, the Second World War, Korea and Vietnam might just as well have been movies. They know less about their own history than they know about Star Wars."

Clifton seemed to be warming up. "An example can be found in our reserve forces," he continued. " Each year four million men and women in this country reach the age of eighteen, yet our military reserve is forced to operate with a constant deficit of nearly half a million. In a conflict of any duration we would find our combat forces over a million men short within the first ninety days."

"Those are pretty powerful statistics," said Mattson, scribbling on his pad. "What I don't understand, if your estimate is accurate, why hasn't Congress done something already. Why do they still insist that the military is up to strength?"

"Congress is filled with idiots, fools, and liars." said Clifton, in a flat, matter of fact, tone. "The Army and Marine Corps have never been up to acceptable strength for a full scale engagement. At one point, in an effort to maintain desired quotas, tests had to be downgraded across the board to accommodate high school students with a fifth grade reading level. The army is saturated with the poor, the uneducated, and minorities that have no other place to go"

"That paints a pretty bleak picture," observed Mattson.

"Of course, it's bleak," said Clifton. "When national defense depends on the least educated, when it depends on people who have no other place to go, it's damned bleak. If you add that to the number who quit…"

"Quit?" Mattson looked startled. "I don't understand. How do you quit? Are you talking about desertion?"

"The word 'desertion' is becoming lost to the Army's vocabulary." said Clifton. "Do you realize that, back in the eighties, seven out of ten volunteers gave up and went home before their first tour of duty was complete?"

"No, sir, I didn't realize that." Mattson made a note in his book. "I didn't think that they could."

"It's true," said Clifton. "These young punks today don't find the incentives offered by the military good enough for them. They'd rather sit in some damned cubicle and play with a computer. As a result, our reserve forces are dangerously depleted and the regular army has to depend on accommodation to maintain strength."

"By 'accommodation' you mean things like lowering standards?" asked Mattson.

"What else would you call it when enlistment requirements are downgraded, and drill Sergeants are turned into babysitters. How do we maintain discipline if a recruit, can simply declare himself gay, pack up and go home? My God, with the bonus and educational benefits offered, you'd think they'd be grateful." The more Clifton talked, the more irritated he became. He began chewing on his lower lip as he jerked off his glasses and began wiping them for a second time. Retired or not, Clifton was still one hundred percent military.

Mattson was taking everything Clifton said with a grain of salt. He nodded in agreement, and chose his words carefully. "I agree with you about the kids today. They just don't seem to give a damn, anymore.

61

Maybe a draft would turn them around. Are there any particular guide-lines you would like to see followed when it is reinstituted?"

The suggestion that the draft was a forgone conclusion, and the assumption that Mattson was in agreement, seemed to mollify Clifton. He replaced his glasses and almost smiled. "Rather than classify it simply as a military draft, I personally feel that there should be a compulsory program for national service, starting with those four million who turn eighteen each year. Those unable to qualify for the military should be diverted to other fields of public service."

Mattson's head snapped up at the mention of 'public service'. Was this the break he was looking for? Or was it just coincidence? "That sounds like a pretty big job," he said, "What about exemptions?"

Clifton considered the question for a moment, and then shook his head. "Except for absolute physical and mental disabilities there should be no exemptions. It's to everyone's benefit. Everyone should participate. It's disgraceful the way this country is falling apart, and there's absolutely no need for it.

"With all of the technology available do you think a massive army is necessary? I mean, with all of the 'smart missiles' nuclear weapons, and…"

"A strong standing army will never be replaced by 'smart' weapons," snapped Clifton.

"I think that was adequately proven during the Gulf War. Missiles, bombs and planes have their place, but as we learned in Desert Shield and Desert Storm, until the ground troops hit the beach there is no victory. You don't conquer an enemy by long distance. You conquer by occupation. Before long we'll find it necessary to engage in limited conflicts all through South America. Limited conflicts are not beyond our capabilities, but eventually this gas-guzzling society will also get us into another land war in the Middle East that will be more devastating than anything the world has ever known. Unless we are capable of launching and sustaining a massive offensive force we'll be backed into a nuclear corner. Without a strong conventional Army our only recourse for survival will be reliance on nuclear weapons."

"God, what a wacko!" thought Mattson. Aloud, he said, "I see your point, sir, but frankly, one of the first things the average man on the street is going to be concerned with is the cost. The price tag to train four-million people a year would be astronomical!"

"Naturally," said Clifton, contemptuously. "I would expect the man on the street to place a monetary limit on his survival." He took a deep breath and peered out the window, as though expecting someone. After a moment he turned around. "Mr. Mattson, they would not all be trained for the military. The infrastructure of this country is crumbling. Buildings are falling apart. Oil pipelines, the life-blood of this country, are rotting and bursting underground. Our medical system is in a shambles. Honored veterans lie forgotten and neglected, literally wasting away in hospitals and nursing homes because they can't get enough qualified people to care for them. The highway system in most of our states is an unending series of potholes.

Forest fires are consuming our national forests because we don't have the manpower to fight them..." Clifton snorted with contempt, "It's a disgrace."

"So you would use ..."

Clifton held up a hand to interrupt Mattson. "I would use the cream of the crop each year to replenish our military forces. The remainder would be trained to provide assistance in all the areas I have mentioned."

"I hate to belabor the point," said Mattson, and I totally agree with you, but again, I have to ask about the cost for something like this?"

"It's costing over half a billion dollars a year just to maintain tactical weapons in Europe. It's costing over four and one half billion to attract low caliber volunteers. The cost for making combat ready, those who turn eighteen each year, would cost a fraction of that figure."

"That would make one hell of an Army," agreed Mattson, "and it would certainly provide the manpower for the other things you mentioned, but how do you get the public to accept something like that?"

Clifton leaned forward, and stared directly into Mattson's eyes. His voice was little more than a whisper but the cold eyes and the intensity of the whisper sent shivers up Mattson's spine. "There will be no room for refusal. Mr. Mattson."

For the next ten minutes Clifton carried the conversation like he was talking to a class of junior officers. He threw figures out like a computer. In spite of himself, Mattson found his arguments convincing. He was impressed with Clifton's air of conviction. His command of statistics made it seem like they were glued to his fingertips.

"To sum up, Mr. Mattson, you may quote me as saying that I am in complete agreement with reinstating the draft. And the sooner the better. If it were brought back tomorrow, it would be a minimum of five years before we would even approach what I would consider an adequate Army."

"Five years? That's a long time, Major. Why should it take so long?" Mattson flipped a page of his notebook. "I mean, it's not as though we're starting from scratch. According to the Congressional records..."

"Mr. Mattson," Clifton broke in again, "As a reporter, I'm sure you're aware that there are some things known to the Military that is not available even to Congress."

"Boy, that's an understatement," thought Mattson, thinking of the Hedgerow papers. Aloud, he said, "Well, sure. I know the military has their share of secrets, but if things are as bad as you say, I don't know how they could keep Congress from knowing about it.

"It's not the best way," said Clifton, "but it's essential for security purposes." He stood up suddenly and went to the window where he peered out as he continued talking. "I'm afraid that informing some members of Congress would be tantamount to putting it on the prime time talk shows. The effect would be the same."

"But five years?" insisted Mattson.

"When I say five years, Mr. Mattson, "I am taking into consideration situations of which you are not even aware. For example: Russian strength. Even with the ostensible break- up of the   Soviet Union, their military is still estimated at six and a half million men. U.S military forces are placed at about two million. Russian tanks outnumber ours five to one. Our medical capabilities are not sufficient to meet combat needs, and our troops, which we say are the best in the world, are nothing more than a mob of deficient delinquents."

As he talked, Clifton became more agitated. He pulled his glasses off for the third time, glanced at them and pushed them back on his face. "I might add", he continued, "Strong national defense requires combat readiness on twenty-four hour notice. We cannot meet that requirement."

Mattson shifted nervously on the chair and scratched his forehead with the tip of his pencil.

"When you look at it that way," he said, "it looks like the Russians are missing the chance of a lifetime by not attacking us right now."

"The Russians don't start wars there is no hope of winning," snorted Clifton. "If they launched an attack at this time it would leave us no alternative but to retaliate with nuclear weapons. The losses would be incalculable on both sides. They prefer to wait until they have the capability to effectively neutralize our offensive weapons. When that day comes, I promise you, we damned well better be ready to defend our shores on a man-to-man basis."

You certainly make a convincing argument from the military standpoint," said Mattson, "but I don't think the public would understand the need for a compulsory national public service program. Do you really think they would accept something that drastic?"

Clifton's eyes flashed behind his glasses and Mattson saw his jaw muscles tighten. "When national survival is hanging in the balance, Mr. Mattson, I don't give a damn about public acceptance. We do what has to be done. Every citizen has an obligation to this country, and it's time they understood it." His eyes burned across the room, challenging the reporter.

Mattson shrugged as he flipped a page in the notebook and jotted down the last statement.

Clifton continued to glare for a moment, then apparently remembering that his remarks would likely become a matter of public record, his face softened and he lowered his voice. "Of course, I'd like there to be some other way, but what would it be, Mr. Mattson?"

He waited, but Mattson remained silent. Clifton attempted a smile, but it fell flat on his tight lips. "I think I should make it clear that there is a lot more at stake here than just the threat of military confrontations beyond our own shores. This country has been gorging itself for the past fifty years. Nature's storeroom is just about empty. New standards have to be set ... right across the board. The sooner people understand that, the better off they'll be."

"If you're referring to the oil situation," said Mattson, "I think we all realize…"

"It's not just the oil." said Clifton, "It involves every aspect of our lives as we know it today. The statistics speak for themselves."

"I'm not sure I follow you?"

Clifton sighed, dropped into his chair and brought his clasped hands up to his chin, thinking. After a minute he gazed up at Mattson like a teacher talking to a dull pupil.

"Let me put it this way. When we were a nation of only one hundred and fifty million people, back in the forties, between twelve and twenty million of those people were farmers. We not only had an abundance of food for this country, but our stockpiles supplied a major portion of the rest of the world. Those stockpiles are gone now, and so are the farmers. This country has shrunk to less than two and a half million privately owned farms. Most of those farms are forced to rely upon illegal aliens sneaking across the border to meet their production quotas. Why, in god's name should that be happening when we have a workforce of nearly two million able bodied men and women sitting in prison cells?"

"Are you suggesting that we put the prisoners out in the field?" asked Mattson

"Why not?" demanded Clifton. "As they are, these people are totally worthless. Their numbers should be utilized for a nationalized farming system and other projects that could benefit the country."

"Would something like that be legal," asked Mattson "It sounds a little like forced labor."

"It will have to be made legal." said Clifton firmly. "At the present time there is minimal government involvement in the farming industry and that should be expanded. When you consider that we are now dealing with a population of over three hundred million people there is no logical reason that those convicted of crimes against society should not be compelled to contribute their share."

That's an interesting thought," said Mattson, as he continued taking notes. "Many of the southern states have had prisoners in the cotton fields and chain-gangs working on the roads for years, but I wonder how the northern states would react?" He also wondered about the Constitution, but he thought it best not to mention it.

"I think it would be considerably better than simply turning dangerous prisoners loose on the streets, because they lack space and have no room to keep them." said Clifton. "I should also point out that a good portion of the farming industry of this country is under the control and management of giant corporations who not only grow the food, but also market, transport and set the price for the commodities they produce. It would be a small step for them to incorporate a prison workforce into that system. Over the years those giant food corporation have built a power structure as formidable as the oil industry."

"I've always held a sneaking suspicion that they were the same people," said Mattson, smiling, but serious.

"There is a definite crossover," admitted Clifton, "In the past seven years over fifty thousand independent gas station owners have been driven out of business through financial pressure from the oil companies. The process is identical to that used by supermarket chains to drive out small grocers and farmers." Clifton glanced at his watch. Mattson knew his time was running short. His main purpose in coming here was to find out if Clifton was the man that had warned him about Hedgerow. Unfortunately, he was now convinced that Clifton would be one of Hedgerow's strongest advocates.

"Well," said Mattson, "In summing up, I guess it would be safe to say that you are in favor of reinstituting a military draft and that it should be wrapped into a program for national public service. Is that your feeling, sir?"

"I think that's an over simplification," said Clifton, but essentially, it's accurate. I do think we are going to need a mandatory public service program. And we are going to need this country's absolute commitment to that program. American people are suffering from a blind spot and it's got to be corrected. We've known for years that there were going to be shortages, but the public has refused to cut back on their greed. They insist on bigger and heavier automobiles, central air conditioning and piped- in music with carpeted floors in supermarkets..." his voice trailed off and he raised his hands upward as though to say, "and who knows what else?"

"I can't argue with you there," said Mattson. "Some people think we've been marching backward for the past thirty years and calling it progress."

"Exactly," said Clifton, bobbing his head up and down. "And that march is coming to a crashing halt. It's time for the people to give something back."

Clifton looked at his watch again and stood up. "I'm afraid that's all the time that I have, Mr. Mattson. I hope some of the things I've said will be of help to you with your article?"

"You've given me a lot, sir, and I want to thank you." Mattson came to his feet. "I'm not sure what I should call you. "Mr. Clifton or Major?"

"My name will do just fine, "laughed Clifton. " I've been out of the military a long time."

Mattson nodded, sticking out his hand, "Well, thank you for talking to me. It's been more helpful than your know."

"No trouble at all," said Clifton, leading the way to the door and pulling it open.

He stood watching as Mattson went down the narrow sidewalk and climbed into the beat-up Toyota. He stood there until the engine ground to a start, then closed the door, and walked quickly into the kitchen where he picked up the telephone. It rang twice before someone on the other end answered.

"Saunders, here," said a voice in a clipped tone. "Who's calling?"

"This is Clifton, let me speak to Jacobs."

The line went dead, but a moment later another voice came on. "Yes, Colonel. This is Jacobs."

"Jacobs, I've just had a visit from a fellow named Mattson. He claims he works for the Capitol City News. Do we have any information on him?"

"Just a minute, sir, I'll check." The telephone went dead again, but in just over a minute the voice came back on the line. "Yes, sir. Mattson is a reporter for the Capitol City News. He's been with them for approximately eight and a half years. He came to our attention a few years ago because of a story he did on the sound barriers. Apparently his concern centered on what he considers a wasteful use of taxpayer's money."

"I'm familiar with the story," said Clifton. "What do we have on him personally?"

"He's Caucasian, Catholic, twenty-eight years old and, at the present time unmarried.

I think he's pretty much of a loner. He graduated from the University of Minnesota. After graduating, he tried to start a small neighborhood newspaper on the east side of St. Paul, but he couldn't keep it going. He's been working for Capitol City News ever since." The voice paused for a moment, and then continued. "We have a complete file on him, Colonel, but nothing subversive and no known connections or

72

affiliation with subversive groups. We've given him a class 'C' rating because of his article and his type of work, but don't feel that he requires special monitoring."

"He's working on another story about the barriers and I want to know how deep he intends to go." snapped Clifton, "Keep me informed on everything he writes."

"Yes sir."

Clifton, gnawing irritably at the inside of his lip, set the telephone back on the receiver. "Those damned reporters," he thought. "Why the hell do they always get involved and complicate things?" He made a mental note to talk to Berghoff about Mattson. There was something about that wimpy bastard that didn't seem right. Finally Clifton shrugged it off and walked into the bathroom. Berghoff would know how to handle him, he decided.

Chapter Six

When Benny left Harry's office at the Capitol City News he walked directly up Fourth Street. He stopped for a minute on the corner of Wabasha, waiting for the light, then dipped his head against the wind and ran the last half block to the entrance of the Courthouse. Inside, he found the lobby crowded with a tour of school children inspecting the gigantic marble statue of an Indian that dominated the huge room. The group of children brought back a fleeting memory of his own school days when he had taken this same tour, some twenty years earlier. Seeing the monstrous sculptured piece of marble for the first time, hearing its history and seeing it turn on its pedestal had been a tremendous experience. Ironically, now that his work brought him to the Courthouse nearly every day, he realized that he had forgotten its history and he seldom even noticed the statue anymore.

Skirting the children he made his way to the elevators. He would have been surprised if a group of people hadn't been standing there. From long experience he knew that by the time one elevator closed and left with one group of people, another group would be waiting when the next elevator opened its doors. When he first started coming here he had gotten into the habit of waiting. An invisible hand seemed to regulate courthouse transportation and never allowed half filled elevators to move. Now he simply squeezed in wherever he could.

Council meetings were held on the third floor. He managed to push the number as he got on, and when the doors opened a moment later he was surprised to see people milling around in the halls. By this time of the morning they should have been in the Council Chambers. Either a recess had been called, or something very unusual was happening. His eyes wandered over the crowd looking for his friend, Chuck Sauerly. He was about to give up when he finally saw him near the Chamber doors, talking to two other men. Both men were bobbing their heads in agreement with what he was saying, but neither man looked pleased. Benny moved forward until he was sure that Chuck had seen him, and then stopped. This would not be the best time to interrupt. He pulled a notebook from his pocket and pretended to write. In a few minutes, the conversation finished, Chuck broke away from the two men and came over. He walked with a swaggering 'I don't give a damn', attitude, swaying his wide shoulders as though they were hinged directly to his feet.

"Benny!" Chuck gave him a wide, big-toothed smile, and stuck out his hand. "I thought you were getting off this beat?"

"I'm doing double duty," said Benny, disgustedly, taking his friends hand. "Someone said there was some action up here today."

"Some action!" scoffed Chuck. "Do you know what those pea-brains are doing now?" Without waiting for Benny to answer, he continued. "They've hired an outside investigator to investigate the investigation!"

"Are you serious?" Benny laughed.

"I'm not shitting," said Chuck, angrily. Glancing around he suddenly saw

75

that people were looking at him and he lowered his voice. "They did it yesterday. That's why all these idiots are down here. He waved his arm, taking in the entire area.

"Two weeks ago they were ready to drop the whole thing," said Benny. "What the hell happened?"

Chuck shrugged. "They got a thorn up their ass because someone said we put a bug on a couple of them."

Chuck's words were said in such an off-handed way that it took Benny a minute to realize exactly what he was saying. "You What? "

Chuck shrugged again.

"Did you?" asked Benny. "No shit?"

"Fuck, we could have bugged the confessionals in the Cathedral and we wouldn't get this much heat. First they want us to investigate this liquor bullshit, and now they hire someone to investigate us."

"They must be worried about something," said Benny, "but, holy shit, bugging a city council member…?" his words trailed off.

"What's the big deal?" asked Chuck, really not understanding Benny's concern. "One of them's a coke-head… we been watching him before he was on the council. That broad that worked on the Mayor's staff… Shit, she has more baggage than Northwest. Hell, they all got something to hide."

"One of them is an ex-cop," reminded Benny

"Fuck, you think that gives him a free pass? I could tell you some shit about that guy that… Ah, screw it. They just damned well better be careful. Before this is over we just might have a few of them hanging by the balls."

"How much weight has the new investigator got?" asked Benny. "Is he taking over the whole show?"

Chuck swore softly and looked around the hall, his eyes narrowing as they landed on certain faces. "At two hundred and fifty bucks an hour, I'd say he is the show. Can you beat that? He brought his eyes back to Benny. "They're paying this guy about two grand a day for the next sixty days!" He shook his head in disgust and took Benny by the arm. "Do you have to stay here?"

"I'm just roving today," said Benny, "and you've already covered everything for me up here."

"Good," Chuck moved to the elevator, pulling him along. "Let's get some coffee or something. I've had enough of this crap for awhile."

Benny chuckled and they got on the elevator. They were both aware of the eyes that followed them. They rode the elevator to the basement and got their coffee out of a machine in the cafeteria. When they were seated, Chuck lit a cigarette and tilted back on his chair. "If I were you, Benny, I'd get on their ass about blowing all that money on the investigator just to make themselves look good. That's the kind of story that the people ought to get. That kind of money would put a couple more cops on the force."

"I can give it some ink," said Benny, "but what the hell good will it do? Look at the story we just covered about the tax money being wasted sending retarded kids to hospital psyche wards just because they have a behavior problem. We got over a thousand letters on that one, but they're still sending them there."

"That's different," said Chuck, dismissing it with a wave of his hand. "That's federal money. This investigator is digging right into your pocket. "Cluck flicked his ashes on the floor and took a sip of his coffee.

The statement was made lightly, but Benny knew that his friend Chuck was really worried about the investigation. He decided to change the subject and get to the real purpose for this meeting.

"They've got me doing another story on those damned freeway sound barriers. They're blowing millions of dollars on that shit. You think our screaming about it will do any good?"

Chuck gave him a strange look, and then set his cup down. "Same as the kids in the psyche wards." he shrugged. "It's federal money. Don't waste your time."

There was something in the off-handed way Chuck was attempting to dismiss the subject that clicked an alert button in Benny's brain. "Chuck, as far as I'm concerned, the money is the same whether it's state, county or federal. It's still out of our pockets." He made a few notes on a scrap of paper. "This story is going to be on government fraud, waste and corruption, so maybe I'll throw in something about this new investigation and the money the county is wasting. But, dammit, those walls are soaking up millions and they don't even make any sense.

Chuck shrugged. "So, some construction company is making dough. So what?" He finished his coffee and crunched the paper cup in his hand. "It's keeping a lot of people working. They're keeping a lot of poor slobs off the welfare rolls." He flipped the crumpled paper cup in the general direction of the wastebasket, missed, and ignored it. "Why all this sudden interest in the sound barriers?"

Benny took a sip of his coffee and shrugged. "Ever since Mattson wrote that series a few years ago, people have been complaining. It just hasn't died down. A lot of them seem to think it's some kind of conspiracy."

"A conspiracy?" Chuck perked up. "What kind of conspiracy?"

The single word created a reaction that was totally unexpected. It might only be the result of a policeman's mind at work, but Benny felt that he had touched something and he decided to pursue it. "Price gouging." Benny smiled, "Have you checked the price on lumber lately? A lousy eight foot 2x 4 costs damned near three bucks! Can you imagine what it cost to build a home today? A lot of people think it's just a way to artificially inflate the price of lumber. And, for what? To put up a bunch of wooden walls that nobody gives a shit about?"

At the mention of 2x4, Chuck laughed, took a last drag from his cigarette, dropped it on the floor and stepped on it. "You newspaper guys find a conspiracy in everything. Do you think the oil companies are in on it, too? Those cranes they use to raise the pilings must burn up a hell of a lot of fuel." He continued chuckling, "Maybe

79

even the cement people are in on it. I notice a lot of the new walls are made out of blocks."

"Go ahead," said Benny, sullenly, "make a joke out of it, but I'll tell you one thing. There's more behind those damned sound barriers than we're being told. Somebody's making a pile of dough, but there's more to it than just money and I'm going to find out what it is."

"Hey, take it easy, Benny." Chuck made a half-hearted attempt to pacify him.

"I don't think it's funny," said Benny. "People have a legitimate beef. They don't appreciate looking out their windows and seeing fifteen-foot walls going up in their back yards. They especially don't like having to pay for something they consider useless."

"And you guys figure a few stories in your paper is going to stop it, huh?" Chuck pulled another cigarette from his pack and lit it. An older blond haired woman with horn-rimmed glasses sitting across the room yelled something about this being 'a no smoking area', and Chuck glanced in her direction. He seemed about to say something to her, but caught himself, and simply muttered the word, 'bitch' under his breath as he turned his attention back to his friend. "Forget it, Benny. Those walls are federal, and they're here to stay. You're not going to change anything."

His smugness burned across Benny's nerves like a piece of coarse sandpaper. He couldn't be sure if Chuck was aware of the real purpose for the walls, but his attitude suggested that he knew more than he was saying. "What makes you so sure?" asked

Benny. "Newspapers have been changing the world for years. It's the power of the press."

"But in this case it's the power of the press fighting the power of the almighty dollar," snorted Chuck. "Believe me, the dollar is a lot more effective. Besides, this is too big."

Benny's heart took a sudden leap into his mouth. He leaned forward, not sure he had heard correctly. "What do you mean, too big?"

"Just what I said." Chuck laughed again, enjoying the way Benny was hanging on his every word. "Have you ever heard of the 'O.E.C.D'?" He asked.

"No," Benny shook his head. "What is it?"

"It's the 'Organization for Economic Cooperation and Development' said Chuck. "It's based in Paris."

"Paris?" Benny was confused. This was something that he hadn't been expecting. "What does some organization in Paris have to do with building sound barriers in Minnesota? Who the hell are they?"

"It's a think-tank full of egg-heads that sit around dreaming up ways to spend government money ... any government. Their latest kick is that we're running out of wildlife and our drinking water contains too many chemicals." Chuck grinned his toothy grin, obviously enjoying himself. "They even say that our agricultural land is decreasing too rapidly and they're trying to come up with a solution for that."

"I don't get it," said Benny. "How does that fit in with the sound barriers?"

"Damn it, you're not listening. Those egg-heads," he seemed to hiss the word, "have their fingers in everything." They're the ones that decided noise pollution was worse in this country than anywhere else in the world. Naturally, a lot of big shots and weirdo's in this country saw a golden opportunity. Presto, sound barriers!"

"How do you happen to know so much about this?" asked Benny. "You sound like you've just taken a course."

"If you really want some news, Benny, you should try watching television or reading a newspaper besides your own. You'll be amazed at what you can learn." Chuck glanced at his watch, and stood up suddenly. "Look, I've got to get back upstairs in case they call me. Are you doing anything tonight?"

"Nothing special," said Benny. "What you got in mind?"

"I thought we'd go out cruising for awhile. Maybe have a few drinks… see if there's any broads around?"

"Sounds good to me," said Benny. "I'll be home around seven. Give me a call and I'll meet you. Okay?"

"Will do," promised Chuck, walking to the door. "See you later."

Benny watched him out of sight, then walked to the machine and got another cup of coffee. He carried it back to his table and sat down. Pulling out his notebook he began writing down some of the highlights of their conversation while they were still fresh in his mind.

Chuck really hadn't said that much, but his remark about the Paris based organization was something worth checking. It would be a great excuse to stop at the library and see the little fox in the reference department again. She looked hot...it would be a good chance to ask her out. He should also stop back at the office. He wondered if Harry had turned up anything at the credit bureau. He thought about it for a moment, and then decided against doing either one.

Mattson would be able to handle anything that came in from the credit bureau and the librarian could wait. He probably wouldn't score with her, anyway. When he met with Chuck tonight he had to be on his toes. From experience he knew that Chuck, on his rare nights out, drank like a fish and expected his companions to do the same. He made a mental note to coat his stomach with buttermilk before he went to meet him.

The more he thought about their conversation, the more he thought he might be on to something. He had a feeling that his friend knew a lot more than he was saying. Chuck's story about the O.E.C.D. had been a little too pat. If something was mentioned on television it wasn't likely that he would have remembered it that well. Who in the hell remembers what they hear on television, unless they have a particular interest in the subject? It sounded more like a prepared statement. Something that Chuck had been instructed to say in case he was asked. Damn it, thought Benny, in sudden frustration, this damned thing is making me paranoid! He forced the thought from his mind. If Chuck did know something, maybe he would get drunk enough to talk about it. Putting the notebook back in his pocket he swallowed the rest of his coffee and dropped the empty cup into the trash barrel on his way out of the cafeteria.

Chapter Seven

The call from Chuck didn't come until nearly eight o'clock. He was at a bar on Rice Street, and from the sound of his voice he had started the party all by himself. At first, Benny considered begging off. Chuck could be wild when he was drunk. Then Benny realized that this was exactly what he wanted. When Chuck offered to pick him up, Benny agreed, and in fifteen minutes he was waiting outside when Chuck drove up, bouncing against the curb as he swung the car into a parking space. He was laughing, filled with unusually good humor, and though he was not what would be considered drunk at the moment, Benny suspected that he was not far from it. They began the evening bar hopping across the East Side, having one drink here, another there, and sometimes doing nothing more than taking a quick peek in the door.

"No women, no point wasting our money," laughed Chuck.

It might have been the weather, which was unseasonably cool and drizzling, or the fact that it was in the middle of the week, but it wasn't until almost midnight that they finally found what they were looking for. On the far East Side, almost in Woodbury, just off I-94, they pulled into the parking lot of a new Disco and found it packed. As they made their way to the door, Benny saw that there was a cover- charge, and reached for his wallet.

Chuck pushed past him, "Forget it, Benny, I'll take care of this."

Benny watched as he took out his wallet and flashed his badge at the bouncer.

The bouncer, a huge man towering over both of them, narrowed his eyes as he looked at them, dropped his eyes to the badge for a second time, and then stepped meekly aside.

Chuck grinned as he took Benny's arm and led the way inside. "Just one of the fringe benefits for being a cop," he laughed.

The huge barn-like structure was crowded, but they were able to get a drink at the bar and finally found a small table in the corner near the dance floor. "Can you beat this," said Chuck, "every joint in town is dying and in here they're packed like sardines.

"New joints always pack them in for the first few weeks," grunted Benny.

Chuck nodded, as his eyes darted around the darkened room. His left hand tapped lightly on the table, keeping time to the beat of the music. "The trouble with a place like this is that you never know what you pick up until the sun comes up." He had to shout over the sound of the music. "Man, you should see some of the dogs I've gone home with!"

At that moment a waitress passed by on her way to the bar. Chuck caught her by the arm. "Hey, honey, how about a little service here?" He grinned at her, his hand brushing lightly up and down her arm. The girl, a tall blond with eyes blackened by makeup, flashed her white teeth in a phony smile and pulled away. Without speaking she stood there, pen poised over her order pad, waiting.

"Two Hudson Bay," said Chuck, "no rocks." Then glancing at the crowd again, he said. "Better make it four; we might not get another chance."

The girl wrote the order and left. Chuck watched her walk away, almost leering, then turned to Benny, "Not bad, huh?"

"Shit," said Benny, "I don't think I can handle a double." He hated Hudson Bay, but he knew it was Chuck's favorite drink, and since Chuck was paying, he had been forcing them down.

"Sure you can," laughed Chuck. "It's late. We'll be lucky if she gets back with these." His eyes went back to the dance floor. "Fuck, with a crowd like this you'd expect to see a few single broads, wouldn't you? Where the hell are they?" Suddenly his eyes brightened and he stood up. "I'll be right back," he said walking over to another table. Two girls sat at the table. They looked up, smiling as Chuck approached. Benny watched him talk to them for a few minutes, then pull out a chair and sit down.

The waitress suddenly appeared with the four drinks. Benny glanced over at Chuck who was laughing like he had just heard the funniest joke in the world. He had completely forgotten him. Disgustedly, Benny reached into his pocket, pulled out a twenty-dollar bill and gave it to the waitress. She glanced at it with a bored look and walked away. He knew she wouldn't be back. Benny poured both of his drinks into one glass and sat silently sipping, wishing he had remembered to drink the buttermilk. He had only had three drinks before this, but he was beginning to feel them.

In a few minutes Chuck returned, looking less happy than when he had left.

"Both bitches are married, "he complained, bitterly. "What the fuck are they doing in here?" Then suddenly he grinned. "You picked a hell of a night, Benny."

"I didn't pick it," said Benny. "You did."

"Well, it's still a horseshit night." He looked across the table at Benny. "Thanks for the drink."

Benny nodded, without speaking.

"What the hell's the matter with you tonight? asked Chuck, "You're not even drinking." He took a long swallow from his own glass.

"It's just one of those nights," said Benny, making small circles on the table with the bottom of his glass. "I guess it's that damned story that I'm working on. I'm supposed to do some kind of follow-up on what Mattson wrote, but I don't know where the hell to start."

"You mean that crap you were talking about this morning?"

"It's not crap, Chuck. It could be a damned good story. Something the public will really lap up. I just wish I could get more information on how those walls got started in the first place."

"I already told you," Chuck grinned at him. "The O.E.C.D, in Paris."

"I know what you told me," said Benny. "I'm checking on it. I just think there's more to it than that." He was beginning to feel reckless. He took a long swallow from his glass, and decided to take a chance. If Chuck did know something, he had to find out. "You know something,

Chuck. I think maybe it doesn't have anything to do with noise at all.

"You're drunk," said Chuck, dismissing him with a wave of his hand. "Come on; let's see if we can find some broads." He started to stand up, then seeing that Benny was not moving, just sitting there brooding, he sat back down. "Look, Benny. You've got to get off of this kick. Forget the story. Write about something else. This is none of your business."

"None of my business?" stormed Benny, pretending to be more drunk than he actually was "What the hell is that supposed to mean? Of course it's my business. I'm a reporter. It's my business to make it everybody's business. Some of those walls look like their building a fucking prison!"

Chuck drained his first glass, pushed it away and pulled the second one closer to him. He studied Benny across the table, but said nothing. The humor was gone from his eyes, and Benny thought that somehow he seemed less intoxicated now than he had been just a few minutes earlier.

"Don't look at me like that," said Benny. "The last time I saw walls like that they were in East Germany. Did they have a lot of noise over there, too?" He made a show out of taking another drink, slopped it on his shirt, and grinned, as he leaned forward conspiratorially. "Tell me the truth, Chuck. What's really going on?"

"You're getting squirrelly," said Chuck, "nothings going on." He leaned forward, suddenly, and grabbed Benny's arm. "Listen, Benny. I'm your friend. Leave it alone. This is over your head."

"Over my head? Shit, Chuck, I'm a reporter…I've got a right to know what's going on."

"You have A Right?" Chuck tilted back on his chair, gave a disgusted grunt, and grabbed his drink. "You figure you got rights?" He gave a humorless laugh, "Shit, you could get busted tonight and if we didn't want you found for a week, no one would find you. When we were finished we'd let you go, and if you got a lawyer and complained… fuck it. We'd apologize and do it again next week. That's your fucking right!" Chuck pulled a pack of cigarettes from his shirt pocket and lit one. Blowing the smoke across the table, his face grew cold, no longer the least affected by alcohol. "We've been friends a long time, Benny. I'm telling you now, for your own good, keep away from this thing. It's bigger than you think, and it'll suck you up like a piece of spaghetti." It was out in the open now. The need for pretense was over. They stared at each other across the table until Chuck finally looked away.

"You think it's too big to be stopped?" asked Benny

"What is it you want to stop?" asked Chuck

"I'm going to level with you," said Benny. "I read some papers that said those walls were being built for crowd control."

"So?" There was no surprise in Chuck's voice or face.

. "So, I want to know if it's true?" said Benny. His head had a distinct buzz, and he silently cursed himself for drinking so much

"Why come to me?" asked Chuck.

"Because the State Crime Bureau was specifically mentioned," lied Benny. "And because I figured if anyone would tell me the truth, you would."

"Where did you get the papers?" asked Chuck.

"What the hell difference does that make?" said Benny. "Is it true of not?"

Chuck didn't answer immediately. He sat his cigarette in the ashtray, picked up his drink and sipped at it while he studied Benny across the table.

"Well?" asked Benny.

"Benny, have you ever been in a riot? Have you ever covered one for your paper?"

"No." Benny shook his head.

"Well, I have, pal. I've been in three of them. In the last one I saw a cop get a busted back from a guy with a car jack. A little while later another cop had the top of his head blown away by a guy sitting on a roof. We never did get that son-of-a-bitch because three hundred college kids were rushing thirty of us with baseball bats."

"What are you trying to tell me?" asked Benny. "I'm sorry about those cops, but doesn't that go with the territory?"

"It goes with the territory," admitted Chuck, "but I'm telling you those two guys got the shitty end of the stick. I'm telling you that it's time we have a way to keep a Saturday night brawl from turning into a civil war against the police force."

"And you're telling me that the way to do it is by locking up the whole fucking city, is that it?"

"I didn't say that," protested Chuck. "Nobody intends to lock anything up. We're just looking for ways to keep riots from spreading out of the area they start in. What the hell is wrong with that?"

"You don't really expect me to believe it's going to stop there, do you?" asked Benny.

"What do you mean?"

"Well, for starters, I don't see the government pouring millions of dollars into a hunch. What makes them so certain that we're going to have riots so big that we need walls to control them? Why aren't they using the money to prevent them in the first place?"

"Benny, do you have any idea how many gangs and groups there are in this country that do nothing but sit around thinking up ways to fuck us up?"

"Oh, bullshit," snorted Benny. "If things are that bad, why aren't they telling the people the truth about the walls? I'll tell you why." Because they know damned well we'd stop it."

"Who's going to stop it?" asked Chuck, "those monkeys out there?" He gestured toward the dance floor with his glass. "The only thing they give a shit about is getting laid tonight and finding a gallon of gas tomorrow. And they probably won't get either one." He laughed as he finished off his drink and looked around for the waitress.

"Better take this one," said Benny, sliding his own glass across the table. "It's too late to order again."

Chuck picked up the glass and drained it. "We should have started earlier," he grumbled.

"I've got a bottle at the house," said Benny. "

Chuck thought about it, and then shook his head. "Nah, I guess I've had enough. I've got an early day tomorrow." He pulled a five-dollar bill from his pocket and dropped it on the table for a tip. "Let's get out of here."

Back in the car they rode in silence. The night had been bad from the start, but the conversation about the sound barriers had finished it. The cold air and the rain spattering against the windshield did nothing to lift their spirits. As they were nearing Benny's street, a car suddenly shot out from the curb, its wheels screeching. The car swerved, righted itself, and roared down the street. Chuck swore, but made no attempt to follow. Instead, he turned to Benny. "I don't suppose I can talk you into dropping the story?"

"I don't know why you would want to," said Benny. "If there's nothing to hide, what difference does it make?"

"I just don't like getting caught in the middle, that's all."

They reached Benny's building and Chuck pulled to the curb. He switched off the lights but kept the motor running. "About six months ago," he said, "eight of us were given a special briefing by some ass-hole from Washington. I don't know

93

who he was, but he had enough authority to keep even the big shots hopping while he was here."

"What was the briefing?" asked Benny

Chuck leaned forward and turned the key, cutting the motor. "It was weird. He talked to each one of us separately. His name was Jacobs, and he said he wanted to meet personally because we would probably be working together in the future." Chuck took out a cigarette and lit it. "I couldn't figure it out. I know all the Fed's, around here, and he wasn't one of them. He seemed more like the Military. The bastard walked like he had a broom stuck up his ass."

"Did he mention the walls?" asked Benny.

"Not directly." Chuck took a long drag, inhaled deeply and held it as he flicked the ashes out the window. "He just said there was definite information that certain groups were making preparation to instigate full scale riots here in the mid-west, and the government was taking appropriate measures to counter them. He told us our police defense measures were inadequate and that advanced riot control training would be stepped up. He said they would be putting less emphasis on putting down the riot, and a lot more on keeping it bottled up."

"Any specifics on how they intend to do that?" asked Benny,

"All right," growled Chuck, irritably. "If you want specifics, here is exactly what he said. 'Were not taking any more shit from the militant son-of-a-bitches. And we're not wasting any more good cops. If they want to burn up their neighborhoods, we'll let them do it. We'll even give them the matches, but the bastards will be in it when it goes up'. Is that what you wanted to hear?" he asked Benny.

"Is that what he said?"

"Those were his exact words," said Chuck. "Then he told me that eight of us had been selected for advanced special training. I'm supposed to leave for some place in West Virginia next week.

"Maybe you'll come back as a Commissar," said Benny, glumly.

"I only saw the guy once," said Chuck, ignoring the remark, "but I'll tell you something. After he left, the department started operating under a set of standards so damned rigid that Internal Affairs is called in for everything. Suspensions are passed out like popcorn. God help the cop that..." Chuck stopped suddenly, flipped out his cigarette and rolled up the window.

"What were you going to say?" asked Benny.

"It doesn't matter." Chuck shook his head. "The point is, we've always been a quasi-military organization, but lately it seems like I'm back in boot camp. Damn it, discipline is so strict that even I'm afraid to question anything." He half turned in his seat, facing Benny.

"Benny, I honestly don't know what the hell is going on. I've got three years to go for retirement and they're sending me to Virginia for special training... does that make sense? Why don't they send some younger guy? Someone that's going to be around for awhile?"

"Did you ask them?"

"Of course, I asked them," snapped Chuck. "They just said I was qualified and that was the end of it." He turned again in his seat, facing the front, and put his hands on the steering wheel staring out the window. "I want to get the hell out, damn it!" He turned again to look at Benny. "Do you know I'll be getting almost as much in retirement as I get now? In the past few years they've come up with a retirement package that's un-believable. It's almost like they're trying to buy us older guys out of the service. So why in the hell are they giving me special training?"

"Maybe it's because of your military record?" offered Benny. He knew Chuck had served in Special Forces and had a stack of medals.

"Nah," Chuck brushed it off with a wave of his hand. "That shit's over."

"You're still in the Reserves, aren't you?" persisted Benny

"Yeah," Chuck nodded, "but that's just bullshit." He took a deep breath and exhaled as though it were an effort. "Look, Benny, What I'm trying to say is, I know something is going on, but I don't want to get involved. I've got three years left and I don't need the hassle."

"You think I'd blow the whistle on you?" asked Benny.

"No, I know you wouldn't, Benny, but I might do it to myself. Do you know they started giving us random lie detector tests in the department?"

"I never knew that," said Benny. "How often? Is that legal?"

"It is, if you want to keep your job. Anytime they doubt your word about something they can order the test. Sometimes the commander will order it just from spite. The way things are going you never know what's going to happen. It's different with you, Benny. You're always looking under rugs and in back alleys, trying to dig up something. You enjoy that. I guess your job depends on stirring up a lot of bullshit. My job depends on not stirring it up."

Benny said nothing and Chuck took a deep breath, almost in resignation. "That's why I'm going to forget that we ever had this conversation. If you want to keep digging, that's your business, but until it's over, one way or the other, just treat me like any other cop. No special favors, okay?"

Benny shrugged. "I can't drop it, Chuck."

"I think you're in way over your head, pal, but that's your business." He held out his hand. "No hard feelings?"

"No hard feelings," agreed Benny, taking his hand.

"Okay," Chuck leaned forward and switched on the ignition. "One other thing, Benny. Be careful who you talk to. They're getting so many new young cops that it's almost like they're cloning them. And they're tough, Benny. They aren't like the cops in the old days. They aren't out to make friends with the neighbors. Drive by some morning when they're lined up outside and you'll see what I mean." Chuck turned and looked at Benny, as though he wanted to add something, but he stopped himself, shook his head, and said simply, "I've got to get going."

"You bet." Benny opened the door, and stepped out of the car. "Thanks, Chuck." He shut the door and stood waiting, watching as his friend pulled the car from the curb and drove slowly down the street.

Chapter Eight

The next morning Mattson and Harry were already waiting in the office when Benny arrived. He smiled sheepishly as he closed the door and crossed the room to the coffee pot. "Had a tough night," he said. "I overslept." His hand trembled slightly as he filled a mug.

"I wish I was still young enough to survive nights like that," observed Harry, seeing the bloodshot eyes of the young reporter.

"I was out with Chuck Sauerly," explained Benny. Making his way to the sofa, he sat down, sipping at the hot coffee. "Believe it or not, I didn't have that much to drink. I just couldn't get to sleep when I got home."

"Sauerly's the cop, isn't he?" asked Mattson.

Benny nodded. "We had a pretty good talk." He told them about his conversation with Chuck.

"You figure he was telling you the truth?" asked Mattson.

"I'm sure he was," said Benny. "Actually, I was surprised that he opened up as much as he did. He kept telling me to get off of it, but I got the feeling he really would like to see something done. He just doesn't want to be involved himself."

"Nobody wants to risk losing a pension," said Harry. "It's not easy throwing a big part of your life down the drain." He had been standing at the window. He left it now, crossed the room and opened the door.

He stood there for a minute looking out. Then shaking his head, he closed the door and went back to his desk.

Mattson and Benny looked at each other, and then at Harry. "What the hell was that for?" asked Mattson.

"I don't know," Harry seemed confused. He waved his hands in the air, shaking his head. "Since this thing started I've just had a bad feeling, I don't know what the hell I'm doing lately."

Mattson turned to Benny. "You intend to talk to him again?"

It took Benny a minute to realize that he was talking about Chuck. He shook his head. "Not for awhile." He said. "Chuck's been a cop a long time. You been a cop as long as he has, you get a tendency to look the other way when your pension's involved." He tried to sip at his coffee, but it was still too hot. "I don't want to press him. I was glad he said as much as he did. At least we know now that something is really going on. Maybe when he gets back from Virginia I can talk to him again." His eyes went from Harry to Mattson. "What about you guys? You come up with anything from the Credit Bureau?"

"We found out about Clifton," said Harry. "Mattson went out to see him."

"You did?" Benny stared at him, "What happened?"

"Nothing much." Mattson shrugged. "The guy's a nut on the Military. You've heard about hawks? Well, this guy would swallow one. That might be the reason he's not in the service now. He might have been too much even for them. He sure as hell isn't the one giving me information."

"You think maybe he's involved in this as a civilian?" asked Benny.

"Maybe," said Mattson, without enthusiasm.

"I've been doing a little research of my own," said Harry. "I read that most of the police departments in the country are under pressure during riots because of poor equipment. In some situations, they've actually been out-gunned. You remember that shoot-out in L.A. a few years ago?"

"Yeah," said Benny, "I remember that. A couple of bank robbers. They had so much fire power the cops couldn't do anything except hide behind their cars."

"They knew it was coming," said Harry. "It's been coming for years. In fact, it was so bad, back in the late sixties, that they tried to get M-16 rifles issued right here in St. Paul."

"What?" Mattson's laugh was uneasy. "That's crazy. In the sixties people were bitching about the cops using dogs to patrol the streets. They used them up on Selby and Dale and a few people got bitten. They sued the hell out of the city. How could they seriously expect to get an M-16?"

"Never the less," insisted Harry, "the cops asked for them and they damned near got them. They were even on back- order. And," his eyes narrowed, "that was a long time ago."

"I believe it," said Benny. "That was about the time that cop got ambushed up there. Someone made a phony call for help and when the cop showed up, they nailed him in the back with a shotgun. That was really the first time anyone really went after the cops." He shrugged his shoulders and took a gulp from his cup. "We have to face the fact that times are changing. God knows what they have in their arsenal now, but if I were a cop, I'd want everything I could get. There's a hell of a lot of sick bastards out there today".

We use to bitch about the Chinese and the Russians holding life so cheap," grumbled Harry, "but we're not a damned bit better. Like it or not, this country promotes violence. We abort babies; we execute criminals... why are we surprised when they start shooting cops? Hell, we're not even honest about it. We don't hit babies...we 'spank' them. We don't say the old man kicked the shit out of his kid. We say, 'he took him out behind the woodshed'. If we can't use our brain to make someone do something ... we use our fist. Face it; from the cradle to the grave, we live with violence."

"I'm not for spanking kids," grinned Mattson, "but it's not the same as going after a demonstrator with an M-16."

"You're missing the point, said Harry. "It's not the weapon; it's the insane thinking behind the weapon."

Benny's coffee had cooled and he walked over to refill it. "I think you're right, Harry. We've turned into a violent society. And it started when I was growing up. Remember that guy, Fob James, or James Fob, or whatever the hell his name was."

"You mean the guy that was Governor of Alabama?" asked Harry.

"That's the one." Benny carried his coffee back to the sofa and sat down. "Remember when he told the independent truck drivers to arm themselves against striking truckers? He said, 'it's time to put the Billy back into the Billy-stick. I'd put a shotgun beside me and go, and I'd kill anybody that tried to stop me!' Benny spread his hands, "Now what kind of statement is that for a Governor to make?"

"That was a long time ago," said Mattson. "A lot of the truckers were hot. They were losing a lot of money."

"So what the hell do we have the police for?" asked Benny

"They couldn't handle it," said Harry. "It was too widespread."

"Which brings us right back to where we are now," said Mattson. "Call in the Army."

They sat for a few minutes without anyone saying anything. Finally Harry coughed, breaking the silence. "You know, this reminds me of something I heard when President Reagan was in office." He looked at the two reporters, making sure he had their attention. They were both watching him, waiting. "I guess he made a comment to someone one day that, 'Morning is finally here.' One of his aides responded with, 'It's not morning, Mr. President. It's Midnight and it's getting darker by the minute'. Harry smiled, "I think that pretty well sums up our situation.

Tearing a sheet of paper from a pad on his desk, he passed it to Mattson. "Walls or no walls, we still have a paper to put out. The bus company is going to raise the rates again. I want you to go out to the high-rise on Hamline Avenue and talk to a few senior citizens. See how they feel about it. Besides, if anyone is watching you it may help to throw them off the track."

"I can tell you how they feel about it", snorted Mattson, pulling himself back to the present. "When Regan was elected we had three ex-presidents that put in a total of twelve years work. For those twelve years, they were each guaranteed about a million bucks a year for the rest of their lives. That was about the same time the bus company decided to start charging senior citizens for their rides. The only thing that increasing the rates will accomplish is that this winter those old people won't have enough money to even ride the bus."

"Do they really get that much?" asked Benny, "ex-presidents, I mean?"

"Figure it out yourself," said Mattson. "They get a retirement fund, an office fund, a special fund for re-adjustment to private life, Secret Service agents to run errands, and usually pensions for the time they spent in Congress and the Military. I don't know what else there is, but you can bet your ass that isn't the end of it."

"Not a bad haul," laughed Benny. "Maybe I should run for office?"

"What pisses me off," said Mattson, "is that the average guy on the street can work his ass off for thirty years. When it's over they give him a pat on the back and send him on his way.

He's lucky if can he pay for his food and rent. When it gets a little tough on politicians they just vote themselves another pay raise." Mattson began walking to the door, but Harry stopped him with a wave of his hand. "Come back here, Ron. I've got something else." He pulled a newspaper from a basket on his desk. "This was in the Press this morning. Either of you read it?"

Both men shook their heads.

"I think it's something that might fit in with this 'Hedgerow' thing. Apparently the Corrections Department wants to refurbish all of the county jails in this state. They claim it will cost about a hundred and ten million."

Benny puckered his lips and let out a low whistle. "They were just complaining about the ten million dollar cost over-run on the new prison. What's all this crap about jails lately?"

"The commissioner said it's a critical problem and has to be dealt with." said Harry.

"That's not all he said," cut in Mattson, as he looked at the paper. "He claims that 'if we don't act, someone else will'. Listen to this, 'federal courts have taken over state prisons in at least a dozen states because of antiquated facilities, overcrowding, inadequate staff, and inhumane living conditions.' Mattson gave the paper to Benny.

"Can they do that?" asked Benny. "I mean just come in and take over?"

"It fits with what you told us about Chuck," said Harry. "They said that they would be coordinating local law enforcement agencies. That must include the correction department as well."

"According to this," said Benny, looking at the newspaper, "The commissioner said he hopes the Governor and the Legislature will take a look at whether the state should take a more active role in the jail improvement business, and at what is politically salable. He suggested a fourteen year jail re-construction program."

"They're laying it right out in the open," Said Mattson. "You just have to know what to look for. A lot of cells can be put together in fourteen years."

"The public really wants the jails." Said Harry. "They just don't want the cost. If we didn't know about Hedgerow, we'd be the same way. You know that, Ron."

"The trouble is, we do know about Hedgerow."

'They don't have to know anything to be concerned," piped in Benny. "All they have to do is listen. I caught the Energy Secretary on television last night. He said this country is going to have to get used to discipline, social control and sacrifice… what does that tell you?"

"I heard him," said Harry, but the statement was too general. When the government talks about social control and discipline, most people don't think it's something that will affect them personally."

"Usually," said Mattson, "those statements are made just to gage public reaction. They test the ground to see how far they can go with something. If public opposition doesn't hit a ten on the scale, they all climb on the band wagon."

"I just don't understand why the public lets something like that slip by?" said

Benny. "Anytime a politician even mentions 'social control' they should grab him by the collar and make him explain just what the hell he means."

Harry shrugged. "The only part of his statement that the public heard was the word, 'sacrifice'. They figure they're already doing that, with the gas situation. Besides, you'd be surprised how quickly people adjust. I can remember when we used to get mad if we had to stand in line for something. Today you can walk into any supermarket and see how quickly we've learned to accept it."

Mattson walked to the door again. "I'll see you later. I've got to run home for a minute and then I'll go out to the high-rise and talk to a few seniors about the bus company." Harry and Benny, still intent on their conversation, hardly noticed his leaving.

Chapter Nine

The telephone was ringing as Mattson opened the door to his apartment. Flipping his

Jacket on a chair, he kicked the door shut behind him and picked it up. "Hello?"

"Ron," said a now familiar voice, "do you know who this is?"

"Yeah," said Mattson, feeling a rush in his blood. "I was hoping you would call. Are you still in Washington?"

"No, I'm here in St. Paul. I'm at the Kelly Inn on Rice Street. Can you meet me?"

"Hell, yes," said Mattson. "Who do I ask for?"

"Just come to room 423. I'll be waiting for you."

The Kelly Inn was on the other side of the Cathedral, just across I-94. It was well within walking distance, but the Marion Street Bridge was closed for repairs. Mattson grabbed his jacket and raced down the stairs to his Toyota. He checked the rear view mirror for traffic, then made a quick U-turn from the curb. Five minutes later he pulled into the parking lot of the hotel and came to a stop in a parking space in front of the Rice street entrance.

The lobby was nearly empty when he stepped on the elevator and pushed the button for the fourth floor. When the elevator doors slid open he glanced at the sign on the wall, turned to the right and walked quickly down the hall to room 423.

The door opened on his first knock and he found himself facing a tall lanky man with short blond hair in a rumpled suit and stubble of beard on his blotched face. He appeared to be in his early thirties.

"You didn't waste any time getting here." He said,

"We're only a few blocks from my apartment." said Mattson.

"I know," the man nodded, and closed the door. "That's why I came here. We don't have much time."

Mattson dropped into a chair by the window and studied him. "Now that I'm here, don't you think it's about time that I know your name?"

The man hesitated, and then shrugged. "Call me, Paul." And then, "You think I'm being overly cautious?"

"You know more about it than I do," said Mattson

Paul nodded and sat on the edge cf one of the two large beds in the room. "Have you done anything with the material I gave you?"

"Not yet," said Mattson. "I've talked to my boss and we're still checking on it. Did you have any luck in Washington?"

"More than I hoped for," said Paul. He stood up and went to the closet. Bringing out a large brown briefcase, he unzipped it, pulled out a four inch thick leather bound manual, and   dropped it on the bed. "This is called, 'Operation Lock-Down'. It's a synopsis of the Hedgerow Project."

"A synopsis?" Mattson stared at the book. "How the hell much is there?"

"This book comprises eighteen years of extensive research and preparation. It contains two thousand pages. Before editing it was close to thirty-thousand."

"My god!" gasped Mattson. Are you telling me the sound barriers take up that much space?"

"No," Paul shook his head. "Those walls are only a part the Hedgerow Project".

Paul went back to the closet and brought out a small digital camcorder, and a package of cartridges. He set them next to the book, "We have one problem," he told Mattson.

"What's that?"

"This book has to be back in the file by Monday morning. If they find it missing it will lead directly to me."

Mattson pulled a pack of cigarettes from his pocket and lit one. He took a long drag, blew the smoke out slowly, and considered the book on the bed. "Where do we start?"

"We photograph everything," said Paul. "As we go along I'll try to answer any questions that you have.

"Do the pages come out?" Mattson looked at the leather bound book with skepticism. "Can we take them out?"

"Sorry," Paul shook his head. "Each page is sealed."

"What about the pages you already gave me?"

"Those were made from photographs. I was nearly caught taking those pictures. That's when I decided it would be safer to take the whole book."

Mattson looked at the book, shook his head, doubtfully, and then shrugged as he shook himself out of his jacket. He dropped it on the floor next to his chair, and leaned over to pick up the camera. It was a Sony Digital 8 Handy cam, with a 450 digital zoom. More than enough for what was needed, he decided.

"You already have the first twelve pages," said Paul. "We can start with thirteen." He saw the ash hanging from the end of Mattson's cigarette, and went into the bathroom. A moment later he emerged with a soap dish in his hand. "Sorry, Ron, we don't have ashtrays." He gave it to Mattson. "You said you were going to check those papers," he said, "how will you do that?"

Mattson set the camera back on the bed and crushed out his cigarette as he put the soap dish on the desk next to the television. "My editor and another reporter ran a check on a few of the names that were mentioned. We found out that General Sleighton is dead and that his aide, Major Clifton lives here in Minnesota, right out in Edina."

"I could have told you that," said Paul.

"Frankly", said Mattson, "we weren't all that sure about you. Anyway, I went out to see Clifton."

"You talked to him?" Paul's voice seemed to crack and he turned slightly pale. "What did you say to him?"

Mattson shrugged and recounted his conversation with Clifton. As he talked he was surprised at the concern growing on Paul's face. "What's wrong?" he asked.

"Was that all that was said?" demanded Paul

"As near as I can remember," said Mattson. "I could check my notes."

Shaking his head in obvious displeasure, Paul walked to the closet and brought out his suitcase. For a minute Mattson thought that he might be leaving, but he only set it on the floor, opened it and took out a bottle of Vodka. Without speaking he carried the bottle to the dresser where he tore a fresh glass out of its paper wrapper. Still without speaking, he poured a shot in the glass and gulped it down.

"What's the difference?" asked Mattson. "Clifton's retired. He's got a real estate office in Minneapolis."

Paul poured another shot into the glass and sat down on the bed, cupping it in his hands. "The difference," he said quietly, "is that when General Sleighton died, they decided to step up the Hedgerow Project. Clifton's knowledge was invaluable. He was promoted to Colonel and transferred to a special domestic intelligence unit spearheading Hedgerow. His retirement was nothing but a cover. You," he gestured with the glass to Mattson, "have just had a conversation with the top military man in Minnesota." Paul brought the glass to his lips and took another sip.

"You're joking!"

Paul held the Vodka in his mouth for a minute before swallowing. He didn't bother to answer. "Shit," Mattson grumbled, disgustedly. "You think I've blown it?"

"It sure as hell doesn't help," grunted Paul. "Have you seen anyone following you?

Any strangers hanging around?"

Mattson shook his head. "I haven't noticed anyone." He was totally deflated. His voice was barely a whisper.

"Nothing we can do about it now," said Paul. "It's my fault, I should have warned you." The Vodka was beginning to hit his blood stream and he could feel its soothing effect. "Clifton is sharp," he said, "but he has no way of putting you and this report together. How much did you actually say about the barriers?"

"We hardly mentioned them." said Mattson. "He's so hung up on getting the draft restored…"

"What do mean, getting the draft restored?" He gave Mattson a strange look. "Clifton doesn't want a draft. Hell, restoring the draft is the last thing he wants."

"No," Mattson shook his head, firmly. "He's all for a draft. Shit, you should have heard him."

Paul shook his head in exasperation. He opened his mouth to say something, then caught himself and took a deep breath. "Let me read you something." He picked up the book, thumbed quickly through it and began reading. "U.S. military forces have been substantially reduced- from a total of 3.3 million personnel in 1989 to 2.7 million in 1994. The Department of Defense plans to further reduce its forces to 2.4 million by the end of 1997."

Paul set the book back on the bed. "Why would they want to institute a draft when they have been intentionally downsizing our forces? I'm sorry, Ron, but Clifton was playing you."

"That son-of-a-bitch!" Mattson's eyes flashed. "And I lapped it up."

"It's not your fault", said Paul. "There are things I should have told you. Let me try to run this down for you real quick." Paul pulled a pair of wire-rimmed glasses from his shirt pocket and slipped them on. "Colonel Clifton is assigned to a special part of the military that is completely separate from all other branches. It's called USORSC. It stands for, 'United States Ordinance Resource and Strategy Command'. "Think of it as you would the Allied High Command in World War Two. They run the entire Hedgerow operation. They coordinate activities between the Military and the individual states, and they supply everything from monetary funding to military hardware and personnel."

Paul opened the book. "Next, you have what they call, 'DOC's'. These are the individual Departments of Correction in each state. Collectively they are called, US DOCs. Individually they are known as DOC, followed by the abbreviated name of the state. For example, Minnesota would be 'DOCMN'. Are you following me?"

"I'm getting the general drift," said Mattson

Paul nodded. "These are not what you normally think of when you hear 'Department of Correction', he said. "These organizations are being put together to coordinate activities between local police and military units during civil disorders. They include civic leaders, politicians, and even religious leaders. They have CEOs from some of the largest corporations. There are teachers, health care representatives…" Paul spread his hands in a gesture of completeness. "You name it, they have it."

"And those people agree with this?"

"They only have a small part of the picture," said Paul. "They see this country falling apart. They see the number of street gangs rising. Terrorists are behind every tree. They want to make America safe and they think this is a way to do it. Specialists in psychological warfare have been assigned to convince them we're on the verge of a massive public rebellion. In short, the government is scaring the shit out of them."

Paul thumbed through the book "Let me show you how this thing works." He began reading. "Each state will be responsible for training their DOC forces in basic service skills, such as infantry, armor, and aviation so that they can be integrated with other forces in other states in joint exercises and operations'. Just think of these DOC forces as a private army," said Paul. "They operate much like the National Guard, but the pay is a hell of a lot better and they are sworn to absolute secrecy." Paul began reading again.

'In defining specific responsibilities, the Chairman has designated the Operational Plans and Interoperability Directorate to USORSC as the joint training focal point. The Chairman also assigned certain responsibilities to the Joint Pacification Center.' Paul stopped reading for a second and said, "I was at the Center earlier today. That's where I got this book. The Pacification Center is a Washington

115

'think tank'. It's the control center for the Hedgerow Project. When problems come up, they provide the solution. They control situations."

"What kind of situations?" asked Mattson. "How do they control them?"

"One way," said Paul, "is to provide believable disinformation." "If an underground pipeline explodes mysteriously, disrupting the flow of oil to a certain area, the Center will see to it that the official explanation is natural erosion. The public will probably be told that the pipelines are decaying with age and because they're buried so far underground there's no way to inspect them. Whatever the situation, the Center has the Media capability to deal with it."

"I've heard them say that," said Mattson. "About decaying pipelines, I mean. Do you think the public really buys that?"

"Why not?" said Paul, "They have no other frame of reference. Look, if an American submarine goes to the bottom after being rammed by a Russian Destroyer, do you think the government will tell you the truth and risk international implications? Hell, no! They tell you the seams ruptured during heavy storms. When a plane explodes over a war zone, it's not because of a bomb or a missile. It's because of shearing bolts and metal fatigue. Believe me, Ron, the public buys it." He waited for a response from Mattson, but nothing came. After a minute, Paul began reading again. 'The Chairman recommended that USORSC based forces, comprised of elements of the Army Special Forces, the Blue Atlantic

Fleet, and the Northern Air Combat Patrol, all be combined under a single command responsible for the deployment of these forces in response to civilian disorders, and natural disasters.' "These people," said Paul, "are seasoned, specially trained, military personnel in covert branches of each service. Rather than retirement they are being offered the option of using their military expertise in a semi-civilian capacity. In October 1998, the Secretary turned them over to USORSC. With the overall reduction in U.S. military forces, and the return of some forces that were formerly stationed abroad, USORSC now commands about 200,000 military personnel. That's more than ten percent of all U.S. forces."

"I don't get it," said Mattson. "Is Hedgerow a part of the military, or isn't it?" He shook his head; confused by the seeming conflict in the information he was receiving.

"Hedgerow, is the plan," said Paul. "USORSC is the machine that will put the plan into action. Because of its military components, it is subordinate to the Pentagon, but at the same time, the Pentagon has a hands-off policy concerning USORSC."

"That doesn't even make sense", protested Mattson.

Paul got off the bed and picked his glass of Vodka from the dresser "The hands-off policy toward USORSC is about the same as you find between Congress and the CIA. The people behind Hedgerow believe our real challenge will be right here in the United States. USORSC is being developed for that purpose.

"You're talking about a secret army," said Mattson.

"Exactly." said Paul. "USORSC will be training state forces to react as military units during civil disorders. They plan the strategy and they provide military advisors. They also supply the heavy hardware and the manpower to train the state forces. In return they expect the state forces to react jointly in emergency situations. In other words, regardless of the state requiring assistance, the forces called in would fit together like fingers in a glove. Whether it's fighting a forest fire in California, putting down a riot on the streets of Chicago, or engaging militant groups in the hills of Kentucky."

"It sounds like an army of mercenaries." said Mattson.

"There's a problem," said Paul. He could see that Mattson was having difficulty taking in the full import of what he was saying." Setting the book aside he tried to explain it in his own words. "The National Command has allowed each state to evaluate their own joint exercises, but the states haven't implemented the proper standards to guide those evaluations. The civilian leaders are having a problem making the transition from their way of doing business to the standards demanded by the military. As a result, the National Command hasn't been made aware of some serious problems. They have conducted only four independent evaluations out of the 57 exercises completed in 1999."

"Hold on a minute," protested Mattson, holding up his hand. "Are you saying this is something that's already going on? They're already training these guys?"

"That's what I'm saying," said Paul. "Next year they have scheduled sixty training exercises."

"How the hell can they do it without anyone knowing?" The surprise was evident in Mattson's voice. "Where do they hold these exercises?"

"Mostly in unpopulated areas," said Paul. "Government owned property, State Parks, National Parks." Paul shrugged. "Some of the training takes place during hunting season. Some of it takes place right under your nose in operations labeled, 'Police Stings'. The next time you hear about millions of acres of mountain area being closed because of forest fires, you might ask yourself, what's really going on up there? "Anyway," said Paul, "there are deficiencies. There are problems."

"Do they say what the problems are?" asked Mattson

Paul nodded. "One serious problem is that some states don't want to follow National Directives. USORSC has developed a field training program, but civilian directors are concerned about having their forces trained by USORSC because they won't have control. They also suspect that Command has a hidden agenda."

Mattson snorted derisively, "They sure as hell have that right!"

"They decided to select their own commanders from their own states, and not from USORSC forces." continued Paul, ignoring the remark.

"Shit," said Mattson, "That just sounds like a power play."

"Exactly," said Paul, "They were also skeptical about the soundness of a strategy which requires integrating forces from individual states. Some DOC Directors insisted they were capable of developing their own programs. Two of the Directors said they already had training capability and didn't need assistance from Command. The Directors of DOCMN said they were proceeding with the development of a Simulation Center right here in the Minneapolis/St. Paul area."

"What the hell is a Simulation Center?"

"Just think of it as a Command War Room." said Paul

"Where are they going to build that?" asked Mattson.

"We may never know." said Paul. "These things are usually underground. What they do is bury them under some legitimate business enterprise. They use things like Stadiums, Hotels, Strip malls... Anything that is big enough, and deep enough. They've developed sites out East where they've built cities under cities without public knowledge."

Paul flipped the pages to another section of the book. "Anyway, 'USORSC was really pissed. Some State Directors had gotten big heads because they now have more power than they ever imagined. USORSC went to General Waltham and he went to the Secretary. A few days later each of the State Directors received a personal message from the Vice Chairman. He reminded them that USORSC is in command, and that USORSC strategy requires forces that are highly skilled, rapidly deliverable, and fully capable of operating effectively as joint teams immediately upon arrival anywhere in the United States. He also made it clear that, in an emergency, the National Command, can bring the full weight of the military against a state individually, or if necessary, against all of them collectively." Paul set the book on the bed and smiled at Mattson "The Directors got the message loud and clear."

"I feel like my head is ready to explode," said Mattson, putting another cartridge in the camera. "Let's take a break." He set the camera on the dresser and stretched out on the bed.

Paul, picked up the bottle of Vodka from the dresser, and poured a drink. He started to sit down, then stopped, picked up another glass and poured a shot for Mattson. "This might help." He said.

Mattson accepted the glass, sniffed it, and threw it down in one gulp. The room was warm and stuffy and almost immediately he regretted the action. He got off the bed, walked over to the window where he flipped the switch on the air conditioner. Coming back to the bed, he said, "Let's try something different." He pulled a chair over to the bed and knelt down beside it with the camera. "If you sit on the bed and hold that book up to your chest, I'll be able to rest my elbows on this chair while I take the pictures."

"Okay," Paul sat on the edge of the bed and held the book to his chest. "Just be damned sure you don't get my face in any of the pictures."

Mattson kept filming, emptied the cartridge, and changed it. Paul kept turning the pages for him. As they worked, Paul kept talking.

"When you talked to Colonel Clifton, did you mention the word, 'Hedgerow'?"

"Hell, no," growled Mattson, "I'm not stupid!"

"But you did talk about the walls?"

"Only the fact that I plan on doing a follow-up to the series I did on government corruption." said Mattson.

"The reason I'm asking," said Paul, "is because that part of the project was put on hold for awhile because of political pressure and public protest".

"You mean they aren't going to use the walls?"

"Oh, they'll use them." assured Paul. "In a few years, when the clamor dies down, they'll start building them again. Materials and design will be changed to make them more esthetically acceptable. If they make them attractive they expect the public outcry to be minimal."

"I don't care how pretty they make them," said Mattson. "The public will never accept them."

"The public already has," said Paul. "Open your eyes, Ron. It's been a couple of years since you wrote about them. Do you hear the people complaining now like they did then?"

Mattson had no answer and Paul continued.

"As long as people believe the only purpose for the walls is to stop noise pollution, there won't be a problem. We have to make them know what the walls are really intended for."

Paul watched Mattson peering into the camera, lining up for another shot. "There's a screen on the side if you want to monitor what you're shooting." he said.

Mattson nodded, but didn't answer. He continued snapping pictures for a couple of minutes more before he looked up. "How many do they intend to build?" he asked.

Paul turned to a page in the back of the book. "So far," he said, "they have 22,300 miles of abatement barriers constructed and strategically placed in cities across the country. When the time is right, they'll start building them again and you won't hear a peep from the public."

"How the hell did all this get started?" asked Mattson.

Paul found his place in the front of the book again and held it up to be photographed. "The 'Hedgerow' concept sprang from the rash of riots in the Sixties." He said. "Detroit, in 1967, was a real ball buster. It got so bad that Martial law was imposed, civil rights were suspended and the press was blacked out. Eventually, it was lifted, but many of the things that happened were never reported." He took a sip from his drink and adjusted the book.

"Literally thousands of innocent people were snatched off the streets and held in makeshift detention centers. Hundreds of men and women were held on city buses without food, water or toilet facilities. Hundreds more were held for days in an underground police garage."

"Yeah," said Mattson, "but that was a riot. They were burning down the damned city."

"Most of those people didn't even know there was a riot," argued Paul. "They didn't know what the hell was going on. They were just ordinary people caught in a sewer of insanity. In a single day over seven hundred people were booked into the city jail. On that same day two thousand others were taken from that jail and shuttled like cattle to other detention centers."

Paul tilted the book at an angle. "Do you know why they were able to do the things they did in Detroit?" he asked.

Mattson kept taking pictures, not bothering to answer.

"It was because most of the people were law abiding citizens." said Paul. "All of their lives they had been taught to obey the law. The very numbers of those arrested attests to the fact that there was no organized resistance. Indictments by the thousands were passed out by grand juries that took no longer than three minutes for each case!" Paul shook his head in disgust. "This was something that should have been contained in the neighborhood where it started. Instead, panic set in, the police over-reacted, and the damned thing spread through the city like wildfire. I wasn't there, but I don't find it hard to visualize."

"What about all of those militant groups we hear about. Where were they?"

"They talk big," said Paul, "but it's mostly, blustering, bullshit. When an army tank rolls down the street spraying bullets into apartment buildings, it's pretty hard to find those guys, but eventually, when

Operation Lock-Down begins," Paul shrugged. "Who knows?" Paul thought for a moment and then frowned. "Actually, the Hedgerow Project is counting on militant groups getting involved. It will lend credibility to the need for military troops."

"Did they really do that?" Astonishment widened Mattson's eyes. "Did they fire machine guns into apartment buildings?'

Paul nodded. "That happened in at least one recorded incident during the Detroit riot," he said. "There were others, but that one is documented. It couldn't be hidden." As he talked he continued turning pages. "Anyway," he said, "that's when they new they were going to need some way to contain future Riots. Major cities were being trashed, but you have to remember, this was happening at the same time that the Military was being trashed. The government was frustrated with public opinion concerning war policy. They resented the growing lack of support for the war effort. We had just had our ass kicked in Korea, and we were facing a military disaster in Vietnam. Up until Vietnam, being in the military was a source of pride, but suddenly everything was turned upside down. Instead of supporting the soldiers, the American people were spitting on them when they came home, calling them baby killers! As far as the military was concerned, the protesters were traitors." Paul set the book on his lap for a moment to rest his arms. "There were those who even suggested that some of the riots were just diversions to get out minds off Vietnam."

Noticing the skepticism in Mattson's eyes, Paul smiled, cynically. "I know what you're thinking, Ron, but believe me, it's not as far-fetched as it sounds. During the late sixties, even right here in St. Paul, agitators were sent in to stir things up."

"Damn it," Mattson said, suddenly changing the subject and obviously angry with himself, "It's that bastard, Clifton. He really got me, didn't he?"

"Don't beat yourself up," said Paul. "Clifton's a professional. And he's dangerous as hell." He studied Mattson for a moment. "Not having second thoughts, are you?" he asked.

"Hell, no." growled Mattson. "I'm just kicking myself in the ass for being such a dummy. That ass-hole really got me."

"Clifton was General Sleighton's right hand," said Paul, "but he always resented being in second place. I heard a story not long ago about Clifton and his aide. It seems the aide asked him what his thoughts were, about something, or other. Clifton replied, 'Colonel's don't think, Berghoff. Generals think, Colonel's listen! That's how Colonels get to be Generals.'

I guess he laughed like a lunatic. He thought he was clever as hell"

"Paul, I'm really sorry," Mattson's voice was filled with remorse. "About going to see Clifton, I mean. "Do you think I screwed things up?"

"Forget it," said Paul, "there's nothing we can do about it now." He leaned over and took his glass from the table. "You want another one of these?"

"No, thanks" Mattson gave a little shudder, shook his head and forced his mind back to the issue at hand. "Have you read all of this?" he asked, holding up the book.

"Every word," Paul assured him.

"In that case," said Mattson, gesturing with the camera, "you keep talking and turning the pages and I'll keep snapping. This is going to be damned tough reading."

Paul nodded, set his glass back on the dresser and picked up the book. He began to turn a page, but stopped suddenly and leaned over to unzip his shaving kit. He pulled out a plastic bottle, uncapped it and took out a couple of the white pills and swallowed them.

"So what happened, did the Military just decide to take over?" asked Mattson.

"Not the Military," corrected Paul, "They know if we stand together we're the strongest power on earth. But they also know that we can't fight a war while this country is being torn apart from the inside. It's the people behind Hedgerow that decided on a re-adjustment of priorities."

"In what way?" asked Mattson.

"The military was persuaded that the new plan will be to secure this country from the inside so they won't be distracted the next time they have to engage in a major conflict on the outside."

"You're saying they're going to ban protests?" asked Mattson.

"They're going to limit dissent." said Paul.

"Right," scoffed Mattson. "Limit dissent."

"Something like this was bound to happen," said Paul. "It took Korea, Vietnam, Desert Storm, Bosnia, and, shit, even Haiti, to teach us that we can't win unless we're totally committed. We're not the top dogs in the pack anymore. We still put up a good show, but in reality, the countries we fight have learned that if they hang in long enough our own people will eventually start protesting and win the fight for them. "That bastard, Saddam, sucked us dry!"

"We should have gone in and finished him while we had the chance," said Mattson.

Paul suddenly set the book on the bed and picked his glass off the dresser. He poured another shot of Vodka and continued. "Anyway, the military decided to let the rest of the world have the massive armies. Rather than bulk, we'll have speed. Our Military really is lean and mean, and they are more capable than at any time in our history. The beauty of it, from the viewpoint of Hedgerow, is that it can be turned inward as well as outward. They can engage in hit and run pitched battles anywhere in the world, but they can also put down anything that occurs in this country."

"You ought to lay off that stuff," cautioned Mattson, gesturing toward the bottle. "We've got a lot of work to do."

"I'm okay," said Paul, smiling. Then seeing Mattson's irritation, he set the glass back on the table and turned a page in the book.

They worked quietly for the next half hour, Mattson taking the pictures and Paul turning the pages, each man lost in his own thoughts. Outside the sun had gone down

128

and a light drizzle was gently slapping at the window. Mattson emptied the cartridge in the camera, replaced it with a new one and set the camera on the table. "I've got to hit the can," he said. On his way to the bathroom he stopped long enough to turn off the air conditioner and take a quick look out the window. Looking down he could see bumper-to-bumper traffic, barely moving, in either direction. "This isn't even rush hour," he thought. "What the hell are they going to do in ten years?" He turned from the window and went into the bathroom.

When he came out, Paul was still sitting on the bed. The book lay open in his lap. "I called room service," he said. "I thought you might like a sandwich and some coffee?"

"Good idea," said Mattson, crossing the room and picking up the camera. "I'm starving."

He got into position to start taking pictures again, and then looked up. "Tell me, something, Paul. Are these local people involved with Hedgerow aware of the military connection?"

"No," Paul shook his head. "Only a few at the top. Most of the people involved are just ordinary citizens. Some represent corporations and social organizations. Others are just everyday people going about their daily routine. They attend regularly scheduled meetings with the police and neighborhood leaders and they look at this as a civic duty. You know, making the streets safe, busting drug dealers, fighting terrorism, that sort of thing. They have no idea what the real agenda is." He began slowly turning pages while Mattson worked the camcorder. "If you mentioned

Hedgerow, these people wouldn't even know what you were talking about. "Everything connected to the project itself is held under the highest possible secrecy. Not even some members of the Senate Intelligence Committee have access to this information."

"What about you?" said Mattson. "You have access. Who the hell are you, anyway?"

"What difference does it make?" Paul's voice was cold, almost challenging.

"Mattson shrugged, knowing he was not going to get an answer.

"Of course," Paul continued, "It's a safe bet that some members of Congress are on the inside. There would have to be, but no one knows who they are.

It seemed like a silly question to ask, but Mattson decided to ask it anyway. "What about the President? Does he know?"

"You would think so, wouldn't you?" asked Paul. "I mean, something this big... how could he not know? The truth is, I don't know if he's aware or not. Since the days of Truman, some Presidents have known, and some have not. I don't know what the criteria is, but it seems to require more than simply being President."

"I don't know how he could be kept out of the loop on something this big," insisted Mattson.

"President's have always been protected from knowing too much." said Paul. "Harry Truman thought the President would have access to all information, but after taking office he realized how wrong he was. At one time he told some close friends,

"There's a group out in Virginia that not even the President of the United States can control."

Mattson laughed. "My editor told me that, just the other day." He raised the camera to his eye, zeroed in on the page, and pushed the button. "But Truman wasn't talking about these guys," he said.

"Are you sure?" asked Paul. "Truman was talking about the CIA at Langley, but what the hell's the difference? It's all part of the same stew."

The sudden sound of knocking caused them both to stiffen and turn to the door. Mattson's eyes flashed from Paul, to the door and then back to Paul. "Who the hell is that?" he whispered. There was a hint of panic in his voice.

Paul put the book on the bed and stood up. "Take it easy," he held up a cautioning hand as he walked to the door. "It has to be room service."

Mattson watched as Paul opened the door, revealing a bus boy with a food cart. He felt the tension flow out of his body. Leaving the camera sitting on the chair, he stood up and walked to the desk where he picked up the soap dish he had been using as an ashtray. He carried it to the other empty bed and flopped down. He lay there, breathing deeply, forcing himself to relax. Reaching into his shirt pocket he pulled out a cigarette and lit it.

He had gone through three and a half cartridges and more than halfway through the book. Even without the tension and the worry about being caught it would have been exhausting work, and he wished, briefly, that he could forget the whole damned business and go home. He watched as Paul gave the waiter a tip, wheeled the cart into the room and closed the door.

Swinging his feet off the bed, Mattson sat up, kicked off his shoes and rolled to his side, leaning on his elbow. "I could use a little of that, now," said Mattson, as he watched Paul go to the dresser and pick up his glass. "Do we have some ice and mix?"

"Plenty of ice," said Paul, "and we have a couple of Cokes. Will that do?"

"That will do just fine," said Mattson. He got off the bed and made himself a drink. He took a quick sip, added coke and sat back down. He took a long deep drag on his cigarette.

"Are you going to eat?" asked Paul, gesturing to the dishes on the cart

"In a minute," said Mattson, sucking the smoke into his lungs. "I just want to unwind a little. What do we have?"

"I ordered you a salad and a steak sandwich," said Paul, "Okay?"

"Great," said Mattson. He took another drag and crushed the cigarette out in the soap dish as he got off the bed and came over to the table."

"You know," said Paul, "the ironic part of all this, is that these guys are halfway right. Something has to be done." He was putting steak sauce on his sandwich as he spoke, but he set down the bottle and held up his hand to forestall Mattson's protest as he saw the other man give him a startled look. "Wait," he said. "Hear me out." He took a bite of his sandwich and sat down on the edge of the bed.

"You see, essentially, Hedgerow is based on the premise that, in the not too distant future, this world is going to run out of, quite literally, everything. Not just a temporary food or fuel crises, mind you, but shortages of water, timber, wildlife, housing, farmland, seafood, medical services…the list is endless. It even includes the air we breathe. The only thing we're guaranteed not to be short of is population. And the population is becoming increasingly more violent." Paul took another quick bite from his sandwich and set the dish on the dresser. In almost the same move, he snatched up the book, opened it and began searching. It took only a moment to find what he was looking for.

"There's been an increasing level of terrorist activity in this country", he said. "This has given USORSC an opportunity to funnel money into local law enforcement special weapons teams. Not the regular police, mind you, but special teams within the police force. It also provides an excuse to create hundreds of special military units to combat terrorism proactively. Did you know that the ban on Federal troops, acting as police, has been lifted? Did you know that national security now allows those troops to act… without executive order… on a shoot first, ask questions later, basis?"

Mattson was changing the cartridge in the camera. He shook his head, "No, I didn't know that. But, hell," he said, "After the bombing at the Federal building in Oklahoma City, who can blame them?"

"That's exactly the response they're expecting from the public." said Paul. "And if I were the average guy on the street, it's the response I would give. But let's take a look at both sides of the issue." He began reading the book.

"The Government is saying that the increase in domestic terrorism is the result of anti-government sentiment resulting in the increase of self-styled militia and paramilitary groups with extremist positions. According to recent ATF reports, bombings, or attempted bombings, have had a 52 percent increase. They say there is a growing threat to government facilities and federal employees throughout the nation. Let me read a few of the statistics they cite:

"**March, 1995,** right here in Minnesota. Two members of the 'Patriots Council' were convicted of making a batch of Ricin. A toxic derivative that they planned to put on doorknobs in federal buildings.

October 1995, an Amtrak train is derailed in the Arizona desert. A section of track had been removed. A note left behind claimed credit for an unknown terrorist group called 'Sons of Gestapo'.

November 1995, in Muskogee, Oklahoma, anti-government terrorists, led by Ray Willie Lampley were found guilty of plotting to bomb abortion clinics, homosexual gatherings, welfare offices, and offices of the anti-defamation league and the Southern Poverty Law Center. They had plans to blow up federal buildings in several cities.

December 1995, Ellis Hurt and Joseph Bailie tried to bomb the Reno, Nevada office of the Internal Revenue Service.

January 1996, A bomb exploded outside of a U.S. Forest Service headquarters building in Espanola, New Mexico

April 1996, The Department of Labor, Mine Safety, and Health office in Vacaville, California had a bomb explode in the truck of one of their employees. A phone threat came in from a caller who said, 'all you guys are dead. Timothy McVeigh lives on.'

May 1996, A bomb blew out the fifth story windows of an FBI field office in Laredo, Texas. The office was staffed by 12 agents. A caller claimed credit for a group called Organization 544.

August 1996, Charles Ray Polk was sentenced to 20 years for plotting to bomb the Internal Revenue Service in Austin, Texas.

October 1996, Seven members of an anti-government paramilitary group in Clarksburg, West Virginia were arrested for plotting to bomb the Criminal Justice Information Services Division. The arrests occurred while members of the West Virginia Mountaineer Militia were putting together huge quantities of explosives and blasting caps. Explosives were later found at five locations in West Virginia. The list is endless," said Paul, reaching over to pick up his sandwich. He ate with one hand as he continued reading.

"In New Mexico, a District Attorney's office is hit with a Molotov cocktail. In Tampa, a Florida a man is taken off a flight with five handmade explosives and 180 rounds of ammunition… A member of the Freeman Group was arrested in Topeka, Kansas when a bomb-triggering device was found in his car. This year two

135

members of the Georgia Republic Militia were arrested while making dozens of pipe bombs. They claimed they were preparing for a war against the United Nations and the New World Order.

"In June, twelve members of the Phoenix Militia were arrested for making bombs and other weapons. In July, the FBI arrested four people belonging to an anti-government militia in Bellingham, Washington for possession of guns and explosives."

Paul closed the book and smiled at Mattson. "People like these are all over the country." he said.

Mattson sat with his head bowed in silence. He had never heard of most of the cases cited. Finally, he raised his head and looked at Paul. "I think you're making a pretty good case for the government," he said.

The truth is," said Paul, "the guys behind 'Hedgerow' couldn't care less about a few bombs. It fits with their strategy. They also intend to utilize Media sources to foster panic. They know if they can hold the public at the appropriate level of fear they'll be excused for any tactics they employ."

"They're right about that," said Mattson. "When people are afraid they'll accept a lot of things,"

"Still, it's going to take something big," mused Paul, staring out the window. "Some colossal tragedy to jump-start this thing." His voice was low, almost as though he was speaking to himself.

"How's that?" asked Mattson

"Oh, it's nothing," said Paul, purposely avoiding Mattson's eyes. "A thought just struck me. I guess I was thinking out-loud."

Mattson had heard the statement, but he let it pass. "You said something about the Media?" he prodded

"Yes," Paul nodded. "Hedgerow is going to depend heavily on the movie industry and the news media to get their message across. The movie industry has cashed in for years by making unreal situations appear real. In this instance the process will be reversed. They'll portray things that are really happening in a way that makes them totally unbelievable. A good movie can make most people think that black is white"

"Are we talking about some sort of brain washing?" asked Mattson

"On a major scale," said Paul, nodding. "It will be less difficult than you might think. Hedgerow operates on the theory that the proper mixture of fact and fabrication, repeated over and over, will eventually become all fact. A television news commentator can sway a listener with a simple gesture or a frown. Imagine what hundreds of them can do when they all zero in on the same subject and are spewing up the same crap."

"I can imagine," growled Mattson. "I've seen it happen right here in the Twin Cities. It happens every time the Twins or the Vikings push for a new stadium. Any idea when they will start it or what their first target will be?"

"It's already started," said Paul. Have you ever noticed how some huge story, something really important, is pushed aside and replaced with some silly chatter about a movie star's divorce?" His answer was immediate, but he did not elaborate. He had finished his sandwich. He stood up now and walked to the table where he picked up his salad. "This looks good," he said. "Aren't you going to eat yours?"

"I'll have it later," said Mattson. "I think we should get back to the pictures. We don't have that far to go."

Paul gave a nod. "I'll be right with you." It took him only a minute to finish his salad. He set the empty dish back on the table, and went into the bathroom. A few minutes later he emerged, wiping his hands on a hotel towel. When he was finished he flipped the towel into a corner, sat on the edge of the bed and picked up the book. "Okay, let's get this out of the way." He said. "What page were we on?"

"Twelve fifty- three," said Mattson. He knelt down and prepared to line up the camera. "This is going a lot faster than I expected."

Paul found the page and glanced at it. "Ah, Transportation," Grinning at Mattson he held the book to his chest. "You asked what the first target would be? Let's start with this one: Our country's mobility is a major problem for Hedgerow. They know that as long as we have unrestricted mobility, complete control is impossible."

"God," said Mattson. "I was just thinking about that when I looked out the window. I was looking at all that damned traffic and wondering what the hell we were going to do in ten years!"

"In ten years that problem may be gone," said Paul. Anticipating Mattson's next question, he continued. "Somehow they have to immobilize this entire county. They can't very well control a population that has the ability to hop in a car and travel thousands of miles whenever the mood strikes them."

"They can't just take the cars away," protested Mattson.

"No, they can't just take them away, but they can encourage people to give them up. The process has already begun with the oil shortages and the rise in gas prices. Blame for this has been so cleverly manipulated that the purpose has been totally obscured. We blame the oil companies; the oil companies blame the Arabs …"

"Hell, I figured it was the Arabs." said Mattson. "I figured the oil companies were just taking advantage of the situation and gouging us at the pumps."

"They are," said Paul. "But what do you think the next step is?"

"Shit, I don't know." Mattson gave a quick shake of his head as he lined up another page. "Cut the oil off altogether?"

"No," Paul shook his head. "That would create the same situation as banning the cars. No," he repeated, still shaking his head. "First, they have to make the public believe it's their choice to give up their cars."

"Give up their cars? Voluntarily?" Mattson laughed scornfully. "Lots of luck with that!"

"It's not such a stretch when you have the media and the movie industry pumping out bile and misinformation," said Paul. "When it comes to driving your car or keeping your house warm, what are you going to choose? When it's drilled into you day after day that each time you pump a gallon of gas you're condemning some old lady to freezing in an empty apartment... how much gas are you going to pump? They'll make it so un-patriotic that you'll chance being stoned at the pump just for driving a car."

Mattson's jaw tightened as he continued taking pictures, but he said nothing.

"Confusion and illusion are the watchwords for Hedgerow," said Paul, holding the book against his chest. "Whenever there's a serious issue at stake the Center will flood the media with seemingly reputable and knowledgeable people. They'll each be touted as experts in the field, but each of them will provide different versions of what happened, why it went wrong and who is to blame. They'll call it "fair and balanced.""

Paul stood up suddenly and set the book on the bed. "I've got to have a little coffee." He walked to the food cart, filled a cup and came back to the bed. "Take the gas stations," he continued. "Most independent dealers are gone. Thousands of them have been driven out of business or have caved in and accepted the terms offered by the conglomerates... Huge chains that manipulate the price have replaced them. And those chains are beginning to tell us the amount that we are allowed to buy. Did you know that some stations are refusing service on sales of less than ten dollars?"

"I didn't hear about that," said Mattson. "If they want people to use less gas, why do they want them to buy more? What's the point? "He was thoroughly confused. "I haven't seen that around here."

"Money is always a part of it." said Paul. "The official version is to prevent tank-topping which they claim increases demand. The real purpose is to create confusion. The truth is that a lot of people can't afford to fill up their tank. They buy gas a few gallons at time when they have the money. As a result, they'll drive less and keep their cars parked. They'll get used to walking where they can, or find other means of transportation. And, no, it hasn't begun here," Paul smiled, "but its coming."

"You know," Mattson frowned, as he lined up the camera for another picture. "This is beginning to make sense. They were building special car-pooling lanes on the off ramps long before we had an oil crises!"

"I'm only hitting the highlights." said Paul. "I'll never be able to cover...."

He was about to say something more when there was a knock on the door. The first time it was only a tap, but a moment later it was repeated more loudly, almost banging.

Mattson jumped up clutching the camera, his eyes darting from the door to Paul. "Who's that?" His voice, bordering on panic, was barely a whisper.

Paul, equally startled, held up a hand to calm him as he stood up and set the book on the bed. He brought a forefinger to his lips in a gesture of silence, then slipped around the food cart and made his way to the door. "Maybe they came back for the cart," he whispered back.

Mattson watched intently as Paul put his eye to the peephole. "Who is it?" he whispered.

Paul held up his hand, still looking through the peephole. "It's some guy in a T-shirt and jacket."

"Is he alone?"

"Yeah, I think so," Paul squinted through the hole, "It's hard to tell." He looked at Mattson as though hoping for an answer, but Mattson could only stare back without speaking.

Paul took another look through the door and turned the doorknob. Outside a short stocky, balding man, in a soiled T-shirt and a worn brown leather jacket stood grinning at him and shifting back and forth from one foot to the other as though he had to go to the bathroom.

Paul gave a quick look up and down the hall and then relaxed. The hall was empty. His eyes went back to the man. "Can I help you?"

"I'm looking for Bob Marshalton, man." He came forward a step, trying to see into the room. "He here?" he asked

Paul moved forward pulling the door with him, blocking the man's view. The eyes confronting him were wild and the man's foul breath forced Paul to turn his head. "There's nobody here by that name." he said.

"You sure?" The man was still trying to look around Paul. "Shit man, he said he'd be here."

Even though Paul had been drinking it did not protect him from the overpowering stench of alcohol and body order coming from the agitated man nervously bouncing in front of him. "I told you," said Paul, "there's no one here by that name."

"C'mon, man," the bouncing man persisted, trying to look over Paul's shoulder. "He said he'd be in room 523!"

"This is 423" said Paul, feeling his anger rising.

The man stopped moving for a minute peering closely at Paul. Slowly comprehension came into his eyes and he backed away. "Ah, shit, man. I'm sorry." He slapped the side of his head with an open palm, "Shit man, I thought this was 523."

"Don't worry about it," said Paul, "No harm done." He tried closing the door as the man started bouncing again, still trying to get one last look into the room. Finally the man turned, and still bouncing with every other step made his way down the hall toward the elevators. Paul stood by the door a minute, waiting, making sure the man had gone. Finally satisfied, he came back to the bed, shaking his head. "There's a good example of what's ahead for all of us," he said. "That poor bastard doesn't know if he's coming or going and he doesn't even know how it happened."

Mattson put the camera on the chair and flopped down on the bed. He lay there stretched out with his eyes closed, his mind swirling as he waited for his nerves to settle.

After a minute he sat up on the bed and looked at Paul.

"You think he was really drunk?"

"Drunk or high on something," He dismissed it with a wave of his hand as he picked up the book, "Where were we?"

Mattson thought for a few seconds, then swung his legs off the bed and picked up the camera. "We were talking about mobility."

"Right," Paul opened the book and held it in position for Mattson. "Getting cars off the road is a priority for Hedgerow. There's a thing called 'built in obsolescence', said Paul. It's a method employed by manufacturers, especially automakers, to keep you coming back. They build an absolutely perfect metal part, and then throw in some tiny little piece of plastic guaranteed to wear out in x-number of months, and make the entire part worthless. Years ago this wasn't a big deal. With a screwdriver, pliers, and a few wrenches most car owners could make their own repairs. Today special tools and computerized equipment is required and repair costs are going through the roof. People, who can afford it, get the repairs. A lot of others can't afford it and are forced to jerry-rig. They wrap tin cans around tail pipes to plug the holes. They use tires until they're ready to blow out. They do whatever they can to keep going and save a few bucks. . As a result, a lot of dangerous cars are on the highways. Pretty soon you'll see legislative bills being pushed in selected states to restrict cars older than ten or fifteen years from using the freeways. The Media will call them gas-guzzlers and cite public safety. They'll demand that these cars be taken off the road.

At the same time a companion bill will be pushed through Congress establishing a special fund to purchase those old, useless, cars from the public. Hedgerow will launch a massive campaign to calm public outrage. They'll praise the buyback as a benevolent gesture by a sympathetic Congress. The issue will totally divide public opinion. The poor bastards who lose their cars will be grateful to the federal government for helping them recoup some of their loss. The more affluent will be incensed because their tax money is funding the program." Paul shook his head, sadly. "It's going to be a hell of a mess, Ron. The government will justify the tremendous expenditure through a media blitz aimed at convincing the public that the unwanted cars will be used to create a new, and desperately needed, new source of energy."

"There goes my Toyota," grumbled Mattson.

"That's not the end of it," said Paul. "Even those who keep their cars don't get off the hook. Other legislative bills will be enacted to place a tax on cars based on the miles driven. It will be regulated by individual states and attached to yearly renewal of license plates. They haven't finalized or clearly established the guidelines for this process, but generally speaking, each state will allow a maximum number of miles to be driven without tax. Say, 500 miles. Anything in excess of that number will be subject to a highway tax. For example: A car wracking up 10,000 miles per year, based on half a cent a mile tax would cost the owner about fifty dollars at the time of renewal. That, of course, is in addition to the normal cost of license plates.

"So if I drive 10,000 miles and they only exempt 500 miles, I have to pay half a cent a mile for the other 9,500 miles?"

Paul nodded. "Half a cent at the pump would cause a little bitching, but it would be taken in stride. Having it attached to your license tab means that you have to pay or you don't drive. This attacks the automobile owner personally. Believe me; a lot of people will have second thoughts about taking those long vacation trips.

"So a guy driving to California could have another four or five thousand miles added to the ten or fifteen thousand he normally drives in a year?" Mattson shook his head, "They'll never get the public to accept that."

"Sure they will," said Paul. "If the people in Minnesota think the rest of the nation is accepting this, they'll accept it, too. We're a nation of conformists, Ron. "If you control the Media, you control the country. Besides, what choice do you think they will have?"

Mattson was growing weary. His eyes were burning and he was getting a headache. He suspected the cause was looking through the view- finder of the camera, but the dull, dry monotonous voice of Paul was also beginning to wear on him. He spoke in a voice devoid of feeling and that bothered Mattson. His emotion and the context of the information he was providing seemed totally disconnected.

"Things in this country are going to change in a way that people can't even imagine," said Paul, suddenly. He pointed to the cigarette that Mattson was holding. "That cigarette, you're smoking," he said. "In a few years if you get caught with one of those you'll get a mandatory jail sentence."

"Sorry, Paul." Mattson started to crush out the cigarette. "I didn't know smoking bothered you.

"No, wait." Paul leaned forward to stop him. "It doesn't bother me. I was just trying to make a point. Under the new rules people will be subject to prosecution at the drop of a hat. They'll tell you that it's your body, but it's our money that pays for your health care when you get sick. You'll go to jail for possession of a controlled substance and for endangering the public health."

"Oh shit," Mattson stood up and crushed the cigarette out in the soap dish. "I need a drink." He went to the dresser, poured some coke into a glass and put in a double shot of Vodka. He went back to the bed and sat down with a disgusted look on his face. "How the fuck much more is there?"

I'm not even scratching the surface." said Paul. "Let's get back to mobility. We can get back to this subject later." Without giving Mattson a chance to object, he continued. "By the time the older cars are off the freeways, government funded light rail systems will be in place all across the nation. That's when the pressure on the rest of the privately owned cars will begin."

"Where the hell is the President during all this? If he's not in on it, why the hell isn't he doing something to stop it?"

"Whether or not he's in on it doesn't matter. A one or two term President isn't in

147

office long enough to change anything. These guys were there a long time before the President and they'll be there a long time after he's gone. When a President tries to make changes, they listen politely, nod their heads in agreement, and then go on doing as they damned well please. The news media will first convince the public that no reasonable person would want to stop it," said Paul. "If those particular cars are a danger to the public, they should be removed. The mileage tax will lead to an artificial and temporary drop in the oil prices. Eventually the pressure applied through the media will gain public support. The illusion will be created that this is the fairest method because people will no longer be paying for the fuel of other gas-guzzlers. They'll only pay for the gas they personally consume."

Mattson had forgotten to put ice in his drink and the taste made him pinch up his face.

He managed to swallow what he had in his mouth, but he put the rest of the drink back on the desk. "Let's get this finished," he said, "picking up the camera. As he began taking the final pictures he laughed sardonically. "I hope they don't have all of this scheduled within the next six months." He said. "I'd sure as hell like to make Florida this year."

"This isn't going to happen overnight," said Paul. "But soon. A verbal slip was recently made by a government official concerning the last census. I think it was a feeler to test public reaction. He said, 'The undercount in the Census won't be completely eliminated until the government tightens up on some of the freedoms

Americans cherish.' His exact words were, 'you would have to restrict mobility for awhile'."

"I didn't even fill out the last census," snorted Mattson. "I received some papers but I didn't fill them out. Shit, they want to know everything!"

"Of course they do. The more information they have, the more power they have." said Paul. "Anyway, that was the first time they came out openly suggesting mobility restrictions. What kind of response do you think it received from the public?"

Mattson shook his head, "No much, I would guess."

"Total apathy." said Paul. "The media ignored it. Nobody said a word. Media coverage that day centered on some minor politician getting arrested for hiring a hooker."

Time was passing rapidly. The book was almost finished and Mattson found himself growing restless. He went to the desk, picked up the warm drink he had left there and took a small swallow. His eyes fell on part of the steak sandwich that he hadn't finished, but he made no move to pick it up. He glanced over at Paul who had picked up the camera and was reviewing his work.

"I don't know if it's the Vodka, the lack of food, or just the whole rotten situation," said Mattson, "but I feel edgy as hell. I feel like smashing something and I don't know why. What the fuck kind of people are they, anyway?"

"You're just depressed," said Paul, laying the camera on the bed. "It's the frustration that I warned you about." He leaned over and picked up the black leather shaving kit from the floor. Unzipping it, he took out a small plastic bottle, uncapped it, and offered two small white pills to Mattson.

"What's this?"

"Amphetamine," said Paul. "Nothing that will hurt you. It'll give you a little lift…help you get through the night without letting it get to you."

Mattson eyed the pills, suspiciously, and then thought, "What the hell." He threw them down with a gulp from his glass. It was not his first time with speed, but it had been a long time.

"As for the kind of people they are," said Paul, "what people are you talking about? If you mean the politicians…well, most of them are just greedy bastards that find themselves in a trap. They may start out with the right intentions, but by the time they get into a position of power where they might do some good, they're so completely compromised from deals they have made that they can't wipe their own nose without permission." Paul adjusted his glasses, peering over them at Mattson. "If you're talking about the Military," he said, "Admirals and Generals are like horses with blinders on." He rose suddenly and walked to the window where he stood gazing out at the traffic flooding the freeway below. "I should point out," he said, "that they aren't all involved with Hedgerow. Most of them don't even know about it."

"You mean the Generals and the Admirals?"

"Yes," Paul nodded. "You have no idea how large and convoluted the military is, Ron. Unfortunately, those that are involved are a lot like the cop on the beat. A General without a war is like a cop without a crime. They're so wrapped up in their own little circumscribed world that nothing else matters to them. Police live, work and play with other police. To them, the public and the outside world is the enemy. Generals are in the same boat. It's impossible for them to keep a rational, objective view of the world. Their world is war and without war, they're lost. Even a war at home is better than no war at all."

In less than half an hour the pills started to kick in and Mattson felt better. He decided that it was probably the lack of food and the Vodka he was drinking that caused the fast reaction. Whatever the reason, he felt better and he stood up. "You know, even with all this information, I still can't see this country just rolling over. Not even to our own military."

"You won't even see the Military," said Paul, "Not until it's too late. Other people will be there. People just like you and me. They'll be constantly creating phony situations to keep the public keyed up and off balance. City, County and State public employee strikes will be promoted to interrupt public service. Outrage will cause riots when they try to break the unions by hiring scab workers as permanent replacements."

"They'll be mapping out mini-riot situations on the drawing boards in the Pacification Center and promoting them in major cities across the nation. Those cities will see rioting so bloody and violent that the people will welcome the sight of federal troops."

"You amaze me," said Mattson, obviously impressed. "I don't know how you can be so cool, knowing the things you do. I don't mind telling you, I'm scared to death. Aren't you afraid of getting caught before this is exposed? Aren't you afraid of being arrested?"

"My coolness is in this glass," laughed Paul waving the Vodka. "Of course, I'm afraid," he admitted, suddenly turning serious. "But not of being arrested. Unfortunately, I know too much. If I get caught, they'll find a much more effective way of dealing with me. It most certainly won't be in a courtroom."

"I guess the same thing applies to me now," said Mattson. He set the camera on the chair and leaned back, stretching. He pointed to the book. "I'm running into a lot of the statistics you told me about."

Paul turned the book and looked at it. "Yes, and we have just about everything we need. We haven't covered the airlines or farming … "he looked over at Mattson. "Are you tired?"

"Hell, No." Mattson laughed, "I'm more wide awake than when we started. I just get a little stiff from leaning over so much. How the hell long have we been at this?" He glanced at his watch.

"It's just after mid-night," said Paul. "We've come a long way since this morning, but you've been doing all the work. All I've been doing is talking." He gestured to the camera, "You want me to take the rest of the pictures?"

Mattson shook his head. "I can do it. I'd rather keep busy and let you do the talking. I'll absorb it a hell of a lot faster listening than by reading."

"Okay," Paul opened the book and waited for Mattson to get the camera in position. "You know," he said, "I've only been skimming the top of things, but I promise you, every form of transportation from sailboats to the airlines is thoroughly covered in this book. It details how each of them are either going to be banned, neutralized, or nationalized. Because of its close ties to agriculture, and its tremendous consumption of fuel oil, the trucking industry is extremely vulnerable. Most private truckers will be completely shut out. In order to accomplish this, the giant conglomerates that own and operate the farmland, will actually form a partnership of sorts with the government." Paul lowered the book for a moment and took a sip from his drink. "You said Colonel Clifton mentioned putting the felons to work. Maybe it was just a slip, or maybe he was trying to get a rise out of you. Anyway, he was telling you the truth. The men and women in prison play a very important role in the Hedgerow project.

"Since 1980 the prison population in this country has more than tripled. Today we have nearly two million people rotting in cells across the nation. Most of them have been convicted of drug and alcohol related crimes. And the fastest growing budget breaker for state government is building and operating prisons to incarcerate these people. State governments are caught in a trap of their own making. Years ago they thought a get-tough policy would scare criminals into becoming law-abiding citizens. But they weren't dealing with ordinary criminals. They were dealing with drug dealers and junkies. Most of them were too hooked to reform. And most of them haven't even gotten off the drugs in prison. The states kept building bigger prisons. They kept filling them with helpless bastards serving longer and longer sentences. The public demands it. They even managed to force through a 'three strikes law' that can put someone in jail for life for a minor offense. As a result, the prisons are flooded to the rafters and the states pay for it with no hope of return for the investment. What they forget is that eighty percent of those doing time now will soon be back on the streets. The scariest part is that the prisons are now controlled by gangs. You either join them or kiss your ass goodbye. Whatever they were when they went in, when they come out, they're going to be more vicious, brazen and violent than they ever would have been if we had just left them on the street."

"Boy, that's a pleasant thought," scoffed Mattson. "Two million hopped up junkies with a vicious streak, running the streets." He motioned Paul to turn the page. "That's going to be a hell of a shock for the public," he said. "They seem to think the system is working. They say the crime rate has been dropping for the past three to five years."

"You bought into that?" asked Paul, expressing genuine surprise.

"You mean it hasn't been dropping?"

"That depends on whose statistics you choose to believe." said Paul. "The next time you read that the crime rate is dropping you might consider the admission made by the National Crime Statistics Bureau." Paul thumbed through the book for a minute, then smiled and began reading aloud. "Due to NIBRS conversion efforts, only limited arrest data were received from contributing law enforcement agencies in New Hampshire and Illinois, and no arrest data were received from Kansas. Because of reporting problems at the state level, only limited arrest statistics were provided from Kentucky and Montana, and no arrest data were received from Wisconsin. Arrest statistics received from the District of Colombia could not be processed because the format was not in accordance with UCR guidelines."

Paul smiled, sardonically. "You see? If something doesn't fit their agenda, they just don't use it. The truth is, regardless of the statistics you get from the media, for the decade 1989 to 1998 arrests for all offenses were up seven percent. If anyone really believes the crime rate is dropping, let them explain why they're building more prisons than at any time in our history? And, it's not just the federal prisons that are bursting at the seams, it's the state prisons."

Paul flipped a few more pages and continued. "The Federal Bureau of Prisons controls 96 institutions and they have a total of 140, 019 inmates. Of those, only 97, 491 are from the United States. 21,330 are from Mexico, 4,266 are from Colombia, 2,919 are from Cuba, and there are another 14, 013 whose citizenship is listed as unknown. The average age is 37 and within five years 16,000 of them are going to hit the streets. Within 10 to 15 years nearly 80,000 of them will be released."

"And that's just the federal system?" asked Mattson.

"That's just the federal system," said Paul. "Now multiply that 80,000 by 20, and you have an idea of what lies ahead for this country."

"So how does Hedgerow fit into this?" asked Mattson

"Hedgerow' is hoping to privatize the entire prison industry and put them to work." said Paul. "Can you imagine the profit generated by a couple of million unpaid laborers?"

"Aren't you forgetting the Constitution?" asked Mattson

"Not at all," said Paul. 'The thirteenth amendment says: 'neither slavery nor involuntary servitude, except as a punishment for crime, whereof the party shall have been duly convicted, shall exist within the United States, or any place subject to their jurisdiction'. Paul smiled, "All of these people have been duly convicted."

"So the Constitution would actually support something like this?" asked Mattson.

"It's a matter of interpretation," said Paul. "But I think they have it covered in Section Two, which states: 'Congress shall have power to enforce this article by appropriate legislation."

"How do they intend to make it work?" asked Mattson.

"Have you ever heard of PPCA?" asked Paul.

"No." Mattson shook his head.

"It stands for, 'Private Prison Corporation of America" said Paul. "This

Corporation is rapidly becoming the owner and manager of more private prisons than any other company in the country. They operate facilities for the immigration service, and they're building, staffing, and operating prisons across the nation."

"Is this part the Hedgerow project?" asked Mattson

"Of course it is," said Paul. "This is how they intend to keep the country functioning when all hell breaks loose. PPCA is hoping to drive out the other companies and eventually take control of every convicted felon in the United States."

"I've never even heard of them," said Mattson. "How long have they been around?"

"They were founded in the early eighties. They were able to convince legislatures in some of the southern states that they could build and run prisons cheaper than the existing system. Even those who were opposed had to admit that states, counties and even cities, will save millions by eliminating public employee contracts. They charge a flat price per head, and they accept complete responsibility. Of course, they also have complete control."

"On the face, it sounds Okay," said Mattson, "but it seems a little too convenient. Something doesn't smell right."

"You're right," agreed Paul, nodding his head. "In the beginning, privatizing prisons was opposed on a moral basis. Auctioning human beings for profit was likened to selling beef in a meat market. The American Civil Liberties Union, the National Sheriffs Association, religious leaders and even the American Bar

Association strongly voiced their opposition. Unfortunately, their voices were muffled in State Legislatures because of the money that could be saved. Some states jumped on the wagon because they had no other solution. Corporate lockups are now holding approximately 100,000 prisoners. Over the next few years analysts expect the private share of the prison market to triple. They compare this enterprise to a hotel that's always at one hundred percent occupancy and booked for as long as people exist."

"It's always the money, isn't it?" Mattson shook his head in disgust. "Screw the people…get the money. What ever happened to rehabilitation" he asked.

Paul sighed, and thumbed through the book. "During the Reagan administration, in 1985," he said, "Governor Lamar Alexander of Tennessee, backed a plan to turn the entire prison system of Tennessee over to a fledgling company called Correction Corporation of America, for $200 million. That plan was shot down because it was considered too risky, but today that company has control of nearly as many inmates as the federal system and they're still growing. And, these prison corporations are not concerned with anything as mundane as rehabilitation. Their job is to lock people up as cheaply as possible. They design and build their own prisons so they can use video cameras to replace guards. They design the control room to enable a single guard to watch three 'pods' of 250 prisoners each. Security windows offer an unobstructed view of each cellblock. They have what they call 'vision blocks' built into the floor so guards can make visual identification of anyone entering the cellblocks. A state of the art control panel can open or close any door in the facility with the flick of a switch. This system requires only five guards to supervise 750 inmates during the day and two guards at night."

"What about activities?" asked Mattson, "How about job training, some kind of education? You sound like all they do is sit in their cells?"

"That's pretty much what they do." said Paul. "Some of the guards say the company contributes to the violence by skimping on activities for the inmates. One of the guards who resigned after only a month on the job said, "We don't give them anything to do. We give them the bare minimum we have to."

"Shit, that's just asking for trouble," said Mattson. "I'd go nuts in a place like that."

"The state of Tennessee did a comparison study in 1992," said Paul, thumbing through the book, again. Finding the section he was looking for, he began reading: "They compared a prison operated by a private provider against two public prisons. The private prison was built at approximately the same time as the state operated prisons with similar designs and inmate populations. Their findings show the private prison is a much more dangerous place than the public prisons. Violent incidents were 50 percent higher. They had higher rates for contraband, drugs, and assaults on staff and other prisoners. A state representative, on reviewing the data, was appalled. 'If this doesn't raise some eyebrows, and give you some indication of what the future holds, I guess those of us who are concerned had better be quiet.' he said.

"Did they make any changes?" asked Mattson laying down the camera and lighting another cigarette.

"They didn't have to," said Paul. "They were doing what their contract stipulated. They were protecting the public and the public didn't give a damn how it was accomplished. The name of the game for these prison corporations is money, and they make no bones about it. Most of them have eliminated guaranteed pensions and offer the employees stock- ownership plans. One guard, who didn't want to be identified stated, "As an owner you don't waste money on things like cleaning supplies and a lot of molly-coddling activities because it's your own money that you're spending."

"Another statement, this time by a prisoner who had spent time in state prisons, summed up the view of the inmates themselves when he said, "I can't get over how many people are just laying around every day. They must know that inmate idleness is one of the biggest problems in prisons... too much sitting around and doing nothing. You definitely know it's a business. Their business is to feed you and count you and that's it."

"Well, if they just lay around every day," said Mattson, "and they aren't doing anything constructive to change their lives, what the hell does the state expect from them when they do get out?"

"The people behind 'Hedgerow' realize that there is a certain percentage of the prison population that are incorrigible and they intend to use them to their advantage. They want them to come out angry and bitter. They want them to come out with a 'get even' attitude. They expect some of them to start joining forces on the streets, and that's part of the agenda. Without military back up, and advanced training with hi-tech weaponry, the average police force will lose control and be swept away."

"I get it," Mattson nodded as he flicked his ashes in the soap dish. "That gives the military an excuse to come in. But why the hell aren't the state legislatures investing money now to rehabilitate those who are not incorrigible? Can't they see what's coming?"

"The concept of rehabilitation has pretty much fallen by the way-side, even with the professionals."

"So they've decided to just give up and ignore what's happening? They just throw these people in cells and forget about them until their time is up?"

"Not at all," said Paul, a slight smirk was playing at his lips. For those deemed worthy of salvage they have developed a program that I think of as, mental castration, but you would probably prefer the more common term of brainwashing."

"What the hell is that?" growled Mattson.

"What is what?" asked Paul, "brainwashing?" He was amused at Mattson's building frustration.

"No, damn it! I know what brainwashing is. I want to know about the 'program'?"

161

"Okay," said Paul, growing serious, "but this gets complicated. We haven't covered this yet, but the 'program' is basically a method that has been developed to mobilize a workforce utilizing the prison population. This workforce has to be absolutely docile and obedient. They will have to obey without question and they will have to be programmed to a point of dependability where a minimum of security is required to guard them. The hard core Cons will have to be weeded out and transferred to permanent prison settings, but the weak and malleable will be shipped to special camps where they will be subjected to a constant bombardment of humiliation and degradation.

"Lawyers can't help them. Their families can't help them. They'll be totally cut off and helpless. Under these conditions you can destroy their hope, you can destroy their spirit. When there's no hope, there's no fight. By the time its over they'll be totally passive and submissive. At this point a religious component will be added to the program and they'll be put on a psychological diet of carrots and sticks. Ministers from the Bible belt will be making regular visits to these private camps, spouting their own special brand of Christian doctrine. Every waking hour will be filled with praying, Bible thumping, testifying, and praising the lord. They are going to be 'born again'. It will work like any other cult."

Mattson shook his head in amazement. "And the legislators are just going to sit by and let this happen?" he asked.

"What choice do they have? Even if they know what's happening they aren't going to buck the tide. They do what they have to do to get re-elected. You have to remember, Ron, private enterprise and public apathy are the engines generating the power for this thing. The people in the Hedgerow think- tanks are directing the trends and preparing for what they expect will be inevitable chaos. They're like buzzards waiting to gorge themselves on the nation's carcass."

"Clifton said they should be using the prison population for farming and public service programs. What about that?" asked Mattson.

"Those who have been indoctrinated," said Paul, "and are considered reliable and truly born again will form the core of the prison work force. They'll be offered early release under a modified parole program and hired by the prison corporation. They'll do whatever job they are assigned, whether it's farming, road building, picking fruit and berries…. It doesn't matter."

"And if they rebel and refuse to go along with the program?" asked Mattson

"In that case, they get whacked with the stick and shipped back to the nearest PPCA facility. But, believe me, they won't rebel. Their days of independent decision making are gone."

"What's the time-table for all of this?" asked Mattson. "Something like this can't be pulled off overnight."

"There's not a huge rush," said Paul. "After all, it's taken over twenty years to get this far. The pace is subject and dependent, not only to conditions here in the United States, but also to world events. Unless something unforeseen occurs it will be phased in slowly. In the event that something happens to necessitate a speed-up it is adequately covered in the contingency planning." Paul waved the book. "It's all in here," he said. "Even as we speak PPCA is slowly absorbing the majority of prisons in this country. Projections indicate they will be successful in driving out smaller companies and buying up the larger ones. When they have enough control they'll offer prison laborers to any company that requests it."

Paul set the book on the bed and opened his suitcase. He dug through it and after a moment his hand came out with another bottle of Vodka. He was silent as he opened the bottle and poured himself a drink. He offered the bottle to Mattson, but the reporter shook his head. Opening the bottle Paul poured some Vodka into his glass and set the bottle on the table. Taking a sip from the glass, he sat down on the bed.

"As far as PPCA is concerned," he said, "California and the Southwest will be the first to feel the impact. It will be a three-pronged attack. The first prong will be to create a market for the prison work force. The target area will be in towns along the Sierra foothills such as Orange Cove, which has been described as a 'virtual labor camp for the citrus industry'. They have 65 packinghouses and employ 15, 000 'pickers' and 'packers'. They produce about 80 percent of the nation's table oranges. Those workers will be removed."

"So they just fire the Mexicans and replace them with prison labor?" Mattson shook his head, skeptically. "The companies that hired them aren't going to go for that."

"In the past,"said Paul, "because of political influence and possible repercussions, the Immigration and Naturalization Service has devoted only 2 percent of its enforcement man-hours to actual work sites. In fact, since 1994 when California became a testing ground for 'Operation Gatekeeper' only about six employers of undocumented workers had ever been prosecuted. That will be changed. These companies are in violation of the law. Under threat of prosecution they'll accept the government's offer of replacement workers without a peep."

"That's bullshit!" said Mattson. "What the hell happens to the Mexicans? And what the hell is Operation Gatekeeper?"

"I'll get to Gatekeeper later." Paul leaned forward, looking at Mattson. "There is going to be a complete reversal of policy concerning immigration in this country. The second prong of this plan will be targeting the actual deportation of at least 50 percent of the illegal immigrants in California within five years"

"Holy shit," exclaimed Mattson, "You're talking about millions of people. You can't be serious?"

"About 30 million Latinos are in this country," said Paul. "Sixty percent of them are Mexican. Current estimates indicate that 4,000 to 10, 000 illegal immigrants enter this country every month. More than 60 percent of the babies born in Los Angeles County are born to women who have entered this country illegally. Illegal immigrants occupy 56% of all public housing in Los Angeles. And that's just California," said Paul. Three thousand miles away, in Dade County, Florida, the bill for educating undocumented children is over $21 million. Through fraudulent identification, illegal immigrants get federal benefits such as Social Security, subsidized housing, public education and assorted Welfare payments. Projections by the Social Security Administration indicate a budget of $8 billion will be required by the year 2026 just for the illegals. Hedgerow says, "They have to go!" Paul stopped talking long enough to take another sip from his glass.

"Are they building walls along the border?" asked Mattson.

"Not walls," said Paul. "Fences are cheaper

"But they can't just kick them out," protested Mattson. "Can they?"

"Why not?" said Paul, thumbing through the book again. "They did before."

Mattson looked skeptical. "What do you mean? They did it before. "When was that?"

"Back in the thirties," said Paul. "In fact about four hundred thousand people are suing the city and county of Los Angeles right now for the loss they suffered when then were forcibly sent back to Mexico during the depression. A law firm in Beverly Hills said that the deportation program at that time was a coordinated aggressive campaign to remove people of Mexican ancestry from California in large numbers. One of the lawyers said that "until we take an honest look in the mirror, none of us is truly safe." Paul flipped some more pages.

It took him a couple of minutes to find what he was looking for. Mattson was silent.

"Immigration authorities say they have deported three hundred–thousand illegal immigrants since 1996. They now have a budget of one billion dollars and fifteen- thousand armed officers.

"I don't understand." said Mattson. "How is this going on and nobody hears about it?"

Paul ignored the question. "The third prong will seal the border with Mexico."

"Lots of luck, there, too" snorted Mattson. "They've been trying to do that for years."

"They can do it," said Paul, ignoring the derision in Mattson's voice. "USORSC working in conjunction with the Gatekeeper Project will effectively seal off the 2000-mile border stretching from San Diego to Brownsville, Texas."

"What the hell is this 'Gatekeeper program'?" asked Mattson

"Anticipating Mattson's question, Paul smiled. "Gatekeeper is a program put together by the Border Patrol and the Department of Defense' Center for Low Intensity Conflicts. Before Gatekeeper there were only twenty miles of fencing in the San Diego sector. Today there are more than 52 miles of primary and secondary fencing, with half of it extending from the Pacific Ocean to the base of the Otay Mountains. This area also has 54% of the border illumination. Even though the death rate has increased dramatically the Border Patrol has extended Gatekeeper by other names into other areas of the Southwest border. In El Paso they know it as, 'Hold the Line', in Arizona it's called 'Safeguard'. The objective is to re-direct illegal aliens away from the cities and into the deserts and mountains minimizing their visibility in high population areas. As a result, deaths have increased 400% and the Border Patrol itself says that no one knows how many bodies lie undiscovered out there. They know that at least 3000 people have died in the deserts and mountains in the last nine years and the border patrol estimates that about 340 died last year."

'You didn't answer me the last time I asked," said Mattson. "So, I'm asking again. How are all these things happening and nobody ever hears about it?"

"Many people know about it," insisted Paul, "A lot of organizations on both sides of the border have been fighting it for years, but they can't do a damned thing about it. You can look up Project Gatekeeper on the Internet. They don't mention Hedgerow of course, but with a little back-ground the pieces fall together."

Paul picked up the book again. "Laws will be changed and strictly enforced." He said. "Hospitals, under penalty of federal prosecution will be prohibited from treating people they suspect of being illegal aliens. They will also be required to provide names and addresses of those people to the INS. Economic assistance will be withheld from any nation that fails to give us their full cooperation. New provisions will be incorporated into laws designed to stop illegal immigration into the United States. One of them will be a bilateral prisoner exchange and an agreement from Mexico to incarcerate or otherwise punish deported aliens returned to their country." Paul set the book on the bed, stood up and walked to the dresser where he poured himself another shot of Vodka. The Vodka was having little or no effect on him at this point. He felt as though he was drinking himself sober, but getting up gave him an opportunity to stretch his legs. Taking a quick sip he set the glass back on the dresser, locked his fingers behind his head and stretched his back, letting a gratifying sigh escape his lips as he felt the crackle in his spine.

"And now," he said, "This country will take a step that will shock the world."

In spite of himself, Mattson leaned forward, expectantly.

"When the time is right, INS agents with the assistance of USORSC will sweep in and gather up the undocumented workers for deportation. Relatives and close friends will be detained on conspiracy and harboring charges. Movable barriers will seal off massive areas in California and neighboring states until the 'Gathering' is complete in the target areas. The Orange Growers Association, and business enterprises that depend on migrant workers along the Pacific coast and mountain states to produce their products will go through the roof, but that's when private prison corporations will step in and save the day with an unlimited supply of cheap labor. The program will then extend along the entire southern border to Texas like a gigantic wave, gathering up every alien in its path, regardless of documentation. USORSC forces drawn from around the country will be there to enforce massive deportations and this will be done without benefit of court hearings. Every border crossing will be jammed with thousands of people being literally pushed into Mexico. Mexican authorities will be waiting on the other side, gathering them up and forcing them into railroad cars, trucks and busses to transport them to the interior where detention camps will be set up to receive them."

"My god!" gasped Mattson. "What will they do to them?"

"Who knows?" Paul shrugged. "That will be up to Mexico. I expect that a lot of them will simply disappear. Mexico's only interest will be in appeasing the United States. Simply put, Mexico needs money. We have the money. If they give us what we want, we'll give them what they want. I can't prove this, but I've been told that Mexico intends to also declare these people illegal aliens and as such they will be sentenced to work farms and massive highway building projects. They will be permanently prevented from returning to the United States.

"But most of them are Mexican! They won't be aliens in Mexico. How the hell can they do that?"

"They'll speak the language," admitted Paul, "but none of them will be able to produce papers proving they are Mexican. As far as Mexico is concerned, these will be Americans that have come across the border illegally. Needless to say, they will have no money and most will have nothing more than the clothes on their backs." Paul slapped angrily at the book lying next to him. "Believe me, Ron. They have everything covered."

Mattson inspected the camera, making certain it was turned off and set it on the bed. He walked to the corner of the room near a window and flopped into a chair. After a moment he leaned forward, resting his elbows on his knees and cradled his head in his hands, massaging his temple with his fingertips. "I don't believe it," he shook his head obstinately. "I can't believe this country would let something like that happen."

Paul watched him, knowing exactly what he was feeling, but said nothing. Instead, he walked to the dresser, picked up Mattson's glass and the bottle of vodka. He poured a large shot into it, poured in some Coke and added an ice cube. Still without speaking, he carried the glass across the room and offered it to the reporter.

"Thanks." Mattson accepted the glass, took a long swallow and dug into his pocket for a cigarette. "I just can't believe it." He repeated

"It shouldn't be that hard to believe," said Paul, sipping his own drink. "I've just told you this country allows a program to exist that literally forces people out into the desert to die."

"Yeah, but… Ah, shit," Mattson shook his head in frustration, not knowing what to say.

After a moment he gathered his thoughts and looked at Paul. "What about the Asians?" asked Mattson, belligerently "I suppose they have a plan for them too?"

"Of course," Paul nodded in affirmation. "They have a plan for everyone. They even have a plan for Social Security and Medicare. Want to hear it?"

Mattson shook his head, and held up his hand. The reporter's face was pale. "Not now, Paul. I've got to have a few minutes to think"

Paul nodded without speaking. He walked into the bathroom, remembering his own reaction when he had first read the report. If Mattson hadn't been equally shocked he would have been surprised. Pulling a razor from his shaving kit, he lathered his face and began shaving. He took his time, giving Mattson the time he needed to absorb all that he had heard.

When he came out of the bathroom, Mattson was still sitting in the chair nursing his drink. The color had returned to his face but his knuckles were white as his hand gripped the glass. After a moment he looked up. "What the hell is happening in the rest of the country while this is going on?" he asked.

"The reaction will be different everywhere," said Paul. "Part of the nation will be in turmoil, while other parts aren't even aware of what's taking place. The media will keep reports from the border areas to a minimum. They'll attribute the riots taking place on the West Coast to terroristic activity. USORSC forces will be dispatched to quell it."

Mattson had heard enough. He took a sip from the glass he was holding, got out of the chair and carried the glass to the dresser. He wanted to ask more questions, but he hesitated, wondering what Paul might tell him next. He decided to take the chance. "You said they had a solution for Social Security."

"They have," said Paul. "They eliminate those who are receiving it."

"What the hell does that mean?"

"It means that they have to downsize the population. They have to eliminate as many people as possible, but they have to do it in a way that does not expose the fact that it is intentional murder." Paul saw the disbelief in Ron's eyes, and held up a hand. "Relax, Ron. I'm not talking about spraying the city with poison gas, or introducing some new exotic poison into the drinking water. It will be much something much more subtle. Something like gradually increasing the price of Insulin to a point where the average person can't afford it. People will try to stretch out their supply and get by on less. Without adequate Insulin, those people will die."

"I can see that happening," said Ron. "I know a lot of the old people are already forced to choose between buying food, medicine, or to pay their heating bill."

"Another clever method surfaced when Reagan was in office," said Paul. "Reagan suggested that a way to ease the housing crunch was for old people to move into nursing homes and make their homes available to a younger generation. Do you remember that?"

"I remember something like that," said Mattson. "It was stupid. All it did was scare the hell out of old people."

"A lot of people living on fixed incomes and living alone took his advice and did that very thing. Subsequent studies reveal that the life span for most people in the age bracket involved is shortened considerably when they lose the security of their own homes. The only thing that keeps most of them alive is being independent and self-sufficient. For many, the biggest fear is that they will become a burden to their children or to the community. When they feel they have nothing left to contribute they just seem to shut down."

"I'm working on a story now about senior citizens," said Mattson. "They live in a High Rise, but they seem to be doing just fine."

"A High Rise isn't a nursing home," said Paul, "but if they're just fine," he asked, "where's the story?"

The question was unexpected. Mattson had to think for a minute before answering. "Actually it's more about the Bus Company raising their rates for senior citizens. It's a small increase, but it makes it tough on a lot of them."

"Exactly," said Paul. "Now imagine what happens when the federal government cuts back on entitlements to states."

"I don't get it," Mattson was confused.

"It works this way," said Paul. "When the Federal Government holds back money from the States, the States hold back money from the Cities and Counties. When the Cities and Counties realize they don't have enough money to meet their obligations they raise taxes." Paul raised his hand and began counting off on his fingers. "Property Taxes, heating bills, gas and electric, water bills, sewer and garbage, the list is endless. Old people living on fixed incomes, even with their house paid for, won't be able to keep up. When they're forced out of their own home and into a nursing home they'll feel worthless. Everything they worked for their entire lives will be gone. They'll be heartbroken and they'll lose the will to live."

"God, that's cold," said Mattson.

Without acknowledging the remark, Paul continued. "Because of State cutbacks in other areas, nursing homes will not be able to maintain the level of staffing and care that most of them require. "Hedgerow" estimates life expectancy at six to twenty-four months for approximately fifty percent of those people."

Mattson smiled cynically. "As a bonus they free up a shortage in the housing market. Is that it?" He was beyond shock.

"We've only scratched the surface," said Paul, "but I'm beat." Sitting on the edge of the bed, he picked up the book and waved it. "If we can't prove our case with this…" he left the sentence unfinished and shrugged, surprising Mattson as he went to the bathroom and poured himself a glass of water, rather than Vodka. Coming back to the bed, his eyes settled on Mattson. . "Any ideas on how your paper will deal with this?"

"Nothing definite." said Mattson. "We'll have to talk it over. It's going to take time to put this thing together. There's so damned much material. Where the hell do I start?"

"I understand," Paul nodded. "I'll let you take my briefcase. You'll need it to carry the camera and the cartridges."

"You want me to keep the camera?"

"Why not?" said Paul. "You'll find a program, some extra cords, and an adapter that you can plug into a computer. It will save you time and I have no further need for it." He gestured to the book. "There's still a lot that we haven't covered."

Mattson leaned over and picked up the book. He raised it up and down a couple of times, as though testing its weight. "I couldn't even get through War and Peace." He laughed nervously. "I listen a lot better than I read."

Paul got the message and gave a slight chuckle. Leaning back he brought both hands to his face and massaged his head. "Okay", he said. "Let me try to break it down. The walls you see around the twin cities are permanent barriers. But twenty-three factories around the country are under contract to mass-produce artificial movable barriers that can be installed overnight by the Corps of Engineers. They're made of a super strong lightweight material that can be set in place by a single helicopter and secured by ground forces. Each section measures sixty feet in length, five feet in width and eighteen feet in height. They'll be placed between the permanent barriers wherever they're needed. Their purpose, of course, will be to confine people to specific areas during civil disorders.

"Special teams trained at the Pacification Center in Washington will intentionally create the disorders necessary to require the need for USORSC forces. Their job is to infiltrate every major union, business, religious and social organization in the United States. They'll attempt to organize, and control, massive paralyzing strikes. Their targets will be airlines, trucking, communications, agriculture and public service. The objective is to keep the country in such turmoil that no one will question the need for USORSC troops when they come in."

"I still can't believe the public will just sit on their ass with their heads in the sand while this is going on." said Mattson.

"When things really start moving the public will be so confused and disoriented they won't know what the hell is happening. And they'll be so occupied with what's going on in their own neighborhood they won't know or care about what's happening anywhere else." said Paul. In fact, they expect most people to favor the barriers, believing that the barriers are keeping the real violence out of their own neighborhoods."

"That's crazy," snapped Mattson, gulping at his drink and smashing his cigarette out in the soap dish.

"From where you sit now, and knowing what you know, it seems crazy," admitted Paul, "but none of this will be obvious to the man on the street. If truckers delivering food to major chain restaurants and hotels go on strike, it's a big deal, but it's not a surprise. It's also not a surprise when the companies involved hire scab replacements to keep the food moving. When this results in violence, its par for the course. People get pissed off and begin picking sides. Some are for the truckers, some are against them, but no one is surprised when the government jumps in to put down the violence." Paul raised his hands in a way that suggested his intention to, once again, count off on his fingertips. "Laws will be radically changed giving greater latitude to police in dealing with crime. They won't be hampered any more by normal court rulings and constitutional issues. In the beginning the new laws will appear to work, but the increased authority given to the police will grow completely out of control. Eventually the lack of court restraint will erode the rights of everyone."

Paul ticked off another finger. "Major changes will be made in the departments of Health, Education, and Human Service. Education, as we know it today, will cease to exist. Incompetent teachers, fostered by lowered standards, will flood the system. School districts will phase out teaching facilities for lack of adequate funding. Parents will rebel against a system that produces high school illiterates unable to read or write. Students will rebel against a system that has stripped them of their rights. Teachers will become thoroughly demoralized by intimidation, physical attacks that go unpunished, low pay and nationwide strikes. Pacification classes will be created for problem children, giving them free reign in choice of time and study. It will be a disaster, and parents will begin pulling their children out of the schools in defiance of the law. They'll teach them at home, away from the violence. When enough of the schools have been shut down, or burned down, the government will step in and salvage what is left.

A new educational system will rise from the ashes, but the new system will be accessible to only a limited percentage of the population. For the general population there will be a dumming-down process. Higher education will be reserved for the elite and those whom the government considers 'Super Students'. Those behind 'Hedgerow' know that an intelligent, well educated population can only be controlled to a certain point before they rebel, so the objective will be to keep the masses ignorant". Paul took a swallow from his glass. "That, in a nutshell is what's in store for the education system in this country."

Mattson said nothing. He sat silently sipping his drink and smoking his cigarette.

"The medical field will be another monster," said Paul. "Medical services will be priced completely beyond the reach of the general population. Standards for the care that is available will be so low that people will scream for a nationalized public health system. Organ donations will surge when the new system allows organs to be taken from mental incompetents, criminals, the elderly, and anyone determined by the courts to be incapable of contributing to the betterment of society.

"The main thrust of medicine, however, will be on mind control. Mood altering drugs are already used for political and social purposes. Ritalin is a good example. Just about any kid in school that exhibits a little spirit or individuality is considered hyper and placed on Ritalin, or another drug, in the same class. The parents have no choice in the matter. The school districts make the determination and back it up with their own doctors. What the parents are not told is that each school district receives a stipend of at least thirty-five dollars for every kid on Ritalin. In one district in Georgia, 85% of the kids were on Ritalin. Who cares if it stunts the kids growth, hooks him and starts him on his way to becoming a junkie? Money is money! Ritalin, incidentally, is not unlike the amphetamine we've been taking tonight. In the future you'll find specific drugs mandated for the entire population. These drugs will be added to the foods you find in your local supermarket. It will probably start with soft drinks. First an addictive ingredient will be introduced to get people hooked. Later, specific drugs to reduce paranoia and aggressive behavior will be added to keep the population passive. The public will believe they're getting vitamin supplements. In time, drugs that we haven't even heard of, drugs in the same class as Thorazine and Compazine will be as common as Aspirin."

"You mentioned something earlier about welfare." Said Mattson. "What part will that play?"

"Welfare, or as it is known today, 'Health and Human Services', has already played its part. The only function it will serve in the future will be food distribution and record keeping. It will be completely privatized. A few hard-nosed supervisors will be kept in place, but the majority of human service employees will end up just like the rest of us. Hedgerow has no intention of tolerating anything as benevolent as public welfare. During the early phase government agencies will institute massive relief programs to provide specific areas with emergency help, but this will be in keeping with their policy of confusion and delusion.

"Later, as Hedgerow develops and gathers strength, non-conformists and anyone deemed incapable of contributing to the new society will be phased out... and I mean that literally. Citizens in good standing will be issued a single identification card. It will be used for all transactions, from buying food to seeing a movie. The citizen's name, vital statistics, address, employment and current rating will be coded into the card. Without that card, you simply don't exist. As Citizens age, become ill or injured, commit transgressions or for any other reason are considered inappropriate for the new society, will be deleted with the push of a button."

Mattson, listening intently, crossed the room and refilled his near empty glass from the bottle on the desk. Flicking the ash from his cigarette stub, he took a final drag, and dropped the butt into the soap dish. "I feel like I'm listening to the script for a science fiction movie." His voice was unusually subdued. "A week ago I would never have believed that anything like this was possible. I still can't believe it. How the hell can they get away with it?"

"As long as they can keep the public frightened and confused, and convince the majority that it's good for the nation… they can get away with anything. This country is molded by television commercials, movies and magazine ads. They tell you everything from which car to buy to how often you should brush your teeth. Remember, confusion and delusion. Today coffee, eggs and butter are good for you. Tomorrow they will be bad. Today x-rays are your best hope of finding cancer at an early stage. Tomorrow they'll cite statistics showing that x-rays are responsible for a large percentage of the cancer being found. Subliminal techniques are already being employed to confuse people and change their pattern of thinking. The media can make you believe whatever they want you to believe."

"So how do they get that kind of control over the media?" asked Mattson.

"To a great extent, they already have it, said Paul. "It's only a matter of time before the government will control all of the communication in this country. They'll purchase what they can from private owners of cable communications and install their own brand of programming. They'll infiltrate those that they can't buy, and through harassment, strikes, new court rulings and litigation they will effectively neutralize anything that they don't control.

"Maybe that's what was happening a few weeks ago?" said Mattson.

"How's that?" asked Paul.

"An article I read said that Minnesota Public Radio's news director had resigned because of what he described as problems in the organizational structure of the network. He said his duties were no longer clearly defined, that his role as news director was becoming increasingly fuzzy."

"He was just letting us that someone else was making the decisions," said Paul. "You'll find that every network and newspaper is going to be restructured. All forms of communication will become increasingly less reliable. And when a crisis develops in one particular area, someone out in Virginia will simply flick of a switch. Satellites will fail, computers will crash, and cell phones will go dead in that area until the situation is stabilized.

Travel limitations will be routinely imposed. Railroads, buses, airlines and shipping will be strictly controlled and regulated by the government. Automobiles, to a limited degree, will continue to operate, but only by select groups and individuals. The final phase of Hedgerow will involve the individual states themselves."

"How's that?" asked Mattson.

"Independent farming will no longer exist. Responsibility for producing the nation's food will be awarded by contract to the huge conglomerates that employ genetic engineering. The government will determine what each state is best suited for, and all the resources of that state will be directed toward producing those particular products for the good of the nation. In other words, areas such as Montana, Idaho, Utah, Wyoming and Colorado might be designated as ranching, timber, mining, and potato states.

"And the mid-western states will be into farming and agriculture?" asked Mattson.

"Exactly," said Paul. "And each state will be designated specific crops."

"How about states that aren't suited to any one particular thing?"

"Nothing will go to waste," said Paul. "States such as North and South Dakota, New Mexico and a few others will become refinery states and sites for nuclear waste. Government owned lands, state parks, and privately owned mountain areas, will be opened for extensive drilling and mining exploration. Yellowstone National Park and other protected areas will be opened up and exploited."

"What's going to happen to the cities?" asked Mattson.

"Some of them will continue to expand and grow." said Paul. "People are already being driven back to urban areas because of the energy crunch. Some, because of the destruction they receive during the riots, will be abandoned. They'll become rat- infested havens for those who have been ostracized from the general population.

"Do you think this really can be stopped?" asked Mattson.

Paul considered the question for such a long time that Mattson thought he might not have heard him. He was about to repeat it, when Paul finally spoke. "I don't know." He leaned back, rubbing the back of his neck. His fatigue was beginning to show. "Unfortunately," he said, "nobody knows there is anything to stop. Except for people at the very top, no one has more than bits and pieces. They only know the part they will play. and they think it's for the good of the country. When the military is called in to put down a riot or to seal off an area, they will be doing what soldiers have always done... following orders from their Commander In Chief. They won't know that the riot was intentionally created. They won't even question it. Our only chance is to get this out in the open so that people will question it."

"That's a question in itself," said Mattson, "Will people believe it?"

"All we can do is try," said Paul. "The odds are against us, but unless we try, none of us has a chance."

"What I don't understand," said Mattson "is what are they getting out of this? The people behind this, I mean?"

They 're greedy, vindictive, evil-minded bastards that think they've been chosen by god to save the world." said Paul, "They've already accumulated all the money they'll ever need, so the only thing left is power. They want their place in the history books, even if the books have to be re-written. They 'd like everyone to think that their actions are necessary for our survival, but what they're doing is a total debasement of everything this country has ever stood for." Paul's voice held a fearful resignation as he continued. "My personal feeling is that, as a nation, we will not survive. I think our days are numbered and time is running out. I'm not a religious person, but I'm beginning to believe that the United States is the 'Wanton Queen' referred to in Revelations. I think we're going to fall to a level so low that even Rome would blush. We'll become so feeble and crippled by our own malignance that the Russians and the rest of the world will attack us out of self-preservation. They'll consider us mad."

"God! You really believe that? Asked Mattson. "The entire world would attack us? Would they win? Could they win?"

Paul smiled. It was a sad smile, and his voice cracked slightly as he spoke. "There won't be any winners. If a nuclear attack is launched against this country we'll have less than thirty minutes warning. We might get off a few missiles, but if all the countries with nukes launch at the same time it would happen so fast that we'd be buried."

"No shit," Mattson swore, "You really believe that could happen?"

"It would make the religious fanatics happy," said Paul. "It would fulfill the prophesy, 'Alas, alas, thou great city, thou mighty city, Babylon! In one hour has thy judgement come"

Paul glanced at his watch and shook his head. "Time is running out for us too," he told Mattson, as he walked over to the bed. "I've got to start getting ready for the plane back to Washington."

"You want me to drive you?"

"No thanks. I'll catch a cab. I don't want to take any chance on our being seen together."

He picked up the briefcase and handed it to Mattson. "Now that Clifton has met you we can't afford to let anyone even think that we know each other."

Mattson accepted the briefcase and opened it. Very carefully he placed the camera and cartridges inside and closed the lid. "Will you give me a call after you get the book back in the file?"

Paul nodded. "Don't worry. As soon as I get the chance I'll call and let you know. It will probably be about nine o'clock tomorrow morning. Will you be home at that time?"

"I'll be there," assured Mattson. "I sure as hell hope nothing goes wrong."

"Relax," said Paul. "The tough part was getting it out. Nobody will be looking for me to smuggle a book into the file."

Mattson nodded, and walked into the bathroom. He threw cold water into his face, combed his hair, and put on his jacket. "I guess that's it, then." He said, picking up the briefcase and extending his hand.

Paul took his hand. "It's been a pleasure meeting you, Mr. Mattson. I hope our meeting accomplishes something."

"I'll do everything that I can," promised Mattson. "I'll be waiting for your call."

Paul nodded and opened the door. He glanced out in the hall and stepped aside for Mattson to leave. "Take care." He said.

Mattson stepped by him and walked quickly down the hall to the elevator. As he pushed the button he glanced back and saw Paul give him a quick wave before disappearing back into the room.

Downstairs, except for the two people working behind the desk, the lobby was empty. They seemed not to notice as he stepped off the elevator and walked outside to his car. The weather was unusually hot and muggy. He set the briefcase in the backseat, rolled down the window and waited a couple of minutes for the inside to cool off before getting in. As he pulled out of the parking lot he thought about going over to Benny's apartment to let him know what had happened. Then, thinking better of it, he decided to go straight home. The first thing he had to do was hide the briefcase.

By the time he reached his apartment he was tired and sweating. The thought of going into the attic in this weather filled him with dread, but there was no way to avoid it. The sooner the papers were hidden the safer he would be. He had no illusions as to what would happen if someone like Clifton got their hands on the film.

Back in his apartment he carried the chair from the kitchen into the hall. Standing on the chair it took only a second to remove the trap door. He had to step back down on the floor to get the briefcase, and then back up so that he could toss it through the hole. Grabbing the edge of the opening he pulled himself up after it, being thankful that today was Sunday. There was little chance of anyone coming through the halls and seeing him.

He had forgotten the flashlight, but it took only a minute to locate the briefcase. He pushed it ahead of him; in the direction he was so familiar with, being careful to avoid the wires. It took him a few minutes to locate the packet of papers that he had hidden earlier, but at last he had them. He pulled the envelope from under the insulation and stuffed it in the briefcase, then placed the briefcase back under the insulation. When he was satisfied, he backed slowly to the opening and let himself down.

Replacing the trap door was no less a problem this time than it had been before. Finally, after struggling until his arms were about to give out from the strain, and just as he was about to give up, the door dropped into place. Sweat was pouring off of him as he picked up the chair, carried it into the apartment and closed the door. He tried the knob, making sure it was locked before he carried the chair back into the kitchen.

Mattson thought again about calling Benny, as he walked into the bedroom. He sat on the edge of the bed looking at the telephone, wanting to call, to share his excitement, but finally decided that he was just too damned tired. The pills had stopped working and he had all that he could do just to get his clothes off and crawl into bed. Even the insulation clinging to his sweaty

skin didn't bother him. In a few minutes he
was snoring.

Chapter Ten

Paul was as good as his word. At exactly nine o'clock the telephone began ringing.

Mattson was still sleeping and he woke with a start. He jerked upright in the bed and for a minute he just sat there staring at the blank wall. The telephone gave another shrill blast and he suddenly remembered where he was. He leaned over and snatched it up.

"Hello?"

"Ron, this is Paul. You wanted me to call you."

"Yeah, Paul." Mattson shook his head trying to clear it. "How'd everything go?"

"Everything is fine." Said Paul. "I took care of it. No problems. I'm in a pay phone now so I can't talk long, but I wanted you to know that everything is okay on this end."

"I really appreciate the call, Paul. Did you get any sleep?"

"Not enough," said Paul, "but I'll get some more after I have breakfast. "When I get back to the Twin Cities, I'll get in touch."

The line went dead before Mattson could respond. He looked at the phone, surprised at the abrupt ending to the conversation, then shrugged and hung it up. In a few minutes he was once more sleeping soundly.

Less than an hour later the phone rang again. This time Mattson was instantly awake. He grabbed it on the second ring.

"Is that you, Ron?" It was Benny's voice and he sounded agitated.

"Yeah, Benny, what's up?"

"What's up?" growled Benny. "How the hell do I know what's up? You're the one that's been missing. You tell me what's up?"

Mattson laughed and swung his legs over the side of the bed. "I'm sorry about that, Benny. I planned on calling in, but I just didn't get a chance. I was with Paul Stoddard at the Kelly Inn since Friday."

"Who's Paul Stoddard?" asked Benny. "Do I know him?"

"My friend from Washington," said Mattson, lighting a cigarette. "He brought me the whole damned report. We spent the weekend video taping it.

"No shit?" Benny's voice changed from agitation to awe. "How the hell did you pull that off? You should have called me, damn it. You should have called me!" His voice was shrill with excitement, and then suddenly the tone changed to quiet concern. "Have you got the tape?"

"I've got a briefcase filled with them." laughed Mattson.

"Oh god! You've got them with you?" The concern was evident in Benny's voice.

"I've got them hidden," assured Mattson. "Don't worry about it." He took a long drag off the cigarette and flipped the ashes toward the ashtray sitting on his nightstand. "We can go over all of this later, Benny. I want to get some more sleep."

"More sleep?" Benny's voice was an anguished cry. "Ron, you've got to get the hell out of there!"

"Why the hell would I do that?" Mattson was unconcerned. "Oh, by the way. Paul told me that guy Clifton, out in Edina, is not really retired after all. That's only a cover. He's supposed to be in charge of the whole operation here in Minnesota."

"Oh shit." Benny's voice was little more than a whisper. He was silent for a moment, and then he said quietly. "Ron, do you trust me?"

"Of course, I trust you." said Mattson. "Why?"

"Because I'm going to tell you something, and I don't want you to get hot about it." said Benny.

"Go ahead," said Mattson, cautiously.

"I've been doing a lot of thinking. I think this is too big for you, Ron. It might be too big for all of us."

"So?" said Mattson.

"What I'm saying," said Benny "is that these guys are professionals. We're nothing more than a snack for people like this. Sooner or later they're going to put you and this guy Stoddard together. When they do, all hell is going to break loose."

"How are they going to put us together? No one saw us. Besides, I've got everything hidden."

"Yeah," scoffed Benny. "And I'll bet you've got it hidden right there in the building, haven't you?"

"Mattson didn't answer.

"I thought so." said Benny. "Listen, Ron. When those guys get a line on you they'll tear that place to pieces brick by brick. You've got to get that shit out of there, and you've got to get out of there, too!"

"Come on, Benny. You're freaking me out. How the hell could they know?"

"I told you, Ron. They're professionals. It's their job to know. If Stoddard made any mistakes at all, they'll find them, and they'll find you. Something like this is just too damned big!"

"Okay," Mattson got off the bed. Without even being aware of it he glanced nervously at the door. "Okay, what should I do?"

"Get everything you've got and meet me outside. I'll be there in fifteen minutes." Benny hung up before Mattson had a chance to answer.

"Damn it!" Mattson slammed the phone back in its cradle. "Doesn't anyone say good-bye, anymore?"

Whether it was because he had done it so often before, or it was a sudden surge of adrenalin, the climb into the attic and the retrieval of the briefcase, even replacing the trapdoor, took only a couple of minutes. The things Benny had said and the tone of his voice had gotten to him and he could feel the panic rising. This time he didn't bother returning the chair to the kitchen. He just opened the door and flipped it into the living room. He was at the curb, waiting, when Benny pulled up.

The car was still moving as Benny leaned over opening the door on the passenger side. "Hop in," he shouted.

Mattson, hugging the briefcase to his chest, dropped into the seat pulling the door shut, and Benny hit the gas pulling out onto Summit Avenue. The car had never even come to a complete stop.

"What the hell's the rush?" growled Mattson.

"The rush," said Benny, glancing at the briefcase, "is that I want to get the hell out of this neighborhood." Coming to Western Avenue he turned right, swinging around the little duck pond park sitting on the corner, heading toward Selby Avenue. He kept looking in the rear view mirror and glancing at the occupants of the cars they passed. "Where's that guy, Stoddard, now?" he asked Mattson.

"He called from Washington this morning," said Mattson. "He told me he put the report back in the file and there was nothing to worry about." Mattson slid the briefcase down on the floor between his legs. "Where we going?"

"Over to my place on the east side." said Benny, turning right on Dayton Avenue, heading back toward the Cathedral Church. "We need some time to talk and sort this thing out. We need to find a place to put that stuff." He gestured to the briefcase.

"Shit," said Mattson. "We've got everything we need. Why not take it right to the office and start running it?"

"No way," said Benny, "Harry won't touch that stuff until we have a chance to go over it. Besides, if they put you and Stoddard together, they'll hit your apartment first and if they don't find what they want, they'll tear the newsroom apart. We've got to slow down and do this thing right." Benny maneuvered the car through the streets until he was able to get onto the freeway heading East. "We should also make some back-up disks, just in case."

Mattson was surprised when Benny pulled off at White Bear avenue, turned left back, over the bridge and continued down the street for about six blocks before turning left again. He pulled the car to a stop in front of a small white house with brown trim.

"I thought you lived down by Mounds Park?" said Mattson.

"I moved in with my girlfriend a few days ago," said Benny. Seeing the sudden concern on Mattson's face, he grinned. "Don't worry. She's at work. Nobody's home." He cut the motor, got out of the car and led the way up the cracked, uneven sidewalk, with Mattson following, clutching tightly to the briefcase.

Inside, the house was as small as it had looked on the outside, but clean and neatly kept with family pictures and knick-knacks lining the walls. Benny led the way through the small kitchen to the back of the house where he had converted one of the two bedrooms into an office. He motioned Mattson to a leather love seat while he grabbed a chair in front of a narrow wooden desk holding his computer.

"Not bad," said Mattson, flopping on the love seat and laying the briefcase on a pillow next to him. "How come you moved?"

"Ah," Benny seemed embarrassed, "Sara's been after me for the last six months to get out of that place and move in with her. She says she's afraid of living alone out here." Benny shrugged. "I figured, what the hell. It'll save me a few bucks, and she's a good cook." He motioned to the briefcase. "Let's see what we've got?"

Mattson opened the briefcase and set it on the floor. He pulled out the camera and held it out to Benny. "Know anything about these?"

Benny looked at the camera without touching it. After a moment he nodded, turned and opened a drawer on the desk and pulled out a camera that was almost an exact duplicate. "The guy's got good taste. This is the one I've been using." He flipped open the side of the camera. "Hand me one of those tapes," he said.

Mattson took a tape from the briefcase and gave it to him. Benny inserted it into the camera, pushed a couple of buttons and an image came onto the small screen on the side of the camera. "We've got it," smiled Benny.

"Let me see," said Mattson.

"Wait a second." Benny turned to the desk and flipped on the computer. Reaching behind the machine he brought out a cable and plugged it into the camera. He pushed a few more buttons and seconds later the image on the camera came on the computer monitor. "Take a look," he said to Mattson.

Mattson came off the love seat and peered over Benny's shoulder. "God, that's it. That's really it. Every word." He sounded like someone just witnessing a miracle.

196

"Okay," Benny spun around in his chair. "Now bring me up to date. Tell me everything that happened. Who the hell is this guy Stoddard? How did he get this material, and where did he get it. I want to know everything."

"Everything is right on these tapes. I can't even begin to remember everything he told me." Mattson stopped for a minute, thinking. "Paul said he got this report from some place in Washington called the Pacification Center."

"Just tell me everything you remember." Said Benny. He leaned over and took the cartridges from the briefcase. "You keep talking. I'm going to start making backups for these." He turned back to the computer.

Mattson began filling him in, starting with the initial call from Paul asking him to come to the Kelly Inn. He had no idea what Benny was doing with his computer equipment. His own knowledge of the machine was limited to turning it on and typing his stories. If something went wrong it was his habit to call Benny or someone else from the office to fix it. When he got to the part in his story where the man had come to the door, Benny turned and looked at him. "Was he really drunk? Are you sure?"

"Paul was certain that he was either drunk, or on drugs. I only got a glance at him."

"Well, nothing happened so he probably was, but that was a hell of a coincidence. I'd have gotten the fuck out of there."

"Paul didn't seem that worried about him." Said Mattson.

"Okay," Benny nodded. "What happened then?"

"Well, I kept taking pictures and Paul kept talking. At one point I asked him if the President knew what was happening, and he said he couldn't be sure. He said some President's knew about it and some of them didn't. He said something about it being an exclusive club and that just by being the President was not a guarantee that you would get in. I thought that was weird."

"This whole damned thing is weird." said Benny. "Did he say when all of this is going to start?"

"Not exactly," said Mattson, furrowing his brow. He said some of it has already started. But at one point he told me that something was not yet in place. Something about having all of the right people in all of the right offices. I assumed he was talking about something political."

"Maybe he was talking about Congress?" suggested Benny

"I don't know," Mattson's voice was suddenly grumpy. "Damn it, Benny, I'm really beat. I haven't eaten or anything. How long is this going to take?"

Benny pulled a cartridge out of a small machine next to the computer and inserted another cartridge from the brief case. "This doesn't take long," said Benny, "But I want to print out a copy for Harry to look at. That's going to take some time."

"Do I have to be here?"

"You do look like hell," admitted Benny. "Tell you what. This stuff is pretty safe for now, and I've got a lot of work to do on it. What if I drive you home and you get some rest?"

"You think it's safe for me to go home?"

"As long as you don't have this material with you," said Benny, "it's as safe a place as anywhere. That doesn't mean that they won't come, but at least they aren't going to find anything."

"Okay," said Mattson, "I'll leave this stuff with you. You can drive me home and call me later. After I get some more sleep and something to eat, I'll feel better. I've still got to turn out a column on that Senior Citizen Bus issue."

"Have you talked to any of the seniors?"

"Nah, I'll just have to wing it."

"Why not," shrugged Benny. Nobody really gives a shit anyway. The only time they count is on election day." He stood up and walked to the door. "C'mon, I'll drive you home."

Chapter Eleven

Colonel Norman Clifton sat, silently brooding, staring at the paper in his hand.

A rainy drizzle whipped lightly against the living room window, bringing an early chill to the air.

After a moment he put down the paper, leaned forward, put his elbows on the desk and cradled his head in his hands.

The paper had arrived an hour earlier by special courier. The contents had jolted him. "That wimpy son-of-bitch. Damn him! I knew he was going to be trouble," cursed Clifton. He gave himself a minute to relax, then reached across the desk and grabbed the phone. Pushing only a single button it was not more than three seconds before he heard a familiar voice.

"This is Saunders. Who's calling?"

"This is Clifton. Get me Jacobs."

"Yes, sir."

The phone went dead, but a moment later another voice came on the line. "This is Jacobs, sir."

"I want you to move that guy, Mattson, to a Class B rating immediately!" snapped Clifton. "Now get me Berghoff."

"Yes sir. Immediately." The line went dead again and Clifton sat impatiently drumming his fingertips on the desk. It was nearly three minutes before another voice came on the line.

"Sorry sir. This is Berghoff. I'm out of the office. They had to reach me on the Cell phone."

"We've got a situation." Said Clifton. "I'll explain everything when you're on a secure line, but it concerns that fellow in Washington. Do you know who I mean?"

"Yes sir." Snapped the voice without hesitation.

"It seems he suffered a heart attack as he was leaving his hotel this morning. Apparently he had a long history of heart ailments. He's dead. "

"Unfortunate," said Berghoff,"

"Yes, very unfortunate." said Clifton. "He had a name in his pocket."

"What name?" The voice on the phone suddenly became concerned.

"Someone named Mattson." Said Clifton. "Talk to Jacobs and he'll fill you in. Give this your full attention, Berghoff. We have reason to believe the dead man was here in the Twin Cities over the weekend."

"Yes sir. I'll get right on it."

Clifton hung up the phone. He sat staring at the paper on his desk for a full minute, then, shaking his head in disgust, he snatched it up and pushed it into a small paper shredder sitting on the floor beside him.

An hour later Clifton was in his Minneapolis reality office waiting for Berghoff to deliver his report. The drive in from Edina had taken longer than usual due to new construction, and the continuing drizzle had put him in a foul mood. "Come on, Berghoff," he said impatiently, "Get on with it. I've got a lot to do today. What do we have?"

Berghoff glanced at a small black notebook in his hand as he spoke. "Stoddard flew into International airport at 12:53 Saturday afternoon. He took a cab directly to the Radisson South hotel and checked in. He had only one piece of luggage with him." Berghoff suddenly frowned at the notebook he was reading. "He checked in, but apparently, he never went to his room."

Clifton had been idly thumbing through messages, but at Berghoff's words, his head snapped up. "What do you mean he never went to his room? What happened?"

"According to this," Berghoff waved the notebook, "Radisson South was the site of a huge convention. Stoddard mixed in with the crowd and our people lost him. They didn't pick him up again until the next day when he came back to the airport to catch his return flight to Washington."

Clifton banged his fist on the table. His face had turned beet red, but he said nothing. He sat glaring across the desk at Berghoff.

Berghoff shifted uncomfortably in his seat. He let his eyes meet Clifton's, briefly, and then let them drop meekly down to the book he was holding limply in his left hand.

"Who was in charge of the surveillance?" Clifton's voice was calm, but anger burned in his eyes.

"Agent Aldrich," said Berghoff. "He's out of the office in Washington"

"Shit!" Clifton spun in his chair and sat staring at the blank brick wall of the office building across the courtyard. Over his shoulder, he spoke to Berghoff.

"Where did he spend the night?"

"We can't be sure," Berghoff's voice had lost its usual air of confidence, and he seemed embarrassed, even though the loss of Stoddard was not his responsibility. "We have a line on a cab driver who picked up someone matching Stoddard's description at the Radisson that day, and driving him to the Kelly Inn in St. Paul. The time frame seems to be about right, but no one by that name was registered."

"So, he used an alias," said Clifton in a flat voice.

"We think so," agreed Berghoff. "The Kelly Inn is about a mile from where this guy Mattson lives."

"I knew it!" Clifton swung around in his chair. "That little bastard was Stoddard's contact."

"I don't think it's a coincidence, sir." agreed Berghoff. "We have no way of knowing what Stoddard had in his luggage, but he may have brought him something. Before coming to Minneapolis he spent the morning at the Washington Pacification Center. And he went to the Center immediately upon his return to Washington, Sunday night."

"What the hell was his clearance?" demanded Clifton.

"He had total clearance concerning the Hedgerow Project, Colonel. No restrictions."

Clifton appeared to totally deflate. "That means he could have had anything in that bag. He had to have something. He didn't fly all the way out here just to talk."

"And he would have had adequate time to return it when he came back to Washington," added Berghoff. A barely perceptible smirk pulled at the corners of his mouth. A part of him enjoyed watching Clifton squirm.

Clifton let out a long sigh and cupped his chin in his hand. "What do you think it might have been?" Is there a way to find out?" His voice was low, almost pleading, hoping that Berghoff would have an answer.

"We can check with the center and find out what Stoddard was working with that day." Berghoff glanced at his watch. "Other than that, I think our best bet is to apply a little pressure to Mattson."

"Do it." Clifton slapped his hand on the desk, obviously pleased that Berghoff had given him some direction. "Yes, do it. Take whomever you need and see if you can crack that son-of-a-bitch. We have to know how much Stoddard told him, and whether or not he gave him anything. Get back to me as soon as you know something."

"Yes, sir." Berghoff slipped the notebook into his pocket and stood up. His back stiffened to attention for a moment, and then he spun on his heel and left the room.

Chapter Twelve

There was no knock, no warning, no sound at all. The door just seemed to explode! Mattson, sitting at his computer with his back to the door didn't even have time to turn before they were on him. A huge meaty hand, with the force of two hundred odd pounds, crashed against the side of his head, driving him off the chair and onto the floor.

Stunned, his brain alive with brilliant, flashing lights and his ears ringing violently, he rolled to his side trying to crawl to his knees. He was dimly aware of a foot being placed against his shoulder and pushing, as he rolled helplessly onto his back.

Seconds later one hand grabbed the front of his shirt and another caught him by the hair and jerked him to his feet. Expecting to be hit again he tried to raise his arms to protect his face, but he was spun around and slammed against the wall. Hands began patting him down, tearing at him, searching, while he leaned against the wall silently praying for his head to clear. Feeling a tug at his pocket he heard the sound of tearing cloth as his wallet was ripped out. A moment later he was spun around and found himself facing two men.

Still dazed, uncomprehending, he stood there, using the wall against his back for support. Gradually the shrill ringing in his ears became a low buzz. His head began to clear and at last he was able to focus on his attackers.

One of them, a thin shallow faced man with pockmarks and dark, short-cropped military style hair, was idly fingering through his wallet. He appeared casual, almost indifferent, with his thick lips puckered in a way that made him look as though he was about to whistle.

"What the hell is going on?" screamed Mattson, "What are you guys doing…what do you want?" The sound of his own voice surprised him. He had meant it to be a roar, but it sounded more like a screech.

The second man grinned as he placed the palm of his huge hand against Mattson's forehead and jammed him back against the wall.

"Shut up." he ordered. The raspy voice was surprisingly quiet. It came from a face as expressionless as wood, but there was no mistaking the unvoiced threat in the cold, black, piercing eyes. They held Mattson like a magnet.

Mattson tore his eyes away and forced them back to the first man in time to see him drop the wallet into his pocket. He returned Mattson's glare for a moment, then without speaking, walked to the bedroom door. "You find anything in there?" he asked.

"Nothing so far," answered a voice.

Take your time," said the man with the pockmarks. "When you finish in there, take a look around out here. See what's in his computer. We'll take him with us." He turned and motioned to the man with Mattson.

Suddenly a handcuff snapped on Mattson's wrist. Before he could protest he was spun back to the wall and both hands were clamped behind his back. The moves were so smooth and swift that he felt like a puppet.

Mattson's mind raced, but it was less thought, than panic. In total confusion, unable to resist, he was hustled between the two men, out the door, through the hall, and down the back stairs to a shinny black Ford van waiting in the back yard.

They pushed him into a seat facing the rear. The back windows had been blacked out and there were no windows on the side. He tried turning his head to the front, but a sharp piercing pain shot through his wrist and arms as someone jerked up on the handcuffs, forcing him to look toward the floor.

For at least ten minutes they rode in silence, stopping only for what Mattson guessed were stop signs. The annoying buzz in his ears was replaced by a dull throbbing ache somewhere near the base of his skull. At last they came to a complete stop and the engine was shut off. In the distance he could hear what sounded like garage doors closing. After a couple of more minutes they hauled Mattson out of the van and he found himself standing on the cement floor of a basement garage. Still without speaking, they led him to an elevator and pushed the button for the fourth floor.

A minute later the elevator doors opened directly into a large room, lined on both sides with steel desks and filing cabinets. Four men stood in a quiet conversation at the far end of the

room, giving little notice as Mattson went past them and was pushed into a small office. Inside, the man with the pockmarks waited for the other man to remove the handcuffs, then motioned Mattson to a straight-backed wooden chair sitting in front of a heavy metal desk.

"Sit down, Mattson."

Having no choice, Mattson stalked over to the chair and flopped down, glaring at them.

His bravado was nothing but a bluff intended to conceal the apprehension he was feeling. It fell flat. The silent minutes in the car had conjured up scenes in his imagination of being driven somewhere out in the woods and dumped into a worm infested grave without even knowing why?

Now, reasonably sure that they were cops and not just some street gang members out to rob and kill him, the apprehension was still there, but not nearly so close to the terror that he had felt a few minutes earlier. "Look," he said, "If you guys are cops, I want to know what the fuck is going on? I haven't done anything!"

"You don't have anything to worry about, then, do you?" The one with the pockmarks sauntered over to the desk and sat down. He sat there watching Mattson, silently studying him.

Mattson shifted nervously on the chair, saying nothing.

The second man, arms folded across his chest, stood leaning against the door. Neither man spoke, and it became apparent to Mattson that they were waiting for something. He glanced around the room without really seeing it. Ten minutes passed before the sharp shrill ring of the telephone broke the silence.

"Berghoff, here," said the man with the pockmarks, as he picked up the phone and listened. His finger began toying with a crack on the desk, but his eyes never left Mattson. His head bobbed in agreement with whatever he was hearing. "Okay," he said finally, "we'll wait. Bring everything with you." He set the phone back in the cradle and gave an almost imperceptible nod to the man at the door.

Another silent, boring, ten minutes passed. The initial shock was gone and Mattson's fear was slowly being replaced with anger. He was about to speak when the door suddenly opened and another man came into the room. He ignored Mattson and walked directly to the desk.

"This is all I could find," he told the man named Berghoff. He dropped a roll of papers on the desk. "You want me to go back and have another look?"

"Not right now," said Berghoff.

Without a word the newest man turned and left the room as Berghoff came around the desk holding the papers. They were loosely rolled, and he slapped them lightly in his palm, as he glared at Mattson. "I think we can start now," he said. He opened the roll and thumbed lightly through the pages. "How many copies of this did you make, Mattson?"

Mattson's heart skipped as he recognized the papers. At almost the same instant he realized why the name, Berghoff, had sounded familiar. It was the name Paul had mentioned in the story he had told about Clifton. Berghoff was Colonel Clifton's aide! It took all of his strength to force his voice to remain calm.

"Copies of what?" he asked innocently, wondering how in the hell they had found the papers so quickly.

Berghoff sighed, wearily, and dropped the papers on the desk. "Mattson, let's quit playing games. These were found rolled up in your window shade. Do you deny putting them there?"

Mattson stared at him defiantly. "Listen, I don't know what this is all about, but I know that if I'm being accused of something, I've got some rights." He knew his face reddened with guilt, but his voice rose indignantly, "I don't even know who the hell you guys are?"

Berghoff smiled indulgently and turned to the other man. "I guess you'll have to read him his rights, Carl."

The man named Carl pushed himself away from the door and came forward. His black piercing eyes bore into Mattson as he chucked him under the chin with his finger. "Here are your rights, Asshole. If you don't open up, I'm going to crush your balls."

Mattson jerked his head away from the man's hand. The coldness of the voice was more threatening than the statement. The black eyes staring at him out of the pale face exuded pure hate. He watched with relief as Carl turned and walked back to the door.

"Now," said Berghoff, "I'm going to ask you again. How many copies of this did you make, and where are the originals?"

Mattson shifted nervously on the seat but said nothing.

Berghoff stood rubbing the stubble on his chin, observing Mattson. He seemed

210

to be undecided about something. Finally, he walked behind the desk and sat down again.

"You know, Mattson. It just might be that you're too dumb to realize the trouble you're in. You're probably going to be charged with violation of the espionage act. You'll make things a lot easier on yourself if you start to cooperate."

"Listen," said Mattson, angrily. "You guys broke into my apartment, kicked the shit out of me, hauled me down here in handcuffs, and now you're telling me that I should cooperate? What the hell am I supposed to cooperate about?"

"You can start by telling us about these papers," said Berghoff, completely unimpressed by Mattson's outburst. "What are you doing with them?"

"I'm a reporter," said Mattson. "I'm working on a story. What's the big deal about that?"

"The 'big deal', said Berghoff "is that these papers were copied from highly sensitive government documents that you had no right to have. We want them back, along with any other material in your possession. What you're doing can be considered a direct threat to the internal security of this country. Are you familiar with the laws dealing with treason?"

"Treason?" Mattson forced a laugh that sounded hollow in his own ears. "You guys are nuts. I'm doing a follow-up story on government waste. How the hell can that be considered treason?"

"All right," said Berghoff, "maybe I'll buy that. If that's all there is to it, where did you put the originals to these?" he indicated the papers on the desk.

"That's all I ever had," lied Mattson. "I've never even see the originals." In the back of his mind he was wondering why they weren't asking about the film and the camera.

"Are you telling me that Stoddard sent them to you this way?"

"Who?"

"Stoddard," snarled Berghoff, "Paul Stoddard. Are you going to tell me you didn't know he was the one supplying you with this information?"

Suddenly Mattson realized they didn't know about the meeting with Paul in the hotel. "I never heard of anyone named Stoddard," said Mattson, "someone just sent the papers to me."

"These papers?" Berghoff held them up.

"Yes," Mattson squirmed in the chair, feeling that guilt must be written all over him.

"Mattson, you're trying my patience." Berghoff looked at Carl as he rolled the paper back into a tube and slapped them in the palm of his hand. After a moment his eyes came back to Mattson. "We know these were typed on the typewriter in your apartment. We also know where you got them. What we want to know now is, where did you hide the originals?"

"I didn't hide anything," insisted Mattson. He flinched inwardly as he spoke, expecting at any moment to feel Carl's hand crashing against his face.

"Maybe you'd like to explain how these came to be rolled up in your window shade?"

"Okay," Mattson spread his hands, palm up, in a gesture of resignation. "I found some papers in my mailbox. There was no stamp or return address, so I just figured someone dropped them in the box. Anyway, I took them upstairs and laid them on the table. While I was reading them I accidentally spilled a cup of coffee. The papers were ruined so I typed another copy."

"And the originals?" persisted Berghoff

"They were ruined, I threw them out." Mattson shrugged.

"You make a lousy liar," said Berghoff, disgustedly. "Tell me, what did you think when you read them?"

Mattson considered the question, wondering how to answer it. His mind flashed back, trying to remember exactly what it was that the first twelve pages contained. Berghoff apparently was unaware of the film that he had. He would have to be careful not to say the wrong thing.

"I was against the idea of tax money being wasted on those sound barriers," he said, finally. I once wrote an article on that subject. When I read those papers and found out they would also be used for riot control... hell," he shrugged, "it put a whole new light on it. I was in the process of writing another article retracting some of my earlier statements."

"That's all?" Berghoff smiled, cynically. "I didn't think reporters were that

213

willing to retract things that they've written. You're a regular little patriot, aren't you?"

"Well, why not?" protested Mattson. "It was an honest mistake. Hell, I think it's a great idea. To use them for riot control, I mean."

"But why write another article?" asked Berghoff. He hung in with the tenacity of a wood- tick "The first one you wrote was years ago. Why stir it up again? Why not just drop it?"

"Because the first story generated a terrific response. Besides, this was a whole new angle. If I didn't do it, someone else would." The lies were coming easier, but Mattson knew that Berghoff was only toying with him.

"But no one else knew about it, that's what you told me." Said Berghoff.

"I had no way of knowing that," said Mattson.

"And your only interest, in the beginning, was because you figured it was just another, what did you call it, 'a rip-off'?"

"That's right." Mattson heard shuffling behind him and he glanced, uneasily, over his shoulder at the man standing by the door.

"Why were you talking to Clifton?" Berghoff dropped the name on Mattson like a bomb, delight dancing in his eyes as he watched Mattson squirm.

"What?"

"I think you heard me," said Berghoff. "I asked why you went all the way out to Edina to talk to a retired Army officer. What does he have to do with this?"

Mattson straighten up in the chair and folded his arms across his chest. He shook his head, stubbornly. "This can go on forever," he said, "I don't know who you guys are, but I'm not saying another word until I talk to a lawyer."

"I thought you didn't have anything to hide?" taunted Berghoff.

"I'm not trying to hide anything," said Mattson. "I just think I should see a lawyer, that's all."

"Do you deny telling Clifton you were in possession of classified government documents?"

"What?" Mattson was shocked. "I didn't tell him anything like that!"

"You deny it?"

"You damned right, I do." Snapped Mattson.

"But you did imply it, didn't you." Insisted Berghoff

Before Mattson could respond, the telephone rang again. Berghoff snatched it up and listened. After a moment, he nodded, still watching Mattson.

"Yes, sir. I'm talking to him now."

He nodded again and hung up. Pushing himself away from the desk, he stood up and walked to the door. "The Colonel wants to see me," he told Carl. "I'll be back in a few minutes."

Standing outside the office, Berghoff paused to light a cigarette, then walked slowly to the elevator and pushed the button.

While he waited, he let his mind wander over the events of the past few hours, preparing himself for what he would say to Colonel Clifton. Though they had worked together for many years, except for their original meeting, he was rarely allowed more than fifteen minutes with the man at one time. Regardless of the circumstances, he was expected to keep whatever he had to say, within that time limit. It had always been a quirk with Clifton. It wasn't that Clifton's time was in such demand; he just liked to make it appear that way. They never met without Clifton explaining that he was in a rush and expected somewhere else. The real truth about the time limit, Berghoff suspected, was that it was what he had been required to do when he was an aide to General Sleighton.

The elevator arrived and he took it to the third floor. When the doors opened, Berghoff stepped off, turned to the right and took his time sauntering down the long hall. It was still early, but this floor, unlike the floor above, bustled with activity. Ignoring the people rushing past him on their way to work he reached the far end of the hall, dropped his half smoked cigarette on the terrazzo floor and stepped on it. In front of him stood a frosted glass door, stenciled with the words, Norman G. Clifton, Realtor. He opened the door and stepped in.

"Good morning, Mr. Berghoff." The frowsy middle-aged blond woman posing as a secretary smiled and set aside a magazine she was reading. "Mr. Clifton is expecting you."

It was the same thing she said every morning and for some reason it irritated Berghoff nearly as much as the gum she was perpetually chewing. He acknowledged her with a wave of his hand, crossed the room to a second door and opened it. Glancing quickly around the room, he stepped inside and quietly closed the door behind him.

"Good morning, Colonel."

Clifton, sitting behind his desk, nodded, and without looking up, waved him to a chair. "I don't have much time this morning, Berghoff. I have another meeting with the civil defense people and they're becoming difficult. How are things going upstairs?"

Berghoff sat on the edge of a leather chair, his back straight and stiff, almost as though he was standing at attention. "We found a copy of some of the original report on Hedgerow, sir, but Mattson claims that the original was ruined and he threw it out."

"What do you think?"

"He's lying." Berghoff said confidently. "We found the copy rolled up in a window shade. There's a chance that the original is still on the premises, but so far we haven't been able to find it."

"How much of Hedgerow was covered in those papers?" asked Clifton.

"Only the first twelve pages. Basically, just an outdated outline. Apparently Stoddard got cold feet when he discovered we were on to him. How much verbal information he passed to Mattson is anybody's guess."

"In that case," said Clifton, "Mattson could be more of a liability to us than the missing papers."

Berghoff nodded, but did not speak.

"Ordinarily," said Clifton, "I would say, remove the liability, but in view of the fact that he spoke to me so recently, it might be wise to slow down." Clifton began drumming his fingertips on the desk, frowning. After a minute he looked at Berghoff. "Continue the interrogation of Mattson. I'll leave it to you. I don't want this to come back later to bite me in the ass."

"Yes, sir." Berghoff nodded. A faint, almost imperceptible, smirk was playing at the corner of his lips. "One other thing, sir." Berghoff came to his feet.

"Yes?"

"With Stoddard gone, we don't stand much chance of recovering anything that he might have put together. Mattson might be our only lead."

"What do you suggest?" asked Clifton.

"I'd like some time to work on him." said Berghoff. "Just to tie up loose ends. If he has other contacts, I'd like to know about it. I'd rather not let him know that we know of his meeting with Stoddard in the hotel. If he thinks we're only concerned with the original twelve pages, he might feel cocky enough to make some mistakes. I think I'll go through with the formality of a statement, and then let him go. He might think it's all over and get careless."

"What if he decides to go public with whatever he has?" asked Clifton. "There could be some nasty complications."

"I think we can contain that situation, sir.

"I'll leave it to you." Clifton glanced impatiently at his watch. "I hope you'll be able to clear this mess up, Berghoff."

"I'll do my best, Colonel."

When Berghoff returned to the fourth floor Carl waiting outside the office. "I can't stand bastards like that," he said, jerking a thumb in the direction of the office. "One more minute and I would have smashed his face."

"What happened?" asked Berghoff.

"The same old shit," grumbled Carl. "Bitching about his rights, screaming for a lawyer." He shrugged. "Just the same old crap."

"All right," Berghoff nodded, understandingly. "I'm going to talk to him for awhile. When he leaves here I want him kept under constant surveillance. Take two men. I want you prepared for any contingency. Do you understand?"

Carl's black eyes flashed and his wooden face cracked in a smile. "We'll be ready," he promised.

Berghoff nodded, turned and walked into the office. Mattson was leaning forward in his chair, elbows resting on his knees.

Berghoff walked to his desk and sat down. "Well, Mattson, just a few more questions and you can probably get out of here," His voice was almost friendly.

Mattson straightened up, surprised at this sudden switch in Berghoff's attitude. Before he had left the room he had acted as though this would go on forever. This sudden change was too phony to be real and Mattson knew it.

219

"I told you before. I'm not answering anymore questions until I talk to a lawyer." he said

"Fine," Berghoff smiled. "I understand how you feel. This is a serious situation and even if you don't have anything to hide, if you feel you need an attorney, you can certainly have one. Who do you have in mind?"

"Mattson was unprepared for this response. "I'll have to think," he said. Berghoff had thrown him off balance. He suddenly realized that he didn't have a lawyer to call. He considered calling Harry Bower.

"That's all right," said Berghoff, "take your time. It would speed things up if you simply answered a few questions, but we can wait." He reached for the telephone. "I'll just have someone put you in a cell and whenever you're ready you can make your phone call." He picked up the telephone.

"Hey, wait a minute," protested Mattson. "What do you mean, put me in a cell?"

"We'll have to hold you somewhere until your lawyer get's here," said Berghoff. "I have other things to do. I can't just sit here all day."

"How long will it be?" asked Mattson.

"Well, I guess that depends on your lawyer."

Mattson, thoroughly deflated, sank back in his chair. Berghoff watched him, intently.

"Okay," Mattson said, finally, "What are the questions?"

Berghoff released the telephone and settled back in his chair. Under the desk his foot stepped on a button that activated a microphone concealed in the front of the desk.

"Now then," he smiled again. It was a scene he had played a thousand times. "Your true name is Ronald Mattson, and you're employed by the Capitol City News as a reporter. Is that correct?" Berghoff made a pretense of writing on a pad as Mattson replied.

"Yes."

"And you were working in that capacity when you received certain classified documents, belonging to the government of the United States, from a man named Paul Stoddard?"

"I don't know who sent them to me," said Mattson.

"You never met Paul Stoddard?"

"No."

"But you did have numerous telephone conversations with a man by that name."

"Look," Mattson was becoming frustrated. "I don't know who the hell Stoddard is. I never heard of him until I got here. I talked to someone a couple of times on the phone, but he never told me his name."

"You discussed classified papers with this man?"

Mattson hesitated,

"What was the nature of those discussions, Mr. Mattson?"

"The guy just said he had some papers he wanted to give me." Mattson shifted uncomfortably in his chair. "He never said anything about them being classified."

"But you knew they were classified when you saw them, didn't you?"

Mattson remained silent.

"And did he give them to you?" asked Berghoff.

"Yes." Mattson shifted again and threw up his hands. "Look, you know all this. Why do we have to keep going over it?"

"Its just formality," said Berghoff, "Before we release you we have to have a statement. I'm trying to get it in your own words. Can you tell me where those papers are now? To the best of your knowledge?"

"I have no idea," said Mattson. "I spilled coffee on them. They were ruined so I threw them out."

"After you made copies of them?" asked Berghoff.

Mattson nodded wearily. "After I typed a copy of them," he said.

"Upon learning the contents of the documents you received from Stoddard, did you discuss the matter with anyone else?"

"Damn it," growled Mattson, "you keep coming back to this guy, Stoddard. I told you. I don't know him. I never heard of him until I got here."

"Mr. Mattson, we know that Paul Stoddard is the man that gave you the documents. A warrant for his arrest was issued this morning, and as soon as we locate him, we intend to prosecute. I'm simply giving you an opportunity at this time to clear up your position.

Berghoff began writing again. "Now then, did you discuss this matter, or the material, with anyone else?"

"Only with my editor at the paper," said Mattson, and immediately wanted to bite his tongue. There was no need to have mentioned Harry. But at the mention of the word, 'prosecution', he felt a surge of panic and had answered without thinking. Then the momentary fear passed as he thought of the film itself, and its contents. Berghoff had to be bluffing. They would never dare to bring something like this into court.

Mattson pulled his chair forward and leaned on the desk. "Look, Mister. I've been up all night. I'm tired. How much longer is this going to take?"

"Not long," assured Berghoff. "Just a few more questions." He made some marks on a piece of paper. Mattson could see that it was some type of shorthand.

"What's your editor's name?" asked Berghoff.

"Harry Bower."

"Did you show him the papers you received from Stoddard?"

There was that name again. Mattson decided to ignore it. "No," said Mattson, nervously. "I only let him see the copy."

"And what did Mr. Bower say when he read them?" asked Berghoff

"Nothing," Mattson shrugged. "Harry knew I was working on a story."

"Didn't he find it strange that you would be in possession of classified government documents?"

"He didn't believe they were real." Said Mattson. "He wanted me to wait until they were authenticated."

"Then you did show the originals to him?"

"No," Mattson caught himself. "I only let him see the copy. That's why he thought they were phony."

"And did you?" asked Berghoff

"Did I what?"

"Did you have them authenticated?"

"No." Mattson lied. "I figured they came from some nut trying to put me on." Mattson squirmed in his chair. "How would I have them authenticated, anyway?"

Berghoff ignored the question. "Is that why you hid them in your window shade? It was my impression earlier that it was your intention to use them for a follow-up story to your first article?"

Mattson pushed himself away from the desk. He knew he was making mistakes and his temper flared. "I put them in that damned shade because I didn't want people snooping at them.

I didn't know if they were real, and I had no way of finding out. Now you can put me in that damned cell, or do whatever you want to do. I'm finished talking until I see a lawyer."

"I think we have just about all we need," said Berghoff. He pushed himself back from the desk and stood up. "I'm going to have this statement typed up so you can sign it," he said. "It should only take a few minutes. Can I get you a cup of coffee or something while you're waiting?"

"No," Mattson shook his head. "I just want to get out of here and get some sleep."

"Well, this won't take long." Berghoff left the room and closed the door behind him.

Not long? Mattson shook his head, looking at the closed door. That bastard doesn't think anything is long, he thought. He wondered what time it was, and guessed that it must be nearly nine o'clock. What time had they broken in on him? He had no idea, but guessed that it must have been after three. He never could keep track of time when he was on a story. Suddenly a thought struck him and he grinned, in spite of himself. It was a damned good thing that he had decided to get up and work on the story or he'd probably be sitting here in his shorts!

Almost twenty minutes passed before Berghoff came back into the room. He laid some papers on the desk in front of Mattson. "If you just read these over," said Berghoff, "and sign them, I think you can be on your way."

It was a three-page statement. Mattson read through it quickly. That must be one hell of a shorthand, he thought. There wasn't a word missing. He picked up the pen that Berghoff shoved across the desk and signed each page. When he was finished, he stood up.

"I can go now?" he asked

"You can go," said Berghoff, "but I'm sure I will want to talk to you again. As soon as we locate Stoddard," he added. He slid Mattson's wallet across the table.

"If you do," said Mattson, "just give me a call, Okay? I don't need any more late night visits." He picked up the wallet and walked toward the door.

Berghoff stood up. "I'll have Carl drive you home, if you like. He's just outside the door."

"No thanks" said Mattson, remembering the insane eyes. I'll just catch a cab. Where the hell am I, anyway?"

"Minneapolis," said Berghoff, returning to his seat.

Mattson opened the door and left the office. He knew it had to be Minneapolis. It didn't surprise him. It had been too long a drive for it to be St. Paul. He saw Carl standing near a desk across the room talking to two other men as he walked toward the elevator. They looked in his direction, but made no move to stop him. Out on the street he looked back, expecting to see that he had been in the Federal building, but he was wrong. It was an office building he didn't recognize at all. He looked around for a bus stop, and then suddenly realized that he didn't even know which bus to take. He was somewhere in downtown Minneapolis, but he might as well have been on the moon. There was nothing familiar. He walked for three blocks before he was able to flag down a cab.

On the ride back to St. Paul, Mattson tried to figure out how they had gotten on to him so quickly. They couldn't have known about his meeting with Paul or they would have caught him with the videotapes. It had to be something Paul had done after he got back to Washington. When he called he said he had gotten the book back into the file without any problem, but what if someone had seen him? Could they have somehow traced Paul's telephone call? But Paul had not called from his office. He had called from a public phone. No, Mattson decided, it wasn't the phone call or anything to do with Paul or they would have known about the meeting. It had to be something else. Could it have been something Harry or Benny had done? Questions flooded his brain, but there were no answers.

When the cab finally reached his apartment Mattson paid the driver and went quickly up the stairs. As he reached the door a thought suddenly struck him and he jerked around. The cab was just pulling away from the curb, the driver not even looking in his direction.

Damn it, he thought, angrily. Now he suspected everybody. He went inside and found the door to his apartment closed. He had half expected to find it lying on the floor. He knew they broke it getting in. He looked for his keys, couldn't find them and tried the knob. It was unlocked. He stepped inside and stopped in surprise.

Instead of the shambles he had expected, the apartment was exactly as it was before their visit. Mattson couldn't believe it. He kicked the door shut behind him and walked through his kitchen into the bedroom. Except for a pile of clothing lying in one corner, everything was exactly as he remembered it. There wasn't the slightest sign that they had ever been there.

Mattson went back to the living room, picked up the telephone and dialed the number to the office.

"Capitol City News, can I help you?" The voice was unfamiliar.

"This is Mattson," he said, "Is Benny Morris in?"

"One moment, please."

A few seconds later he heard Benny's voice. "Hello?"

"Benny, this is Mattson. Are you busy?"

"Ron! Where are you? We've been worried as hell."

"I'm at home now, but I had some visitors last night. I'll tell you about it later. I just called to tell you I won't be in today. They had me up all night and I'm tired as hell."

"I'll tell Harry," said Benny, "but he's anxious to talk to you. Who were the visitors?

Anyone I know?"

"Think about it," said Mattson, not wanting to go into detail. "Look Benny, we have to get together, but not now. I can't talk on this phone. Just tell Harry I'll talk to him later." Then, as an afterthought, he added, "Tell him he might have some visitors."

Benny was silent for a moment. Then he said, almost in a whisper, "Is it what I think it is?"

"You've got it," said Mattson.

"Oh shit," Benny cursed. "How the hell did they know? What do they know? What about me.?"

"Damn it," cursed Mattson, "I told you not to talk on this phone!" He took a deep breath. "Look, there's nothing about you. Everything is okay. I'm just beat and I need some sleep. I'll talk to you guys later."

"Okay," said Benny, "but call me when you wake up."

"Will do," said Mattson, hanging up the phone. He walked into the kitchen, filled the coffee pot and turned it on. He started to reach for a cup, then thought, to hell with it. The last thing he needed now was coffee. He turned and went into the bedroom. Remembering that he had not bolted the door, he started for it, and then stopped. What the hell difference would a bolt make? Those bastards could bring up a tank! He kicked off his shoes, pulled off his clothes and crawled into bed. As tired as he was, sleep did not come easy. His mind kept going over his conversation with Berghoff. He thought about calling Paul and warning him about the warrant, but he couldn't. He chuckled as he realized he was drifting off. How the hell could he call Paul? He didn't even have his number.

Chapter Thirteen

When Mattson awoke it was evening and the room was growing dark. He got out of bed, pulled on his pants and shirt and went into the kitchen. He still felt exhausted, but his hunger was getting too strong for him to sleep. He knew before looking into the refrigerator that he would find nothing. A single can of beer sat on a shelf next to a small block of cheese. He took out the beer and opened it.

In the morning he would have to go out and do some shopping. Hell, I'd better do it now, he decided. The idea did not appeal to him, but it was still early and he knew if he didn't do it now, by morning he would be crawling the walls. It took him only a few minutes to wash, throw on some fresh clothes and locate his keys. Out on the street the cool night breeze slapped him in the face, bringing him fully awake. He started the car and pulled away from the curb, paying no particular attention to where he was going. He followed Summit Avenue to Dale Street, and then turned left one block and turned right on Grand Avenue. In less than a block he came to a liquor store and decided to stop for a six-pack of beer.

To get into the parking lot he would have to turn left across the street. He looked in the rearview mirror and saw that there was a car behind him. He slowed the Toyota and angled to the right, expecting the car to go around him, but it also slowed, finally coming to a complete stop, waiting for him. Impatiently he gunned the motor and swung his car to the left, crossing the street into the parking lot driveway. As he got out of the Toyota and entered the liquor store he saw the car slowly start cruising up Grand Avenue.

The street was empty a few minutes later when he came out with the six-pack. He tossed it on the front seat and pulled the Toyota back onto Grand Avenue, trying to decide on a supermarket. As he passed Victoria Street, a City Bus that had been behind him pulled to the curb to pick up a passenger. Another car took its place and Mattson recognized it as the car that had been behind him at the liquor store.

Ahead of him, at Lexington Avenue, the light was just beginning to change as he approached the corner. He stepped on the gas in order to make the light, but it turned red before he finished making the turn. To his surprise the car behind him also came through the red light.

It was closer now and he could make out three people, two in the front and one in the back.

Mattson swung onto Summit Avenue, heading back toward his apartment and saw the car continue to follow. It could be coincidence, but it seemed strange that they were making the same turns that he was making and even running red lights in order to do it.

At Dale Street Mattson turned left. He decided that he had to find out if they were following him. There was a Cub Supermarket out on Rice Street near highway 36. If they followed him all the way out there it would not be because they were going shopping. Stepping up his speed he followed Dale Street to the I-94 ramp heading east.

They were still behind him as he passed through spaghetti junction and took the curve heading north on 35E, but as he was nearing Maryland Avenue the traffic became heavy and he lost sight of them.

At Larpenteur Avenue he got off the freeway and took a left turn to Rice Street where he had to wait again for a light change. He breathed a sigh of relief as he followed Rice Street past Roselawn Avenue. The street behind him was nearly empty. He could see every car on the block for nearly a mile and they were nowhere in sight. As he pulled into the Cub parking lot he felt the tension drop from him like a weight.

He was in the store for almost an hour. He hated shopping, but his spirits got a brief lift when buying a carton of cigarettes the cashier insisted on seeing his identification. He hadn't been carded for years, and never looking as he did tonight, with a two-day growth of beard, but he was soon brought back to earth when he discovered that store policy required everyone to be carded, regardless of age.

Pushing his shopping cart out of the store, his eyes flashed from left to right, taking in the entire parking lot, looking for the car with the three men in it. The lot was filled to capacity and his chances of spotting them were dim, but even as he drove out he continued to look. Not wanting to take the freeway, he drove through the parking lot to Rice Street and took an illegal left turn. He didn't care. It was the most direct route home and he was tired. It wasn't until he reached Roselawn Avenue that he glanced into the rear-view mirror and saw a car coming out of the Cub parking lot, making the same illegal turn that he had made. The car was too far back to make a positive identification, but he knew it was the same car.

"Son-of-a-bitch!" he slammed his open palm on the steering wheel as he realized that they must have bugged his Toyota. "Those dirty bastards." He yelled the words in a frustrated rage.

By the time he reached University Avenue his anger had subsided and he tried to figure out what he could do. If it was their intention to arrest him, there was nothing he could do about it, but from their actions it seemed that they were more interested in playing cat and mouse. Probably hoping that he would panic and lead them to the papers, he decided. "You'll have a long wait, you bastards." The last two days had been a nightmare, but he laughed suddenly, realizing they already had him talking to himself.

As he turned up Summit Avenue he noticed that they had closed the distance. He considered driving past his apartment, but at the last minute he saw a small spot almost directly in front of the building. It was a tight squeeze, but he got in the space with one front wheel riding up on the curb. He left it there. He would probably have a ticket in the morning but he didn't care. He grabbed his bags from the front seat and raced for his building.

Upstairs, with the door bolted, he stood in the dark, looking out the window. From this angle he could see only a portion of the street, but everything seemed quiet. He walked to the door and listened. There was no sound. After a few minutes he began to relax and turned on the lights. What the hell, he thought, if they wanted to come in, they would come in. The bolted door wouldn't slow them down anymore tonight than it had the night before. He walked into the kitchen, put the groceries away, and opened a cold can of beer.

Half an hour passed and still nothing happened. Mattson sat in the over-stuffed chair, sipping his beer, puffing on a cigarette and brooding. They had to be cops. Muggers would never have taken the chance of running red lights the way they had. And muggers probably would have slammed on their brakes and jumped him as soon as he got out of the car. The fact that they hadn't made an issue out of his illegal U-turn, or driving up on the curb could only mean one thing. They weren't out to arrest him; they were out to harass him. They wanted to keep him jumpy, hoping he would make a mistake. Well, they'll have a hell of a long wait, Mattson promised himself.

Leaning over he picked up the telephone and dialed Benny's cell phone. It was picked up on the third ring and he heard Benny's voice. "Hello?"

"This is Mattson. Were you sleeping?"

"Nah, I just been screwing around with the story I'm doing on the liquor probe." said Benny. "How about you? Did you get some sleep?"

"The sleep was great, but when I got up I had to go out for groceries. Guess what?"

"Don't tell me you were arrested again?"

"They didn't arrest me, but they sure as hell followed me." He gave Benny a quick run down on what had happened.

"I don't get it, Ron. What the hell do they want from you?"

Mattson smiled at the question. Benny knew the phone was probably tapped and he was letting him know that he was being careful in what he said. He would not be saying anything to give himself away.

"I don't know what they want." said Mattson. "They were talking about some guy named Stoddard when they pulled me in, and they wanted to know about some papers that a guy gave me. I told Harry about it. I thought he would have filled you in."

"First I heard of it," said Benny. "Harry just told me that you were arrested the other night. What was that all about?"

"Nothing serious," said Mattson. "Maybe we can get together in the morning and I'll tell you all about it."

"Sounds good to me," said Benny. "Why not meet me in the Courthouse? Downstairs, in the cafeteria. I'll buy the coffee."

"Name the time," said Mattson. "I'll be there."

"I have to be in the council chambers at nine o'clock, so how about eight-thirty?"

"I'll be there," repeated Mattson.

"See you then," said Benny, hanging up.

Chapter Fourteen

The next morning at eight-thirty Mattson had already purchased two cups of coffee and was seated at a small table in the cafeteria when Benny came rushing in. His eyes flashed around the room and fell on Mattson. He gave a slight, almost imperceptible nod, and then let his eyes roam around the cafeteria searching for strange faces. Finding none, he came over to Mattson's table and sat down.

"I figured this would be the best place to meet," he told Mattson. "I know just about everybody in here and there's not a strange face in the room. You think they're still following you?"

"They might be," said Mattson, "but I haven't seen anyone this morning." He took a sip of his coffee and pushed the other cup to Benny. "Did you have any luck with that stuff?"

"Everything is backed-up and I have one printed copy. It's stashed in three different places." He raised the cup to his lips and took a drink. "I was reading that son-of-a-bitch all night. I was reading it when you called me."

"And?" Mattson pulled his chair closer to the table.

"I'll tell you the truth, Ron. If this was a movie script that someone wanted to sell me, I'd kick them in the ass for wasting my time. It's so fucking wild I can't believe it." He took another sip of the coffee and pulled out a pack of cigarettes. "I haven't smoked in three years, but last night got me started again." He pulled one out of the pack and lit it.

"You'd believe it if you met the bastards that worked me over," said Mattson, lighting one of his own. "That guy, Carl… he had eyes like a snake." Mattson gave a slight shiver at just the thought of the man. "I think he's nuts."

"They're fanatics," said Benny, "and they are nuts. I've met a lot of those bastards over the years and believe me, if they weren't cops, they'd be in a jail or a friggen looney bin!"

Mattson was surprised at his friend's sudden anger. He had known Benny for about five years, but they had never really gotten close. They worked for the same paper, but Benny was considered a 'loner' and usually kept to himself. He wasn't a great writer, but he was tenacious, and he had the reputation of laying himself on the line for the underdog. Because of his friendship with Chuck Sauerly he was usually assigned to stories covering the police beat and over the years he had gained their respect, but Mattson knew that the respect did not extend both ways.

"If they bust you again," said Benny, "don't argue with them. In fact, don't even talk to them." As he talked, his eyes were constantly searching the cafeteria checking out each person as they entered. "If they let you near a phone, call me. I'll know what to do."

"You think they're going to arrest me again?" Mattson couldn't keep the worry out of his voice.

"Take it easy," cautioned Benny. "I didn't say they were going to… I said, 'if they do." Seeing the anxiety in Mattson's eyes, he leaned over and squeezed his shoulder. "Look, Ron, this really isn't your gig, I know that. These guys probably know it too, so they're going to pressure you, hoping you'll crack."

"Fuck," said Mattson, "I wish I had never gotten involved with this!"

Benny looked at him, but said nothing. He knew that Mattson, for all his bravado around the office, was nothing more than a green kid trying to act the part of a tough reporter. If they came after him again, he would probably give them everything he had. Thank god he didn't have anything left to give them except conversation.

"Okay," said Mattson. "So, I should just go about my business and ignore them. If they pick me up, you want me to call you. Is that smart? I mean, won't that put them on to you?"

"Don't worry about it," said Benny. "I don't have anything, and you don't have anything, so screw them."

"So, have you talked to Harry? Does he know what's going on?"

"I haven't told him anything, yet. There are a few things I have to do before I talk to anyone about this." Benny's eyes had been going around the room, checking faces, but now they came back and settled on Mattson. "Ron, I have to get upstairs. You go home and relax. Take a couple of days off. I'll square it with Harry, Okay?"

"Sure," Mattson shrugged, "Why not? I'd rather be working, but I wouldn't be able to concentrate on anything anyway."

"Work on that other story," said Benny. "The one about the seniors. Stay away from the office a couple of days, and relax. Let's see if anything happens." He pushed himself away from the table and stood up. "Give me a little time to put something together."

Mattson also got up from the table. He put out his hand. "Thanks, Benny."

Benny took his hand and shook it. "Just relax, Ron. I'll work something out and we'll get those bastards." Without giving Mattson a chance to answer, he turned and walked toward the elevators.

Mattson watched him go, then, taking a deep breath, he sank back into his chair and sat staring at his empty coffee cup. Damn it, he thought, they were really screwing with his mind.

"What the hell was he supposed to do now? Go home and watch television? Work on that damned bus story? And, what the hell for? Why the hell should he change his lifestyle just to satisfy those assholes?"

Benny didn't want him to go to the office, and he was probably right. Harry would be there and he would be asking questions. Harry had a right to know what was happening, but he decided to wait for Benny to tell him. Benny was right. This wasn't his gig! He decided to take Benny's advice and go home.

By three o'clock that afternoon he had finished his story on the senior citizens, followed by an afternoon movie on television and he was bored to death. He felt like a hermit and he was sick of it. If they thought he had the papers, they weren't going to change their mind just because he

239

was staying in his apartment. As for involving anyone else, a thought that had crossed his mind… that was ridiculous. By this time they probably had a list of everyone that he knew, anyway. Mattson was holding a remote control and he threw it angrily on the table. To hell with them, he decided. Tonight he was going to enjoy himself. He'd give Carla Jenkens a call. It was still early enough to catch her at the office.

Now that he had a plan of action, Mattson's spirits began to rise for the first time in days. It would be a mistake to change his daily routine. It would make him look guilty, and as long as he looked guilty, they would continue to follow and harass him. Going to his desk, he opened the middle drawer, looking for his address book. It wasn't there. He pulled the drawer completely open and moved aside a pile of old bills, but it wasn't there. Damn it! Did they take it? Slamming the drawer shut he jerked open the bottom drawer and there it was, laying on top of some old watches and cufflinks that he kept in the drawer. Snatching it up he closed the drawer and walked over to the phone. He knew he hadn't left it in that drawer. The screwed up and put it in the wrong place after they went through it. It took only a moment to locate the number. Carla picked up on the first ring. "Carla, this is Mattson. Are you busy?"

"Well, hello, stranger." Surprise was evident in her voice. "Where have you been hiding?"

She seemed pleased to hear from him and Mattson breathed a sigh of relief. He hadn't called her for nearly two weeks, not since their last date, and he half expected her to be angry with him.

"Damn," said Mattson, "I really meant to call you, honey, but I've been up to my ears in this new story and I haven't had time for anything."

"Not even a phone call?" chided Carla.

"I meant to Carla. I really did. Look," Mattson tried to sound like he had a sudden inspiration. "Why not let me make it up to you tonight? Are you doing anything?"

"It's my laundry night."

"I'd really like to see you," said Mattson. "Maybe I can bring over a couple of steaks and," he hesitated, "I don't know, just see what develops. Maybe we can get some beer and watch television or something?"

Carla laughed. "I don't think what you want to develop has anything to do with television." She said.

"Now, that's not fair, Carla." Mattson chuckled. "My intentions are totally honorable."
"They better not be," laughed Carla.

"It's a date, then?"

"I'll be home around five o'clock," said Carla. "You can help me fold clothes."

"Great," said Mattson. "I'll bring a few things of my own. We'll make a party of it." He hung up before she had a chance to object. Walking quickly into the bathroom he started the water in the bathtub.

Chapter Fifteen

Carla stood waiting on the landing outside her door at five-thirty when Mattson came trudging up the stairs carrying a pillow case stuffed with shirts, socks, shorts and a six pack of cold beer. She stood leaning on the banister, dressed in a pair of slacks and a heavy white Alpaca sweater that came nearly to her knees, affectively concealing the lush curves that Mattson remembered so well. A quick unconscious shake of her head fluffed her long blond hair away from her face as she smiled at him.

"Ron, sometimes I think all you want is for me to do your laundry."

Mattson laughed and followed her into the apartment. Dropping the pillowcase on a chair he turned and caught Carla by the arm. Pulling her close to him, he slid his hands under her sweater intending to unfasten her bra. "Honey, if you really believe that, I'm willing to just get rid of the clothes. In fact, let's get rid of them right now."

"Forget it," screeched Carla, playfully, pulling herself away. "I'll settle for doing the laundry."

"Want a beer first?"

"I could swear that I heard something about steak," said Carla.

"Indeed you did," Mattson opened two cans and offered one to the girl. "I thought I'd run out and get a couple of T-bones while you're getting things ready here. Do you want a salad with it?"

"I'd love it." Carla took a sip of the beer, set the can on the table and picked up the pillowcase. "For a T-bone and a salad you could talk me into almost anything," she teased.

Mattson made another grab for her, but Carla skipped out of his reach and ran into the next room. "Supper first," she called. "You'll find everything you need in the kitchen when you get back. Take my keys. They're on the table."

Mattson snatched the keys off the table. "Okay," he yelled, taking a final sip of his beer, "I'll be right back."

He was humming lightly to himself as he skipped down the stairs, but he was shocked back to reality as he stepped out the door. Almost directly across the street, two cars behind his own, sat the black van that he would never forget.

The windows were blacked out and he could detect no movement, but he knew they were in there. He felt his hands shaking as he took the time to light a cigarette. He knew he would have to pass them on the way to his own car and he wondered if they would make an attempt to grab him?

As he crossed the street heading for his car he glanced up at Carla's apartment, hoping that she was not watching. He forced himself to look straight ahead as he passed the van, his nerves taught, expecting at any second to have them leap out at him.

In spite of his conscious effort to control them, his hands shook as he tried to unlock his car. He imagined them sitting in the van snickering, and his anger rose. The key finally went in the lock and turned. He slid in and started the engine. Having gone this far without them stopping him, he began to relax. He wondered if he might have been mistaken. Maybe that wasn't the van at all. Hell, he thought, they all look alike. He fought the impulse to turn around and look at them.

A few minutes later there was no doubt as the van began following him. He had to drive all the way to Syndicate and Grand to find a supermarket. Parking in the lot, he went into the store, forcing himself to ignore the van.

Mattson picked out the two largest T-bone steaks that he could find. He grabbed a head of lettuce, two tomatoes, some radish and cucumbers for the salad and was out of the store in less than ten minutes. He looked for the van as he drove back down Grand Avenue to the liquor store, but it was nowhere in sight. When he came out of the liquor store with a bottle of Cold Duck wine, he looked for it again, and still didn't see it. He breathed a sigh of relief. Maybe they've given up? He thought hopefully.

Chapter Sixteen

The sudden appearance of Colonel Clifton on the fourth floor was unusual. Heads turned, fingers poised above keyboards. Coffee sipping conversations stopped and worried eyes followed the ramrod straight back as it moved down the isle between the two rows of gray steel desks. For the full thirty seconds that it took Clifton to traverse the distance between the elevator and Berghoff's office door, an uneasy silence filled the room.

Clifton was not unaware of the sensation he caused and even in his anger took a certain satisfaction from it. Resisting an urge to glance over his shoulder, he pushed open the door to Berghoff's office without knocking, stepped inside and slammed the door shut.

Berghoff, sitting behind his desk reading a report, looked up, irritated at the sudden intrusion. For an instant his mouth went slack and his eyes widened with surprise, but he recovered instantly, scrambled to his feet and snapped to attention.

"Relax, Berghoff." Clifton waved his hand pompously as he crossed the room and came to a stop in front of the desk. "What's the latest on Mattson?"

Berghoff relaxed slightly and shrugged his shoulders. "The situation is unchanged, sir. Carl has him under constant surveillance. To this point in time, no action has been taken. He's nervous as hell and we know he's scared."

"Contact Carl immediately," said Clifton. "Find out what the situation is now."

Berghoff picked up the phone, pushed a couple of numbers and spoke briskly. "This is Berghoff, patch me through to Carl."

They waited less than a minute when Carl's raspy voice broke through the crackling sound of static. "This is Carl. What's up?"

"Where are you?" asked Berghoff.

"On the corner of Summit and St. Albans, in St. Paul. Mattson is in an apartment with some broad. Looks like it might be a girlfriend. He went out a little while ago and bought a couple of steaks and some wine."

Berghoff relayed the information to Clifton.

Clifton nodded and thought for a moment, making small circles on the top of Berghoff's desk with his forefinger. Finally, he looked up. "Tell him to continue the surveillance, but to do nothing until you get back to him."

Berghoff nodded. "Stay with him, Carl, but hold off on everything until I get back to you."

A grumbling curse came over the line, causing Berghoff to frown as he hung up the telephone and looked at Clifton. "I think Carl was hoping we would turn him loose on Mattson."

"I don't think he'll be disappointed," said Clifton, clasping his hands behind his back, and walking to the window. "I've just received word that Paul Stoddard had receipts in his pocket indicating that he purchased a video camera shortly after he signed out of the Pacification Center. He had it with him on the plane when he came here."

"Damn," Berghoff swore softly. "He must have taken something from the center and brought it here to video tape." He spoke to Clifton's back. "What about the Hedgerow report, sir?"

"It's still in the vault, but security records show that Stoddard was in that area before he left Washington on Saturday and again shortly before he had his heart attack."

"Could he have gotten it out?"

"How the hell do I know?" snapped Clifton. "I do know if things had gone according to schedule, he never would have gotten back to Washington!" He spun from the window and glared at Berghoff, as though it was his fault. Then slowly his face relaxed.

He walked over to the desk, sat down on the straight-backed cushionless chair, pulled off his glasses and rubbed his eyes. "We have to assume the worst. We have to assume he got it out of the vault, bought the camera, met with Mattson and spent the night taking pictures. When he went back to the Center he put it back in the vault."

Berghoff sat down on the chair in front of the desk, frowning, as he considered the scenario that Clifton had presented.

"Well?" prompted Clifton.

"I agree with you, Colonel. We have to assume that Mattson has a complete copy.

The question is, where the hell did he put it?"

"The question is," corrected Clifton, "What the hell do we do now? It's one thing to have a couple of pages out of context. We can handle that. But if that son-of-a-bitch has a complete copy ..." Clifton's voice trailed off. He didn't even want to think of the repercussions that were possible.

"We'll have to pick him up again." Said Berghoff. "This girl is the first person he's made contact with since we let him go. He did meet for a few minutes with another reporter from his paper in the Courthouse cafeteria, but they were both empty handed and made no physical contact. Nothing passed between them."

"Who was the other reporter?" asked Clifton.

"A guy named Benny Morris. After having coffee with Mattson he went upstairs to the Ramsey County Commissioner's Council Chambers and spent the entire morning."

Berghoff had his notebook out and was reading from it. "He went out for lunch at Burger King. He didn't talk to anyone. After lunch he went back to the Council Chambers and spent the afternoon taking notes on the Commissioners meeting. After the meeting he went directly home. He didn't talk to anyone or carry anything with him."

"There's got to be a connection." Said Clifton. "I want more information on him."

"Yes, sir." Berghoff made a quick note in his book.

"What about the girl he's with now?" asked Clifton.

"Her name is Carla Jenkens. She's twenty-eight, Caucasian, lives alone and works as a legal secretary in the Ramsey County Attorney's office. We got her name out of Mattson's address book, and we're doing a complete check on her now." Berghoff slipped the book into his pocket. "When Mattson went to her place today he was carrying something that looked like a pillowcase.

We don't know what he had in it."

"I think it's time that we found out." Said Clifton.

"The first papers we found were rolled up in a window shade in his apartment. It's a good bet that everything else is hidden there, too. In the apartment, I mean." Berghoff spread his hands as he talked. "He's not that smart, Colonel. He figures we went through his apartment once and doesn't expect us to do it again. He knows we're following him... I don't think he'd have the guts to move anything." Berghoff gnawed at his lower lip, thinking. "Of course, they may not be in his apartment, but I'll bet he put them somewhere in that building."

"If you're certain of that," said Clifton, nibbling at his lower lip, "destroy the building."

"We may have to do that," agreed Berghoff, "but for the present I think we should concentrate on Mattson, himself. If we destroy the building we'll never know what he had. And there's no way to know if we really destroy everything. There's always the chance that he got it out before we got to him."

"That meddling bastard," cursed Clifton. He stood up again and walked to the window. "Pick him up. Get him before he has a chance to talk to anyone else."

"I think we should pick up the girl, too." said Berghoff.

"Do it." said Clifton, curtly. He had felt himself losing control. Giving direction had never been his strong point. He had advanced in the military because he was able to take direction, and take it without question. While General Sleighton was alive and making the decisions there had been no problems. Now that the General was gone he relied on Berghoff to fill the void. Without Berghoff to keep things in order he would be lost, and he knew it. His calm, cool, acceptance of the situation now, placed things back in perspective and Clifton felt in command again.

"We're going to need some assistance this time," said Berghoff, reaching for the phone.

"From whom?"

"The local police." Said Berghoff. He glanced at Clifton, saw that he didn't understand, and explained. "It's the girl in the apartment with Mattson. She probably has friends in the building. And she works in the County Attorney's office. She knows the law. If strange men in civilian clothes just break in and grab them, the situation could get out of hand. I'm going to arrange for some uniforms and flashing lights to give it some legitimacy."

"Will they cooperate? What about their reports?" Clifton was chewing his lip again.

"Their report will read that they gave assistance to federal officers serving a fugitive warrant. We'll keep it simple and impress them with the sensitivity of the issue." Berghoff smiled. "They'll cooperate."

"All right." Clifton seemed satisfied. "I'll leave that to you. In the meantime I'll contact Washington and assure them that everything is under control."

He turned from the window and walked to the door in a way that could almost be considered a strut. Pulling open the door, he turned to find Berghoff standing respectfully. It brought a gleam to Clifton's eye. "Keep me posted," he said.

"Yes, Sir." Berghoff nodded, waited for Clifton to close the door and dropped wearily into his chair. He had long ago learned how to handle Clifton, but it was becoming increasingly difficult to maintain this attitude of subservience. Clifton had the rank, but Berghoff had the ability, and they both knew it. His mind came back to Mattson and the immediate problem. Picking up the telephone, he pushed a button for a direct line to the St. Paul Police Headquarters. Time was wasting.

Chapter Seventeen

Back in Carla's apartment Mattson took time away from chopping vegetables to peek out the kitchen window. The black van was parked near the entrance to the back alley. Cursing softly, he pulled the tab off a cold can of beer and stood looking at it. Suddenly a thought struck him and he grinned. He almost laughed. They were going to have one hell of a long wait tonight!

"Everything ready?" Carla was standing in the kitchen doorway holding a basket of clean clothes.

"Whenever you are." said Mattson, turning from the window. "I'm ready to put the steaks on. How do you like it?"

"Medium," said Carla, "but give me a minute to fold these, Okay?" She disappeared into the next room.

Mattson enjoyed cooking and the meal was a total success. He intentionally took a seat against the wall where he could not see out the window. He forced the black van from his mind, and listened to Carla's teasing complaints about his faded and worn shorts.

When the dishes were finished they went into the living room and Carla switched on the television. They lay together on the sofa. Mattson's arm was around her with Carla's head resting on his chest.

He tried to keep his mind on the movie, but her closeness, the fragrance of her hair and the soft supple body was too much for him. With the tip of his finger he raised her chin and kissed her. She lay unresisting as he probed the inside of her mouth with his tongue and slid his hand under her sweater. With surprise he discovered that she had already removed her bra. As he touched her bare breast, the passive unresisting body came alive, squirming and moaning.

His hands began moving over her, exploring, touching everywhere, while she writhed beneath him, returning his kisses with a fire and passion that he had never expected. He had the zipper of her slacks halfway down when her hand suddenly clamped down on his wrist.

"Wait," she whispered, "not here."

It took almost more restraint than he could command, but after a moment, Mattson took his hand away, rolled over and stood up. She lay there for a minute, breathing hard and watching him with wide eyes. Then, without a word, she got off the sofa, took him by the hand and led him into the bedroom.

Chapter Eighteen

The buzzer sounded on the car telephone at exactly 10:30. Carl snatched it up. "This is Jacobs," he said.

"Carl, this is Berghoff. Where are you now?"

"Outside the apartment. Mattson is still inside. It looks like he plans to spend the night."

"Good," said Berghoff. "We're going to bring him back in."

"I figured as much," said Carl, disgustedly. "I was hoping to close this out tonight."

"We all were, but this can't be helped." said Berghoff. "The Colonel got word from Washington. Mattson may have a hell of a lot more than we originally thought. We've got to get it back before we say goodbye to Mattson. Understand?"

"I've got you." said Carl. "You want us to bring him in now?"

"Who do you have with you?"

"I'm in the blue Ford in front of the building," said Carl. "Art Bruckman and Phil Richter have the van in back. You want us to go in and get him?" Carl had difficulty keeping his enthusiasm out of his voice.

"No. Hold off for a few minutes. I've arranged for two squads and six local uniforms to assist you."

"We don't need help with this punk!" protested Carl.

"Damn it, I know you don't need help," snapped Berghoff, impatiently. "I'm sending them there for the benefit of the neighbors. I want them to see plenty of flashing lights and uniforms. There will be fewer questions if it's local police in that neighborhood. And I want you guys out of there before any reporters show up."

"I see one of the squads now," said Carl. "It pulled up on the next block."

"Okay," said Berghoff. "You contact Richter and Bruckman. I'll get through to the locals. Wait until it's totally dark, and then flash your lights twice. They'll follow your lead."

"I'll let him get nice and comfortable," promised Carl, and then, "How much do the locals know?"

"Nothing." said Berghoff. "It's all been taken care of. They'll know enough not to ask any questions. I'm cutting off now, but if you run into any trouble you can reach me here at the office."

The line went dead and Carl punched in a new number. "Richter, this is Carl. Get ready to move."

Far down the street a second police car pulled in behind the first.

Chapter Nineteen

Carla was the first to hear the banging on the door. She was out of bed and slipping into her robe when Mattson rolled to the side of the bed, propped himself on one elbow and rubbed the sleep from his eyes.

"What's the matter?" he asked.

"Someone is at the door," she whispered. "Stay here; I'll see who it is." Before he could answer, Carla left the bedroom pulling the door shut behind her.

Mattson waited in the darkened room listening to the faint sound of Carla's bare feet slapping against the hardwood floor of the hallway. His eyes slowly adjusted to the dim light coming from the window and he could make out the dark clump of his clothing piled at the foot of the bed.

Suddenly he heard the sound of angry voices, followed by a muffled scream from Carla and the heavy clump of footsteps making their way through the hall. Mattson threw back the covers and jumped up, reaching for his clothes. With a shock his foggy mind cleared and as everything flashed back, he knew what it was! He was on his feet with his pants in his hand when the door flew open and the bright blinding glare of a flashlight hit him in the face.

"Hold it right there, mister. Don't make a move!"

Mattson froze at the sound of the gruff command, unable to see and half bent over as he tried to slip a leg into his pants.

"I said, don't move!" A hand shot out of the bright light and gave him a violent push, sending him off balance and crashing to the floor.

"There's another one down here," shouted the man with the flashlight.

Mattson had dropped his pants as he fell to the floor. He straightened up now as he heard others approaching. Someone snapped the wall switch and the room flooded with light. A moment later the room was filled with men in police uniforms. Three men in civilian clothes, pushing Carla in front of them, followed.

She fell against Mattson, sobbing. She clung to him, hiding her face against his bare shoulder, making him suddenly acutely aware of his nakedness. His eyes flashed to the men in civilian clothes and he recognized Carl. There was no need to ask questions. He already knew the answers.

Carl returned his glare with icy eyes, a smirk playing at his lips, then turned to the man standing next to him. "I want pictures of everything in this apartment." He jerked his head, indicating Carla and Mattson. "You can start with them."

The man nodded, pulled a small camera from his pocket, and began snapping pictures.

Carl gestured to Mattson and Carla. "You two get your clothes on." He ordered.

Mattson, standing with an arm protectively around Carla, hesitated. "Do you need all these guys in here?" he protested.

"Getting bashful, Mattson?" Carl gloated, enjoying the anger on Mattson's face. "Get your clothes on or we'll take you downtown the way you are."

Mattson fought back his anger, knowing Carl was capable of doing just what he had threatened. "Go ahead, honey." He patted Carla gently on the shoulder. "Get dressed."

"I can't," cried Carla, desperately. "Make them leave, Ron, Please!"

Mattson glared at Carl. "They aren't going to leave, damn it. They enjoy this." He pushed her away, "Damn it, get dressed!"

Carla turned to the dresser, crying, as Mattson bent to pick up his pants.

"Come on," growled Carl, "snap it up." His cold eyes fastened on Carla's shaking shoulders.

Mattson glanced at her as he pulled on his pants and shirt. She was frightened and ashamed, trying to keep her face turned away from the leering eyes watching her. He sat down on the edge of the bed to pull on his shoes, but Carla still stood at the dresser crying, her back turned to them, making no attempt to get dressed.

Carl's patience was at an end. He swore softly, stepped forward and grabbed Carla roughly by the arm, spinning her around. "Save your crying act for the courtroom. You either get dressed now or go the way you are."

"You bastard!" Mattson made a move to get off the bed, but the palm of Carl's hand slammed against his chest, driving him back. "You sit right there." He ordered. "Cuff this asshole." He told one of the men dressed in civilian clothes.

Two uniformed police stepped forward, grabbed Mattson and flipped him on his stomach while the man in civilian clothes applied the handcuffs.

Carl turned back to the girl who still stood sobbing, her head down, and her hands at her sides. Before she realized what was happening, Carl's hands shot out and grabbed the robe at both sides. The movement was so swift that the robe was stripped from her shoulders and pulled down her body leaving her naked. Carla screamed and threw her arms across her chest in a futile gesture of protection.

One of the men in uniform stepped forward preventing Mattson from getting off the bed. Three other uniformed cops stood at the door, eyes narrowed, but saying nothing. The man in civilian clothes took two final pictures and left the room.

Carl watched the girl for a moment, unmoved by her hysterical sobbing, then walked to the closet, pulled a brightly colored blouse and a pair of slacks from a hanger and threw them at her.

"You've got one minute, lady, or you go the way you are."

"You son-of-a-bitch," yelled Mattson. "Leave her alone!"

Carl looked at him and his wooden face almost smiled. "Get him out of here," he told the uniformed cop. "I'll deal with him later." He turned his attention back to Carla. "Well," he snapped, "what's it going to be? You want to go this way?"

"Carla raised her tear puffed face. Her frightened, pleading eyes went from Carl to Mattson, and then back to Carl again. "Please," she murmured, clutching the slacks and blouse against her.

"Get them on," growled Carl.

Her eyes went back to Mattson as he was jerked off the bed and pushed roughly out the door. There was no help and she knew it. Still sobbing she slipped the blouse over her head and sat on the edge of the bed to pull on her slacks. She kept her eyes closed, knowing they were watching her every move.

"Come on, lady... move it!" Carl pushed a pair of shoes at her with his foot.

Biting her lip to keep from screaming again, Carla bent over and slipped on the shoes.

Carl turned to the uniformed cops still standing in the doorway. "You men have been a great help," he said. "I'll be sure to mention it in my report." He pulled Carla off the bed, spun her around and snapped on a pair of handcuffs. He pushed her ahead of him out the door. "We can handle it from here," he told the officers, "but I'd appreciate it if you'd seal up this apartment."

The officers looked at each other and one of them shrugged. "No problem," he said. "The lock is still intact. You sure you won't need us anymore?"

"We can handle it," said Carl, taking Carla by the arm leading her down the hall and out of the apartment.

Outside on the corner the flashing lights of the squad cars had attracted a small crowd of curious spectators. Carl ignored them as he hustled the girl to the unmarked car waiting at the curb. Opening the back door he pushed her inside and slammed it, then spoke to the man in the driver's seat.

"Take her over and book her. Berghoff's waiting for you. Tell him I'll be along in a little while."

The driver nodded and started the engine. "What charge?" he asked.

Carl glanced at the girl, crumpled and whimpering on the back seat, smiled at the driver and winked. "Interstate Prostitution." He said.

Hearing the statement, Carla struggled to sit up, her eyes wild and frightened. Before she could speak, Carl waved the driver on, spun on his heel and walked toward the van parked at the side of the building.

The engine of the van came to life as he approached it. Carl opened the front door and leaned in. Beyond the wire mesh separating the front from the back, he could see Mattson sitting on the seat facing the rear. He half turned in the seat to see who had opened the door.

Carl's face hardened as he spoke to the driver. "Take your time getting there, Art. I'm going to ride in the back."

Art nodded without comment, reached up and twisted the rear-view mirror, blotting out the back of the van.

Carl closed the front door, opened the side door and climbed into the van. He moved to a seat directly across from Mattson and sat staring at him as Art pulled away from the curb.

"You know, Mattson. You're putting us to a lot of trouble." He leaned forward and chucked him under the chin.

Mattson jerked his head away. "You're making the trouble," said Mattson. "I haven't done anything and you know it. And Carla sure as hell didn't do anything. Why did you have to bring her into this?"

"Carla? Is that her name?" Carl grinned at him. "I didn't bring her into this, pal. You did."

"You didn't even know her name?" Mattson stared at him, unbelieving.

"I know that little pig has a hell of a body, Laughed Carl, "you should see some of the pictures she posed for after you left."

"You're the pig," said Mattson, knowing that he was being goaded.

"And you've got a smart mouth," said Carl, "but I'm going to fix that."

Mattson stared at him, but said nothing. The van was going over rough streets, and each time he bounced, the handcuffs behind his back dug into his wrists, causing him to wince. He tried to ignore the pain, concentrating his attention on the insane eyes that seemed to be burning into him.

"You want to know what I'm going to do about that smart mouth of yours?" taunted Carl.

"Why the hell are you doing this?" asked Mattson, ignoring the question. "I haven't done anything to you. I don't even know you." His voice was taking on a note of desperation, and he hated himself for it, but the fear was building in spite of himself. "What the hell do you want, anyway?"

Carl took the time to light a cigarette before answering. Taking a long drag he blew the smoke into Mattson's unprotected face. He grinned as Mattson coughed and turned his head away.

"We want those papers, Mattson. We want everything that you have. And," he said, matter of factly, "we're going to get it."

"I don't have any papers," protested Mattson, weakly.

"That's what I like." Carl took another drag. "You stick with that story. We're taking bets on how long it will take to crack you."

"Go to hell," mumbled Mattson, forcing his eyes away.

"I want you to think about something," said Carl, dropping the cigarette butt on the metal floor and stepping on it. "If you don't tell me everything I want to know before this ride is over, you're going to get out of this van with your nose smashed all over your face. You think about that."

In spite of the pain in his wrists Mattson squeezed himself back in the seat. "You won't get away with it," he said, unconvincingly. "I wasn't hurt when I got in here and a lot of people were on that corner watching."

"They won't be around when you get out." said Carl. "I want you to think about it, Mattson. I want you to know what's coming. Think how it will feel to have your nose smashed, and ask yourself if it's worth it?"

Mattson said nothing. His arms strained uselessly against the cold steel of the handcuffs, knowing the feeling of absolute helplessness.

Carl leaned forward, resting his arms on his legs, his huge hands dangling down between them. "Just start talking whenever you want to, Mattson. It will save us both a lot of time and trouble."

Mattson watched him, warily; ready to throw himself to the side if Carl tried to hit him. It would be a futile defense, but with his hands behind his back, it would be the only thing he could do. His only hope was that Carl was bluffing, hoping to scare him into an admission.

Carl suddenly sat up straight, looking past him out the front of the van. "We don't have much time, Mattson. If you've got something to say, you'd better say it."

Mattson kept silent, watching Carl's hands. He pressed himself as far back as possible, prepared to duck.

Carl, watching him, with eyes narrowed to slits, seemed to know what he was thinking, and almost smiled.

"Now, Mattson!"

Carl's voice was like a hiss. As he spoke he raised his left hand slightly and shrugged his left shoulder, tricking Mattson into ducking in the opposite direction. In a blur, Carl's right arm shot out. The butt of his open palm struck Mattson just below the bridge of the nose and twisted.

Mattson's head exploded in a flash of brilliance. For an instant he felt the blow as it crushed and ground the nose bones together, and then a piercing pain burst in his brain and he screamed. He could feel the warm blood gushing down his face, filling his mouth and gagging him with a thick salty taste. His screaming stopped suddenly as he began choking and spitting.

With surprise he found himself no longer sitting on the seat, but rolling on the floor between the seats. The side door of the van was open and two men were standing there looking at him. In total confusion he saw that one of the men was Carl. It took him a minute to realize that he had blacked out. He tried vainly to get to his knees, to raise himself from the floor, but as his memory returned the pain came with it and he could only lay there and moan.

Carl stood outside the van, looking at Mattson and talking to the man called Art. "We should have seat belts in this damned thing," he said. "The poor guy fell right off the seat. Looks like he might have broken his nose."

"Nah, I don't think so," said the other man. "He probably just a bad nose bleed. I'll give him a towel when I get him upstairs."

"Yeah, you're probably right, Art." Carl nodded. "You take care of him and I'll check in with Berghoff." He leaned over, took one last look at Mattson, smiled and walked toward the waiting elevator.

Art Bruckman pulled a pack of cigarettes from his inside shirt pocket, lit one and stood waiting for Mattson to recover. Waiting was a matter of choice rather than necessity. If a stranger were asked, he would have guessed Bruckman to be either a football player or a wrestler. At six feet five and two hundred and sixty pounds he could have carried Mattson to the elevator like a football.

In his early days he might have done just that, but after twenty years of military life, he had learned to conserve his energy. The sooner he was done with Mattson, the sooner they would find something else for him to do. And so he stood puffing on the cigarette, watching Mattson on the floor, moaning. "These dumb bastards," he thought. They were all the same. Ten minutes ago Mattson didn't have a mark on him. Now his nose was smeared all over his face. Six months from now it would still be nothing but a flattened blob, and the poor slob would breathe through his mouth for the rest of his life. They never learned.

Art wasn't exactly sure what it was that they wanted out of Mattson, but he knew that sooner or later, they would get it. He had seen it a hundred times. In the end, they all talked. First the suffered, and then they talked. They talked so much you couldn't shut them up."

Mattson began to stir again. Art took a last drag from his cigarette and flipped it on the cement floor. Bending over he grabbed Mattson by the shoulders and pulled him toward the door. "C'mon, Mattson. Time to go upstairs."

Mattson felt himself being dragged out of the van and stood on his feet. His eyes were beginning to swell and the blood was still coming into his mouth. It seemed to be coming from the inside. He couldn't be sure, but the taste sickened him and he couldn't swallow. It dribbled over his caked lips, down his chin and covered his shirt.

Leaning back against the van, he opened his mouth wide, trying to suck air into his lungs, then hunched over, whimpering, as the pain came again.

"Come on, Mattson." Art took him by the arm and guided him slowly toward the elevator, being careful to avoid touching the blood. "We'll get you taken care of upstairs."

Mattson shuffled along, moaning softly as each short step seemed to jog the pain. He gave no thought to where he was or where he was going. He couldn't even remember exactly what the hell had happened. His brain felt as though every nerve ending in his body was sending it signals. The elevator moved slowly and he was grateful. One sudden move and he knew that he would throw up. When the elevator doors opened, Art took his arm and guided through an area that seemed vaguely familiar, but keeping his eyes open was too great an effort and he closed them. He let himself be guided by the man holding his arm, listening to doors opening and closing until they finally stopped. At last his curiosity got the best of him. He forced his eyes open for a second and found himself facing a steel-barred cell.

"Get in there, Mattson, and lay on the bunk." Art slid off the handcuffs and pulled open the steel door. "I'll get you a wet towel."

Mattson entered the cell and sat down on an inch thick pad covering a steel bunk that was suspended from the wall by two heavy chains. A sudden sweat broke out on his forehead and he knew that he was going to throw up. Looking desperately for a container he saw a toilet bowl at the end of the bunk.

Hanging onto the edge of the bunk he made it to the bowl and knelt over it, gagging. The fresh taste of blood filled his mouth again as it came up from his stomach.

By the time he was finished and sitting back on the bunk, Art was standing at the steel-barred door with a damp towel in his hand. "Take this," he said, "and try to lay down."It will help the bleeding." He gave Mattson the towel, slid the steel door shut, locking it. He started to turn away, then looked back into the cell. "You can suit yourself, Mattson, but if I were you, I'd tell them what they want to know."

Mattson clutched the wet towel. He wanted to answer, but it wasn't worth the effort. The pain had lessened, and now came only in occasional throbs. Moaning softly, he lay down on the bunk, on his side, holding the towel to his tender swollen face.

Art watched him for a moment, then shrugged and turned away.

Chapter Twenty

Carl stepped off the elevator on the fourth floor and walked directly to Berghoff's office. He saw the girl named Carla sitting on a wooden bench on the other side of the room, but he ignored her.

Berghoff was hanging up the phone as Carl knocked and stuck his head in the door.

"Mattson's in lock-up. Art's taking care of him."

"What took you so long?" asked Berghoff. "That girl has been here for fifteen minutes."

"We had a little incident along the way." Carl shrugged, "Mattson fell off the seat and hurt his nose."

"Too bad." Berghoff was not surprised. "Did he have anything to say?"

"Not yet. He's a stubborn bastard, but he'll come around." Carl picked up the wooden chair in front of the desk, flipped it around and sat down with his arms resting on the high wooden back. "Did you talk to the girl, yet?"

"No," Berghoff shook his head. "I've been waiting for you. She's been sitting out there balling. What's her connection?"

"I'm not sure," said Carl. "Maybe no connection at all. As far as I can see she's just a shack-up job for Mattson. I let her think we're booking her for prostitution. I figure if Mattson told her anything about Hedgerow, she'd think it was so far out, he'd have to be nuts. This will be a good chance to discredit him and scare the shit out of her at the same time."

"How's that?" asked Berghoff.

"I don't know," Carl shrugged again. "Make him look like a pimp… let her think if she doesn't help us she'll be charged. Scare her away from him and make sure she keeps her mouth shut about tonight."

Berghoff considered the idea, nodded in agreement and then gestured to the phone. "I was talking to the Colonel when you came in. He's pissed. He's getting heat and he thinks the whole thing is getting out of hand."

"What does he expect us to do?" asked Carl, anger flashing in his eyes. "They blew it in Washington, not here!"

"It doesn't matter who blew it," snapped Berghoff. "The last one to touch the ball gets the blame. We know Mattson has a complete copy of the Hedgerow report. We have to get that, and neutralize him."

"Why not just burn the bastard like we intended? There's nothing more neutralizing than that."

"We have to get the report first." Said Berghoff, brushing the suggestion aside. "Your idea with the girl is good. We'll just have to amplify it."

"I don't follow you?"

Berghoff stood up and walked to the window. He stood silently looking out for a minute, then turned and faced Carl. "Mattson is a threat only so long as he can get people to listen to him. We've got to put him in a position where no one will listen to him."

"How the hell do we do that? He's a reporter. His column comes out twice a week."

Berghoff came back to the desk and sat down. "I want you to visit his boss at the Capitol City News. The guy's name is Harry Bower. I think with a little of the right pressure he might just fire Mattson. Without his job on the paper he'll be limited in the damage he can do. If necessary, we'll put him in a psyche ward. When we get finished, not even his mother will believe him"

"Suppose this Bower is like Mattson. Maybe Mattson already talked to him. How much pressure do I apply?"

"Do whatever you have to do, but I don't want Mattson working there when he gets out of here."

"How long will I have?" asked Carl.

"You'd better get started on it the first thing in the morning. We'll hold Mattson four or five days and see if we can get anything out of him. Tomorrow I'll arrange for some of our building and fire inspectors to go through his apartment building to see what they can find. If they come up empty, and we can't crack him, we'll have to put a torch to the building. I still think it's the only place he could have hidden the papers."

Carl glanced at his watch and stood up. "Do you need me any more tonight?"

"No." Berghoff shook his head. "Go home and get some sleep. I'll take care of the girl. What's her name, again?"

"Carla Jenkens."

Berghoff scratched it on a pad of paper and walked to the door with Carl. "I'll be here all night." He said. "If anything comes up tomorrow you can reach me at home." He opened the door. Carl nodded and walked to the elevator.

Berghoff watched him for a moment, then turned and walked toward the girl sitting on the wooden bench.

Carla, her face filled with a mixture of anticipation and fear, watched Berghoff approach.

"Carla Jenkens?"

"Yes." Carla nodded nervously and stood up.

"Come with me," said Berghoff, curtly, taking her by the arm. He led her to a desk where a prematurely white haired man in his late thirties sat tilted back on a chair reading a newspaper.

As Berghoff approached, the man sat up straight, slipped the newspaper into a drawer and looked up expectantly.

Berghoff motioned Carla to a chair at the side of the desk and spoke to the man. "John, this is Carla Jenkens. She's just been brought in on the Mattson case. I want you to write up her information and put her in back until I get a chance to talk to her."

"Yes sir." John turned on his computer, "Are we booking her?"

"I haven't decided yet." Berghoff looked down at the frightened girl sitting with her hands clinched tightly in her lap and her head hanging down. "I'll let you know later."

"Possible charge?" asked John, ready to type.

"Prostitution." Berghoff spun on his heel and walked away. It was time to look in on Mattson. The girl would keep.

Chapter Twenty-One

Carla Jenkens, fighting back tears, looked at the man behind the computer, afraid that the tears would start again. "I'm not a prostitute," she said, shaking her head.

John typed the word onto the form and shrugged. "Lady, I don't know anything about it. I'm just here to take down your personal history. What's your full and correct name?"

Carla looked down at her hands.

"Name?" he asked again, impatiently.

"Carla Ann Jenkens." She said softly.

"Date of birth?"

"April third, 1976."

"Minnesota?"

"No," Carla shook her head. "I've only been here for a year and four months. I've lived in South Dakota all of my life. In Sisseton."

"Any previous arrests?"

Carla shook her head.

"Any previous arrests?" he repeated, irritably.

"No!" Carla almost screamed it at him. Suddenly she threw her hands to her face and started sobbing again. Her shoulders shook uncontrollably.

John watched her for a moment, sighed disgustedly, and pushed himself back from the desk. Walking across the room to a water cooler, he filled a paper cup and brought it back.

"Here, drink this." He tapped her lightly on the shoulder, waited until she took the water and then sat back at the desk. Picking a pack of cigarettes from his pocket, he lit one, and waited for her to gain control.

Nearly five minutes passed before Carla set the paper cup on the desk, folded her hands in her lap and seemed ready to continue.

"Ready?" asked John,

Carla nodded.

"All right," John snubbed out the cigarette and turned back to the computer. "I only have a few questions, so the sooner we get them over, the sooner you get out of here. Okay?"

"Yes," Carla nodded again as she rubbed a tear from her cheek with the edge of her hand.

The few questions that John had to ask consumed the greater part of the next hour, ranging from her earliest school days to her present employment. He left nothing out, searching in seemingly trivial areas, knowing that Berghoff would make use of the information in a later interrogation. Finally, deciding he had enough, he pushed himself away from the desk and stood up.

"I think that will cover it, Miss Jenkens. Will you come with me, please?"

Carla came to her feet as John took her arm and led her across the room, through a heavy oak door and down a long, brightly lit hallway, with polished floors. At the end of the hall he took out a key, unlocked a heavy steel door and ushered her into a large white room. The room was completely dominated by a huge camera standing on a pedestal in the center of the floor.

"We'll need some fingerprints for identification." said John, leading Carla across the room to a long metal table against the wall.

Numbness had been creeping over Carla, as though she was sleep-walking, and now she could only stand and watch dumbly as John picked an ink filled roller from the table and ran it back and forth over a steel pad. When the pad was thoroughly covered, he set the roller aside and pulled a fingerprint card from a container on the wall. Inserting it into a steel bracket on the table, he took her hand, held four fingers in a straight line and pressed them to the pad. When her fingertips were covered with ink, he transferred the impression to the card by pressing down on her fingers. He did the same thing to her thumb, and then switched to the other hand. Carla watched, unresisting, as he repeated the process a second time.

When he was finished he poured a small amount of liquid soap into the palm of her hand and gave her a paper towel. "It won't get it all off," said John, "but it will get most of it.

Carla said nothing. She was close to tears again, but she fought them back as she tried to remove the stains.

"I want you to stand over here now," said John, leading her to a spot four feet in front of the camera. "Just keep your toes on that yellow line." He left her for a moment and returned to the table. When he came back he carried a thin flat piece of plastic that he fastened around her neck with a thin chain.

Carla looked down and saw that it was covered with numbers, but before she could read them, John pushed a switch activating floodlights that nearly blinded her.

"Hold your head up and face the camera," he said coldly.

Carla looked up, squinting against the bright lights. She heard a sharp click, followed by a low whirring sound that lasted for about five seconds.

"All right," said John, "Turn to your right and keep your left foot on the yellow line."

Carla started to turn, but in her confusion, she turned to the left.

"To your right, damn it," growled John. "Your right! And keep your left foot on the yellow line."

Carla turned around, making sure that her left foot was on the line as she felt her eyes flooding with tears. This time she didn't try to hold them back and they streamed down her face.

"All right," said John. "Face straight ahead."

Carla heard the click again. In a few seconds the bright lights were turned off and John took her by the arm. "That's all for now," he said, leading her to another door. "I'll have to put you back here until they're ready to talk to you, but it shouldn't be too long." He took the chain from her neck and dropped it on the table.

Carla hung back as she saw that the door opened into a room divided by two cells.

John nudged her in the back, forcing her into the cell on the right. Before she could turn, the heavy door clanged shut behind her. A moment later the outer door closed. Carla looked around her, trance-like. Slowly, as realization set in, she dropped to her knees in the middle of the floor, sobbing.

Chapter Twenty-Two

Mattson heard the footsteps coming and looked up. He was expecting to see the big man again, but it was someone else. His eyes were watery, his vision blurred, and with only the dim light in the hallway outside his cell, it took him a few seconds to recognize the man he remembered as Berghoff.

"How you doing in there, Mattson?"

Mattson pulled the towel away from his face. "You've got to be kidding," he said, bitterly.

"Yeah, I know what you mean." Berghoff's voice contained no hint of sympathy. "Carl told me you fell off the seat. It looks like a pretty bad bruise."

"Fell off the seat, my ass," hissed Mattson. "My nose is smashed, and you know it. I want a doctor. And I want a lawyer. I'm not letting you guys get away with this!"

"Now just relax, Mattson. Everything in good time." Berghoff was totally unconcerned. "You just lay down and take it easy for awhile. When Carl files his report I'll have a talk with him, and then we'll see." Berghoff started back the way he had come.

"Hey, wait a minute!" screamed Mattson. "I want a doctor!"

"We'll have someone look at you in a little while," promised Berghoff, over his shoulder.

Mattson crawled off the bunk and came up to the bars. In absolute astonishment, he watched Berghoff walk out of sight. "My god," he said, in a whimper, "what kind of people are they?" He wanted to shout again, but the sudden movement off the bed caused bleeding to start. Putting the towel back to his face he moved back to the bunk. Maybe if he got off his feet the bleeding would stop again.

Chapter Twenty-Three

John Dickman rapped lightly on the door to Berghoff's office, opened the door a crack and looked in. "You got a few minutes?" he asked.

"Sure," Berghoff pushed himself away from the desk and waved him in. "You finished with the girl?"

John nodded as he crossed the room and dropped a thick brown folder on the desk. "Here's a copy of the arrest report, complete with pictures of the apartment and suspects. I haven't talked to Mattson, yet, but this is the girl's history. She's waiting in one of the cells."

"Take your time getting to Mattson," said Berghoff, picking up the folder and flipping it open. "I think he has a headache." His eyes fell on the photograph of Carla standing naked at the side of the bed, while Mattson, half clothed, sat on the side of the bed being restrained by a policeman.

"What did you think of her?" asked Berghoff.

John shrugged. "I'd classify her as a typical small town girl trying to make good in the big city." He gestured to the pictures. "I wouldn't put much stock in those." He said.

"What does she do for a living?" asked Berghoff

"She's been working as a secretary for her uncle. He's an agent for State Farm."

"State Farm?" Berghoff looked flustered. "Someone told me that she worked for the County Attorney in St. Paul?"

John shook his head. "No, she applied for a position there, as a clerk, but she hasn't heard anything yet. As far as I can see, she's a pretty nice kid. A little dumb, maybe, but definitely not the hooker type. She's pretty damned disillusioned at this point."

"Not as disillusioned as Mattson is right now," chuckled Berghoff, setting the pictures aside. "How the hell could we have been so wrong about where she worked?" He made a mental note to chew out whomever it was that supplied the information.

John turned and walked to the door. "You want me to bring her in now?"

"No," Berghoff shook his head. "Not yet. First I want you to check on her employment... I want to know for certain where she works. In the meantime, I'll read this. Give me half an hour. What kind of shape is she in?"

"Pretty rough," said John. "I don't think she stopped crying since she was brought in."

"Good," Berghoff smiled with satisfaction. "There's no point in wasting time on this girl, but I want to scare the hell out of her before I send her home. I want to make sure she doesn't go blabbing about this to some wise ass and end up getting a lawyer or something. And I want to make sure she doesn't have any further contact with Mattson."

"That shouldn't be difficult." said John. "She's so damned scared now that she'll do whatever you tell her."

"Fine," Berghoff picked up the folder. "You wear the white hat today, John. I'll do the dirty work. When we finish I want you to drive her home and see if you can convince her to get her little ass back to South Dakota where she belongs."

John nodded again and left the office, pulling the door shut behind him. Berghoff opened the folder and began reading. He was on the fourth page when the shrill ring of the telephone interrupted him.

"Berghoff, here," he said.

"Berghoff, this is Clifton." The voice was crisp, tinged with irritation. "What the hell is going on down there?"

Berghoff sighed wearily and sank into a chair. "Colonel, I was just about to call you. We have Mattson in custody."

"Have you talked to him yet?"

"No sir. I'm letting him sit and stew a little while. I'm just getting ready to talk to his girlfriend."

"Do you think she knows anything?" Clifton's irritation was increasing. "Do you think it was necessary to bring her into this?"

"Under the circumstances," replied Berghoff, coldly, "we felt that it was necessary. We didn't want to leave her sitting around asking questions about why we arrested Mattson. At the time we were under the impression that she worked in the County Attorney's office as a legal secretary. Apparently, that wasn't accurate, but we didn't want to leave her alone."

"You have something in mind for her, then?"

"Colonel, by the time she leaves here, she won't give a damn about Mattson or what happens to him. She'll want to forget this night as fast as she can."

"Very well," said Clifton. "I'll assume that you have everything under control. I'll talk to you in the morning. If anything develops that you have doubts about, I want to know."

"Yes sir." Berghoff struggled to keep the sarcasm out of his voice.

"Yes," Clifton hesitated, as though trying to think of something more to say. "Well, goodnight, then, Berghoff."

"Good night, sir." Berghoff hung up the phone, glanced at his watch and picked up the report again. He wanted to be done with it by the time John came back with the girl. He intended to direct his interrogation to the photographs. Make her feel guilty, shame her, turn her against Mattson. He read the report for another ten minutes before the knock came on the door.

John stuck his head into the room. "I've got the Jenkens girl out here," he said. "Are you ready for her?"

"Bring her in," said Berghoff.

John pushed the door open wide and ushered Carla across the room. He seated her in front of the desk.

Berghoff kept his head down, pretending to read. He kept her waiting for nearly five minutes, letting her nervousness grow. When he finally looked up, his face was stern, almost angry.

"Your name is Carla Jenkens?"

"Yes," Carla's voice was just above a whisper.

"Well, Carla," Berghoff waved the report in his left hand and slapped it with the back of his right hand. "You've really gotten yourself into something this time, haven't you?"

Carla shook her head in denial. "I haven't done anything," she said, weakly.

"No?" Berghoff looked at her contemptuously, leaned forward to pick up the photographs and dropped them in front of her. "I suppose these are your graduation pictures?" Without taking his eyes off Carla, he spoke to John. "I want you to schedule her for court in the morning."

Carla recognized the pictures taken during the arrest. Her face flushed with embarrassment as she looked away. "They made me do that," she said, hopelessly.

"Who made you?" demanded Berghoff.

"The police," said Carla, close to tears.

"What?" Berghoff snorted. "You're telling me the police made you pose for nude pictures?"

"No!" Carla shook her head in desperation. "They just made me get dressed. They wouldn't leave the room."

"According to the report I have," growled Berghoff, "this is the way the officers found you when the made the arrest."

"I had my robe on," protested Carla.

"Where was Mattson while all this was going on?"

"I don't know," whimpered Carla, "I think he was getting dressed."

"Getting dressed?" Berghoff scoffed, "In other words, the police found both of you naked. Is that right?"

Carla hung her head, not answering.

"Well," demanded Berghoff, "you were in bed with him, weren't you?"

"Yes." Carla nodded without looking up.

"I think we can dispense with the innocent act, Miss Jenkens. This isn't the first time that we've had Ron Mattson and one of his girls in here." Berghoff turned to John. "Did you get a medical report on her?"

Carla looked up, startled, as John stepped forward, shaking his head in apology. "I'm afraid I forgot it during the rush. Do you think it's really necessary in this case?"

Berghoff sighed and scrunched back in his chair. "You know the procedure, John. We run a check for venereal disease on every hooker that comes in here."

"I don't know what you're talking about," screamed Carla, suddenly losing control. "I haven't done anything. I'm not a hooker!"

"We'll let the court decide that," snapped Berghoff, unmoved. "You may as well take her back, John. Give me a call when she's ready to tell the truth. And have the doctor look her over." He picked up the folder and stood up, as though the interview was over.

"I am telling the truth," protested Carla, desperately. She was unable to hold back the tears at the thought of returning to the cell and sat sobbing in the chair. "Please, don't put me back in there."

Berghoff stood impassively watching her. After a moment he glanced at John, winked, and sat back down in his chair. He opened the folder again and flipped rapidly through the pages. "I don't see a fingerprint report in here, either, John. Has it come back yet?"

"No sir." John stepped forward. "I spoke to the authorities in St. Paul, but they don't have any record on her. We're still waiting on a report from Washington."

"I can't imagine anyone this closely connected with Mattson not having a record," said Berghoff. He leaned back in his chair, made steeples of his finger and looked sternly at Carla.

John, taking his cue, rested a paternal hand on Carla's shoulder. "I might be sticking my neck out," he said solemnly, "but I think she's telling the truth. She hasn't really known Mattson that long."

"She's known him long enough to be screwing him!" said Berghoff, angrily slapping the report down on the desk. "Mattson is one of the biggest pimps that we have in St. Paul. He's got a dozen girls like this working the streets between here and Chicago."

"Did you know that, Carla?" John spoke softly to her. "Did Mattson ever try to get you to work for him?"

"No," Carla shook her head. "He told me that he worked for a newspaper."

"He does," admitted John. "But his main source of income is young girls that he forces into prostitution. We've been after him for a long time, Carla."

Carla's eyes were wide, her mouth trembling, as she spoke to John. "I swear that I didn't know anything about this," she cried.

John watched her for a moment, then turned to Berghoff. "I think she's really in the dark about Mattson, sir." He gave Carla a pat on the shoulder. "I think we should give her a break, sir."

"A break!" stormed Berghoff. "Why the hell should we? What the hell is she doing for us? I can let her go tonight and by tomorrow she'll be back in the sack with Mattson. Within a week she'll be working the streets."

"I don't think so," said John. "I think that this time we got to the girl in time. Now that she knows the truth about Mattson, I think she'll stay away from him." He turned to the girl. "How about it, Carla?"

"Oh, I promise!" Carla's face came alive for the first time, as she began to see a glimmer of hope.

"Ah, shit." Berghoff picked up the folder and then threw it back on the desk, disgustedly. "They'll promise anything to get out of here. You know that."

"No," said John, "I think this girl is different." He gave Carla's shoulder a gentle squeeze. "Anyway, if I'm wrong, it doesn't cost us anything. We can always pick her up again."

"That's true," said Berghoff, appearing to soften, "but I still think we should let the court decide."

"If we do that," persisted John, "this poor kid will end up with a record that will follow her for the rest of her life. I know it's a lot to ask," he continued, "but I'd really like to see her get a break."

"All right," growled Berghoff, pretending to give in. "I'm against it, but if you want the responsibility, I'll go along with it." He leaned forward, picked up the photographs, looked at them closely, and then waved them at Carla. "Young lady, I'm going to tell you something and I want you to remember it. I think you're guilty as hell, but for some reason, John believes you. I'm going to go along with him. If I'm wrong and you keep your nose clean, I'll seal up this file and it will never be seen again." He stuffed the photographs in the folder. "But we're going to keep our eyes on you. If we find out that you're back with Mattson we'll have your tail right back in here. Do you understand me?"

"Yes." Carla smiled weakly, in gratitude, and wiped the tears from her eyes. After a moment she raised them and looked gratefully at John.

"Okay," grumbled Berghoff, slipping the folder into his desk. "Get her the hell out of here."

Chapter Twenty-Four

Mattson lost track of time after the short visit from Berghoff. He had fallen asleep for a while, but his throat clogged and he woke up choking. Easing himself to the side of the bunk he rolled off and made his way to the toilet where he stood gagging and spitting out the blood that had drained into his mouth. Finally, with his throat cleared, and able to breathe again, he stumbled back to the bunk and sat down. He sat there for a minute, catching his breath, then slowly eased himself back until he was resting against the wall. His hand brushed something damp. He looked down, expecting to see the blood soaked towel, but this one was clean. Apparently someone had thrown it into the cell while he was sleeping.

His thoughts were jumbled. He tried to remember the things that had happened, but he had difficulty putting them together. Moaning softly, he picked up the cool damp cloth and pressed it gently against his pain filled face. Every touch to his nose, no matter how gentle, made him wince and he wanted to scream with the pain. Clinching his jaw tight, he continued dabbing at his face. Finally, feeling totally exhausted, he let himself slide down the wall until he was laying on the bunk with his head near the toilet. From this position he would be able to see anyone that passed by the cell. Beyond the barred door, a single bare bulb hung on the wall, casting a dim light into the cell. He watched it for a moment, but even the dim light hurt his eyes, making them water, and he closed them. In the distance he was aware of the faint sound of voices.

"Hey, man, wake up!"

Mattson woke with a start, feeling someone tugging on his leg. Pulling the towel from his face, he sat up and stared at the door, forgetting for a moment where he was. His eyes had continued to swell while he slept, but outside the door he was able to make out a slim, gray haired man wearing a dirty T-shirt, holding a broom and looking at him.

"You want something to eat?" asked the man.

"What?" Mattson rubbed gently at his matted eyes, not fully awake.

"I asked if you want some chow?" The man pointed to the floor. "I slid a tray under your door."

Suddenly memories began flooding Mattson's brain. He looked down and saw a small metal tray just inside the cell door. He leaned over to see what was on it, but all he could see was a large metal bowl filled with something that looked like oatmeal. He felt himself getting sick again.

"Better at least drink the coffee," said the man, sympathetically. "You look like you could use it."

The nausea passed slowly as Mattson wiped gently at his blurred watery eyes with the damp towel. "Who are you?" he asked, without really caring.

"Just the swamper," the man shrugged, and started sweeping the floor outside the cell. "I'll be back for the tray. You can keep the cup." He moved away from the cell, intent on his work.

Mattson started to say something more, but thought, to hell with it. The effort required was too great. Easing himself off

291

the bunk, he bent down and picked up a luke warm tin cup of coffee. He felt the blood rushing to his head, making him dizzy. He straightened up, almost dropping the cup. He took a sip, made a face, and then emptied the cup in two gulps. When he finished, he sat back on the bunk and looked around. The cell was small, not more than five by eight feet, surrounded on three sides by solid steel panels riveted together by thick black bolts. The remaining wall was a solid section of steel bars. Except for the steel bunk and toilet, the only other object in the room was a small metal sink hanging on the wall at the end of the bunk. It had a single push button for water, with a small hole in the top for drinking.

"You want a smoke, buddy?"

Mattson looked up, surprised to see the swamper back again. He was leaning against the bars, his arm extended, offering a lighted cigarette.

"Yeah, thanks." Mattson took the cigarette. It wasn't his brand, but he puffed on it, gratefully. Until now he hadn't realized how much he missed them. "What time is it?" he asked.

"About eight-thirty." said the swamper. "I ain't got a watch." He glanced up and down the hall. Satisfied that they were alone, he set the broom against the wall, took half a dozen cigarettes from his pack and passed them through the bars. Reaching into his pocket he pulled out a book of matches. Looking quickly up and down the hall once more, he put his hand through the bars. "Here, take these and hide them," he whispered. "If you get caught, tell them they were in the mattress."

Mattson grabbed them and slid them under the mattress as the man bent to pick up the tray. "Just don't say you got them from me," cautioned the man. "I got to go now." He grabbed the broom and started to walk away.

"Wait a minute!" Mattson came close to the bars. "Will you make a phone call for me?"

"Can't do it." the swamper shook his head. "They'd have me in there with you." He turned and came back to the cell. "Listen, I don't know what they got you for, but these guys ain't that bad. Tell them what they want to hear, is my advice."

"Forget it." said Mattson, suddenly suspicious of the man.

"It's your neck," said the man, walking away.

"Yeah," thought Mattson. "And you're probably one of the bastards trying to stretch it."

He turned back to the bunk, picked up the damp towel and put it on his face. The cigarette had burned to a stub. He tossed it into the toilet bowl and wondered about the man that had given it to him. Was he really a janitor, or was he actually another cop trying to trick him. Mattson realized that he was probably getting paranoid, but from now on, he wasn't going to trust anyone. The swamper returned with a bowl of hash for lunch, and later that afternoon, with a dry cheese sandwich and luke warm coffee for supper. On both occasions Mattson made it a point to pretend sleep and ignored the man.

It wasn't until the second day that Mattson got his first official visitors.

Hearing their footsteps nearing his cell, he sat on the edge of the bunk holding the towel to the lower half of his face, leaving only his eyes exposed. It was Berghoff and Carl Jacobs.

They stopped in front of the cell and Berghoff smiled in at him. "Feeling better, Mattson?"

"What happened to the doctor you promised?" asked Mattson.

"You mean he hasn't seen you yet?" Berghoff looked genuinely surprised.

"You know damned well he hasn't," said Mattson.

"Now wait a minute," protested Berghoff with an injured expression on his face. "You can't blame me if the doctor hasn't been around. He was certainly informed about your case."

Berghoff turned to Carl who was leaning with both elbows on the bars smirking. "I want you to check on this right away, Carl. See what's holding up the doctor."

"Yes sir. I'll check into it right away." Carl grinned at Mattson.

"Why don't you guys cut the bullshit?" said Mattson, angrily. "When I get out of here you're going to be up to your asses in lawsuits, and you know it. I don't know who the hell you think you are, but..."

"Just hold on a minute, Mattson." Berghoff held up a hand. "I came down here to give you one more chance to come clean before I turn this over to the U.S. Attorney. If I have to file charges, you'll be indicted for conspiracy to commit treason."

Berghoff's voice grew hard, losing all trace of friendliness. "If you force me to do that, I personally guarantee that you'll spend the next twenty years making boots in a federal prison."

Mattson was dumbfounded. The towel dropped away from his face and for a moment he could only gape in open-mouthed amazement at Berghoff. "Are you crazy?" he said, finally. "I haven't done anything. Look at me! What the hell have I done to deserve this?"

"Just settle down, Mattson." Berghoff was unimpressed by either his face or his outburst. Completely unruffled, he continued. "We know that you have a copy of the Hedgerow report. We know that it was given to you by Paul Stoddard at the Kelly Inn. We can prove that you knew the papers were highly classified, and that you and Stoddard conspired to make them public." He paused for a moment to let his words sink in.

Mattson opened his mouth to say something, but Berghoff put up his hand. "Just wait. Let me explain something to you." Mattson remained silent, and Berghoff's eyes narrowed as he continued. "In order to convict you of conspiracy we don't have to recover the report. We don't even have to reveal the contents of the report. A few select government officials will determine its sensitivity, and we'll show that you intended to reveal its contents. Do I make myself clear?"

Mattson brought the towel back up to his face without answering. He had never even considered the possibility that they might be able to squash the evidence before it even got into court.

"I'm going to give you time to think about it," said Berghoff, but there's one other point that I think you should consider. You won't be protecting anyone by remaining silent. Earlier this week Paul Stoddard had a heart attack. He's dead." Berghoff dropped the final statement like a bomb, and without even waiting for Mattson's reaction, spun on his heel and walked away.

Carl stood for a moment watching, and then chuckled. "You're on your own, punk." He winked at Mattson as he turned to follow Berghoff.

Mattson let himself sag back on the bunk, listening to their footsteps fade away. Were they telling the truth? Was Stoddard really dead? My god! He thought. If Stoddard is dead, I really am all alone!" He tried to convince himself that they were bluffing, but he remembered the pills, the booze, and Paul's flushed face the first and only time he had seen him.

His mind switched suddenly to the other things that Berghoff had said. Could they actually take him to Court and convict him of something without even showing a jury the evidence? He tried to remember what Paul had said about the Pentagon Papers. He thought about the Watergate scandal. Only the judge had access to those papers and tapes and there were plenty of convictions.

The towel was drying out and he stood up to rinse it off in the sink. As he stood holding the button on the sink and watching the water falling on the towel, he found himself damming Stodddard for dying. Why the hell, now" he thought. Why now? His brain was twisted with indecision

296

and doubt as he carried the damp towel back to the bunk and sat down.

That night he had a stale bologna sandwich and another cup of lukewarm coffee for supper. He forced them down, more as a way to break the monotony than for nourishment.

The hours drifted by and each was worse than the one that had passed. His mind would not stop turning over the things that Berghoff had said. He wondered about Stoddard. He wondered what it would be like to spend twenty years making boots. He knew they were trying to break him. Why the hell else would they bother with all this? Why not just take him to court? Berghoff was convincing, but if they didn't need that report, why were they trying so hard to get it?

He had already counted all of the bars. To pass the time, now, he began counting the rivets. They were spaced at six-inch intervals from floor to ceiling and all the way around the cell. He could have counted a few and multiplied, but he concentrated on doing them one at a time. He counted three hundred and eighty-five before falling asleep.

Carl came to see him the next day at lunchtime. The food tray had just arrived and Mattson was just getting off the bunk to get it when he heard footsteps approaching. He backed off to wait.

As he had before, Carl stood leaning on the door, elbows resting on the bars, peering in with cold lifeless eyes. His face wore a perpetual smirk. "What about it, Mattson?" he was almost gloating. "You got anything to tell me?"

Mattson picked up the towel, pressed it against his face and said nothing.

"Too bad about your pal, Stoddard." Observed Carl.

"Heart attacks happen," said Mattson, pretending indifference.

"Yeah," laughed Carl, "especially with that much shit shot into you."

"What are you talking about?" demanded Mattson, getting off the bunk.

"Forget it, punk. You know what I'm talking about."

"Screw you," said Mattson. "I don't believe he is dead."

"Believe what you like," said Carl. "Someone had to tell us about the Kelly Inn. Who else knew about it? Who knew about the camera?" As he talked, Carl looked down and seemed to notice the food tray for the first time. "Hey, I'm interrupting your lunch. Damn, I didn't think it was that late. Time sure flies, doesn't it?"

He nudged the tray with his foot, peering down. "What is that? Some kind of stew?" Mattson watched silently as Carl dipped the toe of his shoe into the food, looked up, and smiled. "It really looks tasty, doesn't it?"

"That's one way to get your kicks," said Mattson. "Why don't you eat it now?"

Carl laughed, kicking the tray away, losing interest in it. "Say, speaking of kicks. Did I mention that I stopped to see your boss yesterday?"

Mattson felt his pulse quicken, and forced himself to lean nonchalantly against the wall with folded arms.

"So?" he asked.

"So, he's a hell of a nice guy." said Carl. "A real solid citizen. He's really sorry about the mess you got yourself into. He said you came to him with some crazy story and he asked you to drop it, but since you're such a smart ass and won't listen, he's going to fire you."

"You're lying." said Mattson.

"Why should I lie?" laughed Carl. "You can't really expect someone to face a conspiracy charge just to help a punk like you. Besides," Carl's beady eyes gleamed with delight, "Your former boss doesn't want that junky little paper closed down while he goes through a special investigation. He'd rather drop you and forget the whole thing."

"You guys cover everything, don't you?"

"We try to," said Carl. "That's our job. Now why not make it easy on yourself and tell us where that report is? We're going to find out anyway, and you'll save yourself a lot of bruises."

"I've already got my bruises." Said Mattson.

"You dumb bastard." snarled Carl, displaying sudden, unexpected anger. "Don't you know I can come in there right now and beat you to death and no one will say a word?"

"Get screwed," replied Mattson, with more confidence than he felt. "If you had

299

anything to say about it, I'd be dead already." He snatched up the towel, moved over to the sink and pushed the button for the water. Rinsing the towel, he spoke over his shoulder, "You can believe one thing, you snake eyed bastard. If I do have any papers, you'll never get your fucking hands on them." Wringing out the towel, he carried it back to the bunk and sat down. Ignoring Carl, but safely out of reach, he leaned back on the wall, opened up the towel and covered his face. He sat there, barely daring to breathe, expecting at any moment to hear the steel door slide open and see Carl flying in at him. Finally, with a sigh of relief, he heard the footsteps walking away from his cell. He pulled the towel away from his face, took a deep breath and reminded himself that in the future he'd keep his mouth shut.

The food tray still sat on the floor. He looked at it, bitterly, and then gave it a shove with his foot that sent it sliding out of the cell. Pulling up a corner of the mattress he picked up one of the cigarettes, lit it, and flopped back on the bed.

Had they really gotten to Harry? He wondered. Was Carl lying, or had he really scared the old man into firing him? God knows what kind of pressure they might have applied. They were capable of anything. Without the newspaper to back him up, everything that he was doing was worthless. His only hope was that Harry was only pretending to go along with them.

Late that afternoon the swamper slid another cheese sandwich under the door. This time Mattson grabbed it and wolfed it down without even noticing the staleness. His feelings were fluctuating from one extreme to the other. At one moment he felt like screaming out everything, convinced that there was no hope.   And then he would catch himself. Nothing had changed. The things that were true a week ago were still true today. He discovered that anger was his best defense. He knew they were depending on his own mind to break him. It was sensory deprivation. They removed all outside contact, filled his mind with doubt, and let his own mind do the work for them. Somehow, no matter what they did to him, he had to find the strength to hold out.

Early the next morning Mattson heard footsteps approaching his cell again. Thinking it was the swamper he didn't bother to get up. It had been a sleepless, seemingly endless night, with nothing to do but pace the floor and count rivets on the wall. Worry, hunger, and pain were taking their toll, but the most maddening of all was the solitude. Still, as he heard the footsteps drawing near, he pretended sleep rather than talk to the swamper he suspected was a cop.

"Wake up Mattson, I've got some news for you."

Hearing the voice he had come to hate, he opened his eyes, sat up on the side of the bunk and slipped into his shoes. Carl was leaning against the bars, smiling at him. "You have a good life, Mattson. You get to sleep late every morning."

"You said you had some news." Mattson stood up and leaned against the far wall.

"Yeah, but first I want to tell you about that girlfriend of yours. What's her name, Carla?" He paused, waiting for a reaction from Mattson.

"What about her?" asked Mattson, coldly.

"That's some broad, Mattson." Carl rolled his eyes and smacked his lips, as though relishing the memory of an exceptional steak. "She really knows how to show a guy a good time. You should have seen us last night over at her place. Man, is that bitch hot!"

"You son-of-a-bitch," swore Mattson, "If I ever get out of here, I'll kill you!"

Carl laughed, contemptuously. "I'm glad you said that, Mattson. It makes the news I brought so much better. We're not taking you to court, after all. Berghoff decided that if you don't tell us what we want to know today, he's going to turn you over to me tonight."

His cold beady eyes gleamed maliciously. "Tonight, Mattson. After everyone goes home, I'm coming in there and play with your nose some more." He made a mock grab at Mattson face, and although Mattson was far out of reach, he still flinched and jerked back his head.

Carl broke into raucous laughter and walked away.

Chapter Twenty-Five

After his talk with Mattson, Carl Jacobs went directly to Berghoff's office. He was no longer smiling.

"Any luck?" asked Berghoff.

Carl shook his head, not bothering to hide his irritation. "That fink bastard just isn't giving in. I don't know what the hell keeps him going. He's laying back there now, expecting me to come back tonight and smash his nose again, but I'll lay you ten to one that he won't break." Carl crossed the room and sat down in front of the desk.

"Every now and then you run into one like him," Carl continued, with a hint of admiration in his voice. "The tougher you get, the tougher they get. It's when they haven't got one fucking thing in the world going for them that they seem to be toughest of all. You'd be better off just killing the bastard and starting over."

"Take it easy, Carl." Berghoff pushed aside the telephone and leaned forward, resting his elbows on the desk. "Let's not make this worse than it is. Our objective is to recover or destroy that report. If we can avoid the messiness, so much the better."

"This is the fourth day," grumbled Carl, "and we're no closer to knowing where he hid them than we were on the first day. We don't even know for sure what, or how much, we're looking for."

"All right," Berghoff pushed himself back from the desk and stood up. "I think it's time that we had a change in plans." He walked to the window and stood, for a minute, looking out at the sky.

"You've got something in mind?" asked Carl.

"Yes," Berghoff turned. "We've gone through his car, and we've gone through his apartment twice. The only place they could be is somewhere else in the building. Maybe some other apartment… maybe the basement or the attic… I want the fucking place burned down!"

The order did not surprise Carl, but he frowned.

"Something wrong?" asked Berghoff.

"I was just thinking about the building." said Carl. "It's made of heavy brick and stone. It won't go down easy."

"I don't give a fuck if you use napalm," growled Berghoff, "I want it gone by tomorrow!"

"What about Mattson?" asked Carl, standing up.

"His injuries have to be accounted for." said Berghoff. "Give him something in his food tonight, and serve him late. Knock him out. When you finish taking care of the building, I'll have Art and John dump him in an alley behind some bar in his neighborhood. When someone finds him he'll look like a drunk that got rolled."

"Suppose the papers aren't in the building?" asked Carl, skeptically. "How will we know for sure?"

"We won't," said Berghoff, irritably. "But what can he do? He won't have a home… he doesn't have a job, and he'll stink like a skid row bum. Who the hell is going to listen to him?" Berghoff smiled. "We'll keep a tail on him for awhile. If he makes any moves that we don't like, we'll bring him in again."

"I guess we don't have much choice," conceded Carl. "But, I'd like to get rid of the son-of-bitch permanently."

Berghoff nodded in agreement. "So would I, Carl, but sooner or later he'll make a mistake. Don't worry, we'll get him."

Chapter Twenty-Six

When Mattson opened his eyes his first conscious thought was that he was either dreaming, or insane. Thoroughly accustomed to seeing the barred door during his first waking moment, he was totally unprepared for the scene that greeted him. What he was seeing was vaguely familiar, but the shock was too great. Before recognition could set in, he squeezed his eyes shut again.

He was half sitting, half laying on something rough, something like gravel, with his back propped against something solid. Without opening his eyes he put his hand down carefully, feeling around. It was gravel, gravel and dirt. He could almost taste the putrid stench of urine, vomit and alcohol that seemed to surround him. In dumb amazement he opened his eyes, staring at the gravel he brought up in his hand.

What the hell is going on? He looked wildly around with squinted eyes and this time recognition was instant. To his left he could see what he knew was Western Avenue. Almost directly in front of him and a little to the right he could see the back of a bar that he knew as Costello's and beyond the bar, down a small alley, he could see the top section of the old Angus hotel. Mattson flung the gravel to the ground, brought his hands to his temples and squeezed. What the hell is going on? His brain almost screamed the question. The last thing he remembered was sitting in his cell eating supper and drinking that lousy coffee. How did he end up laying in an alley on Selby and Western?

It was early morning. Too early for the bars to be open, but it was growing light and he could hear people and traffic moving on the street. Still in shock, he put one hand on the ground, rolled to his knees and forced himself to stand up. Something fell from his lap, but a flash of pain raced through his head and he let it fall. Still groggy, swaying slightly, he put out his hand and braced himself against the brick wall he had been laying against. He waited, letting the pain subside, and then slowly opened his eyes.

At his feet lay a brown paper bag. It was the only thing in sight that could have fallen from his lap. Still leaning on the wall for support, he bent down to pick it up. Taking his hand from the wall he tore open the bag. Staring at the contents of the bag, everything suddenly became clear. Shaking his head in helpless rage he pulled the half empty wine bottle from the bag, raised it over his head and let it fly across the parking lot. It shattered against the brick wall of a building that had once been known as the 'Harp Bar', scattering glass and wine across the driveway.

They had drugged him and dropped him like a bag of garbage in a dump. The wine bottle had been intended to make him look like a drunk. He wondered how many people had gone by and seen him lying there. It was pure luck, in this neighborhood, that a squad car hadn't come by checking back doors. They would have taken him to the detox center and thrown him back in a cell. Worse yet, a real wino might have come by and kicked him in the head just to get the wine bottle.

Shivering from the cold morning air, Mattson started walking out to the street.

The stench of the alley followed him as though it had soaked into his skin and he realized they had soaked his clothing with the cheap wine. When he reached the sidewalk he turned to the right, heading for Selby. After almost five days in a cell without shaving or bathing he could guess at his appearance, but not even his imagination could prepare him for the hideous loathsome creature that stared back as he stopped in front of a glass store window.

The swollen purple eyes and cheeks surrounding the flattened blackened nose was grotesque and unreal. A short stubble of black beard caked with flaking patches of dried blood covered the rest of his face, and dried blood formed a solid cover down the front of his shirt. He stood staring in horror, unable to pull his narrow slit-puffed eyes away.

How long he stood there he couldn't be sure, but he gradually became aware of a small group of people gathering at the bus stop on the corner, watching him. Tearing his eyes away from the window, he turned and hurried up the street. They continued to watch, but he kept his face averted as he forced himself into a stumbling jog across Selby Avenue, ignoring the red light and honking horns.

He had felt exhausted even before he had started, but he continued running for the next block. He ran until he could run no further. Gasping for breath, he slowed to a walk, wanting desperately to stop, but afraid that someone else might see him before he could reach his apartment. It was only a short distance now, less than four blocks.

Approaching Holly Avenue, he crossed the street to avoid passing the

Commodore Hotel, and cut through the small park with the duck pond on the corner. Summit Avenue was at the end of the park and he could see that traffic was heavy with people on their way to work early, hoping to avoid the freeway rush.

Mattson skirted around the small duck pond that held the statue of the Indian warrior and his dog, surrounded by four wild geese. Bending his head into his chest, he turned left as he came out of the park and barely missed colliding with a couple of early morning joggers. He kept his head down as he crossed Virginia Street, only a block from home.

The bright morning sunshine had burned away the early morning clouds and dampness, promising a beautiful day, but as he came to Farrington Street, his street, there was something strange in the air. A smell that shouldn't be there. As he came to the corner, he raised his head, and stopped dead in his tracks.

"Oh God!" The exclamation came out of his throat like a strangled scream as he looked at the still smoldering ruins that had been his apartment building. The majestic building that had once sat on the corner was gone. The heavy odor of burned wood and scorched rags hung thickly in the air. The huge wrap-around front porch was nothing more than charcoal, surrounded by a cement foundation and the remains of a single staircase, swaying slightly as it reached upward into emptiness. The two upper stories were gone, having collapsed into a heap of waterlogged trash from the pressure of a fire hose.

Mattson came forward, looking at the pile of rubble with stunned unbelieving eyes. His clothes, his furniture, everything he had in the world was in that building, and now it was nothing but ashes. He walked to the side of the building and touched the charred staircase, as though he had to touch it to believe it. The staircase moved slightly. In a sudden surge of blind fury, Mattson screamed and threw his weight against it. "You bastards!" he screamed.

The heavy staircase swayed inward, hung there for a moment, and then began to topple. Mattson watched the silent giant fall, not bothering to even move as clouds of dirt, ashes and burned boards flew through the air. As the dust began to settle, he dropped to his knees, unable to choke back the sobs of frustration.

"My god, Ron, is that you?" Benny Morris came up behind him. He approached hesitantly, not sure that it was really Mattson that he was seeing.

Mattson looked up, tears streaming down his battered face. He spread his hands helplessly, indicating the rubble around him. "Look at it, Benny, look at it!"

"I know, Ron. I saw it on television last night." Benny knelt on the ground next to Mattson and put an arm around his shaking shoulders.

"How the hell could they do something like this?" Mattson shrugged off his friend's arm and struggled to his feet. "Everything I owned was in this house."

Benny came to his feet, but said nothing. He stood, embarrassed, looking down at the ground, nudging a piece of burnt wood with the toe of his shoe.

Mattson turned suddenly and glared at him suspiciously. "How did you know about this?" he demanded. "How did you know I was here?"

Benny took a step back. "Take it easy, Ron. I didn't know you were here. I've been looking for you for the past four days. When I saw the fire on television last night, I came over, but it was too late to save anything. This morning I figured I'd stop by again on my way to work." He extended a hand, gently touching Mattson's face. "What the hell happened to you?"

Mattson brushed the hand away, flinching. "They found out that I met with Stoddard."

"And they did this to you?" Alarm suddenly spread over Benny's face. "Shit, man, you're freezing! Here, take my jacket." He unzipped the striped windbreaker he was wearing and put it over Mattson's shoulders.

"And they did this, too!" Mattson waved his hand at the scene in front of them. He hugged the jacket tightly, realizing for the first time how cold he was.

"Are you sure?" Benny looked doubtful. Whatever had happened, and something obviously had, this strange bearded, alcohol drenched person with the purple swollen eyes and flattened nose, was not the same Ron Mattson he had seen only a few days before.

"I know it!" insisted Mattson. "They killed Stoddard, too."

"They what?" Benny looked at Mattson, incredulously. "My god, Ron, do you know what you're saying?"

311

"I know exactly what I'm saying," snapped Mattson. "They made it look like a heart attack, but they killed him. Damn it, they bragged about it." He waved his arm angrily, indicating the rubble around them, "and I know fucking well they did this, too!"

Benny looked around, trying to absorb what he was hearing. He had assumed the fire was an accident, but after seeing the condition of Mattson, and hearing what he said about Stoddard, his survival instinct kicked into action. "Let's get out of here," he snapped, taking Mattson's arm. "I'll get you to a doctor."

"No doctor," said Mattson, jerking his arm away. "Just take me somewhere that I can clean up."

"You're crazy," protested Benny. "Your face looks like it's been through a meat grinder. You need a doctor."

"They did this to me four days ago," said Mattson. "Let me get cleaned up. I'll see a doctor later."

Benny shrugged and led the way down the sidewalk to his car. He held open the door for Mattson, made sure he was in, and then ran around to his own side. As he pulled away from the curb he was aware of Mattson turning in the seat so he could look out the rear window. Checking his own rear-view mirror, he could see nothing.

Chapter Twenty-Seven

"How you doing in there?" yelled Benny.

"I'm okay." Mattson answered without enthusiasm as he pulled the damp cloth from his face and looked in the mirror. He had been able to soak away most of the dried blood, but his face was still tender. The process was slow and painful. He could only do a little at a time. Dropping the washcloth in the sink, he picked up the clean shirt that Benny had bought and walked into the room where Benny was sitting and staring out a window.

"Thanks for the clothes, Benny. And for the hotel room." Mattson sat on the edge of the bed to put on his socks and shoes. "How much did they soak you?"

"Don't worry about it, Ron." Benny grinned at him. "I'll send you a bill when you get back on your feet."

Mattson said nothing. On the ride from Summit Avenue, Benny had driven to the Target store across from the Har Mar Mall. He had Mattson wait in the car while he ran inside and purchased a pile of clothing and a pair of shoes. He had to guess at the size, but his guess was fairly accurate and to Mattson's surprise, even the shoes he was now wearing were a good fit. After leaving the store Benny had driven directly to the Twins Motor Lodge on Prior Avenue and registered a room in Mattson's name.

"That shower was a lifesaver," said Mattson, standing up and feeling at the stubble on his face, "but I think I'll wait awhile before I shave. I'm still pretty sore."

"I can believe it," said Benny. "They really did a job on you." Benny turned from the window to look at him. "You look a lot better, but I still think you should see a doctor."

"A day or two won't make that much difference," said Mattson. "Anyway, they'll probably have to break the nose again, in order to set it. I'd rather take it easy for awhile, Okay?"

"Okay," said Benny, not wanting to pressure him. "Are you hungry? You want to get some food?"

"Is it true that I lost my job?" asked Mattson, ignoring the question.

Benny looked startled. "How did you know about that?"

"It's true, then?" asked Mattson.

Benny turned back to the window. "Afraid so, Ron." Benny shook his head, perplexed. "I don't know what the hell happened. One day the word just went around that you weren't working for the paper anymore. I went to see Harry, but he wouldn't talk about it."

"He had a visitor." said Mattson.

"You know about that, too?" Benny was beyond surprise. "He didn't have one visitor, Ron, he had two of them. They came to see him in the morning, and by the time they were finished, Harry looked like he had aged ten years. I've never seen a guy so scared."

"Yeah," grunted Mattson. "I know the feeling."

"I should have known it was about you," said Benny. "Right after that, Harry put out the word that you were fired. I didn't know what to think, but when I hadn't heard from you for a couple of days, I gave Carla a call. I thought maybe you were with her."

"What did she say?" asked Mattson.

"At first she wouldn't talk at all. She was just like Harry. Finally she told me that someone was sick in her family and she was going back to South Dakota. She wouldn't talk about you at all."

"At least she's okay," said Mattson.

"Why shouldn't she be?" asked Benny.

Mattson walked to the window and stood looking out at the parking lot. There were a lot of cars and a lot of people coming and going to them, but then he saw that the Knox Lumber Company had a building next door and most of them were shoppers. He didn't see any black vans.

With a sigh, he turned from the window, sat back down on the bed, and began telling Benny about the past four days. Benny sat with his mouth hanging slightly open and listened without interruption.

When Mattson was finished, Benny could only sit and shake his head. "No wonder Carla is going home." He said, finally. "They must have scared the shit out of her."

"I never figured Harry would cave in so fast," said Mattson. "He wouldn't even talk to you?"

Benny shook his head. "Not a word. I don't know what they said to him, but he sure as hell wasn't the same."

Mattson stood up suddenly and walked to the door. "Gimme a minute, Benny." Without waiting for Benny to answer, Mattson walked out the door, pulling it shut after him.

Benny watched out the window as Mattson walked up and down the rows of cars in the hotel parking lot, glancing in the cars, and then crossed over to the Knox parking lot and did the same thing. He walked all the way out to Prior Avenue and looked up and down in both directions before finally turning around and coming back into the room.

"What is it?" asked Benny.

Mattson shrugged. "I know they're out there, somewhere, Benny. They watch every thing."

"You didn't see anyone, did you?"

"No, but they're around somewhere. You can bet on it." Mattson tipped his head in the direction of the store. "Maybe they're in there."

"So, what do we do?" asked Benny

Mattson thought for a minute, holding his head in his hands and leaned forward on a chair with his elbows resting on his knees. Benny waited patiently until he finally looked up.

"You've got to distance yourself from me." said Mattson. "But I need those tapes."

"Fuck it," said Benny, "let's go get them!"

"Right." Mattson, laughed sardonically, "and by tonight we'd both be laying in a hole out in the woods waiting for the worms."

The vision that Mattson had conjured up snapped Benny back to reality. "Well, what then?" he asked, with much less enthusiasm.

"Somehow," said Mattson, "they missed us when we went out to your place. It must have been before they knew about Stoddard. Thanks to you we got everything moved and I got back to my apartment before they made the connection."

"Yeah?" Benny was listening intently.

"If they thought you had a part in this they would have come after you before they burned down the building. They'd have worked you over first."

"God, that's a cheerful thought," Benny grimaced in mock horror. "But it makes sense." He agreed. . "They probably would have had me in the next cell."

"Okay," Mattson nodded. "So we have to keep you out of this. You're the only one, beside me, that has any fucking idea what's going on."

"You know I made backup files, don't you?" said Benny. "I also got rid of my computer. I deleted everything first, but I think they still have ways to bring it back, so I just got rid of it."

"Good idea," said Mattson, nodding in approval. Then, for a moment he just sat there, as though lost in thought, gnawing nervously at his lower lip. Finally, nodding to himself as though he had made a decision, he looked at Benny. "Okay," he said, "here's what we do. You hang on to the copies that you made, along with the other stuff, in case something happens to me. Just give me the briefcase, and the original tapes."

"How do I do that?" asked Benny.

"Drop me a few blocks from my car." said Mattson. "It's still parked up at Carla's. Then go to work." Mattson leaned over and looked at the watch on Benny's wrist. "It's ten o'clock now… give me a couple of hours. Then go get the briefcase. I'm going to pick up my car and get some money out of the bank."

Benny was hanging on every word, but Mattson stopped talking long enough to look out the window again. When he was satisfied, he turned back to Benny. "I'm sure they'll follow my car. I'm going to drive out highway 61 toward Battle Creek. Somewhere along the way I'll pretend that I'm having car trouble. I'll leave the hood of the car up and I'll unlatch the trunk, and then I'll start hitchhiking back to town."

"And you want me to put the briefcase in the trunk?"

"You've got it," smiled Mattson. "They'll follow me. It's a risk, but I don't think they'll bother with the car. They've already gone through that. They'll follow me. And all I'm going to do is hitchhike back to town and find a mechanic to get my car running again. I'll make sure I don't get back to the car before one o'clock."

"Beautiful!" Benny clapped his hands together gleefully.

"That stretch of highway gives you a clear view in both directions," said Mattson.

"If you see anything suspicious, just keep going."

"What are you going to do then?" asked Benny, suddenly growing serious, again.

"I'm going west," Mattson shrugged. "I've got an uncle that lives about forty miles on the other side of Helena, in a place called Avon.   I haven't seen him in a few years. Now might be a good time."

"I've always wanted to go to Montana," said Benny, sadly. And then, "You'll keep in touch, won't you?"

"Somebody will let you know if anything happens to me," promised Mattson. "As proof, that I sent them, they'll bring you a check for the clothes you bought me today. Okay?"

"Okay," Benny smiled and the two men shook hands.

Chapter Twenty-Eight

Mattson had Benny drop him off on the corner of Grand Avenue and Dale Street. He stood and watched until Benny's car disappeared down the long winding hill heading for downtown to make sure that he wasn't being followed, then turned and walked the two long blocks to Carla's apartment building. He glanced up at her window, but he knew she wouldn't be there. If she hadn't already left for South Dakota, she would be working in her uncle's office. There was nothing that he could say to her, anyway.

Climbing into his car, he put the key in the ignition and waited for it to grind to a start. He still hadn't seen anyone following him, but on the spur of the moment, as he was pulling out, he had a thought. St. Albans Street was a one-way street going south. If anyone was following him he wanted to know. Gunning the Toyota he swung into the driveway across the street, backed up and drove the wrong way, heading toward Summit Avenue. As he neared the corner he saw them. They were sitting across Summit, near the corner in a tan Ford. He recognized Carl immediately, and on an impulse he couldn't explain, gave him the finger as he passed them going in the opposite direction. They pretended to ignore him, but as he crossed Dale Street he looked in his rear view mirror and saw them make a U-turn to follow.

Taking a left on Western, he followed it to Selby and took another left. Without thinking, he glanced into the alley behind Costello's bar where he had been laying only a few hours earlier. Angrily, he

gunned the motor and raced up Selby
Avenue.

At Dale Street he slowed the Toyota
to a normal speed, suddenly realizing that
they might mistake his anger and think that
he was trying to get away from them. They
made no attempt to catch up and kept a
block behind him all the way to the Liberty
State Bank on Snelling Avenue.

It took him less than fifteen minutes
to close out his account. When he was
finished he walked outside to his car and
didn't even bother to look for them. On his
way downtown he stopped at a
SuperAmerica station and filled the car with
gas and got a hot cup of coffee. It took him
only a few minutes to thread his way
through downtown traffic and get on the
Warner Road heading for highway 61.

He took his time now, sipping his
coffee as he drove, not wanting to lose them.
He didn't see the Ford, but he knew they
were somewhere behind him and he
chuckled softly to himself as he remembered
giving the finger to Carl.

He passed around the curve near
Mounds Park, onto highway 61, and could
see his destination about two miles ahead.
About a mile from the bridge at Battle Creek
he began hitting the brakes at intervals and
turning the ignition key off and on, causing
a chugging motion with the car. He began
pulling to the side of the road as angry
drivers began spinning past him and giving
him dirty looks. Finally, he cut the engine
and let the car slowly roll to a stop. Glancing
in the mirror, he saw the Ford pull to the
side of the road about a mile behind him.
Smiling to himself he got out of the car and
opened the hood. After a few minutes of

pretending to adjust something in the engine, he went to the back of the car and opened the trunk. He rummaged around for a minute and his hand came out with a screwdriver. Straightening up, he lowered the lid of the trunk, being careful not to lock it, and walked back to the front of the car.

Once again he pretended to do something, and then got in the car as though he were trying to start it. He let it catch one time and then immediately cut the engine again. If they were sharp eyed, they might have seen a puff a smoke. He repeated the process twice more, left the key in the on position to drain the battery, and then got out of the Toyota and angrily slammed the door.

He looked up the road at the Ford still sitting there and he could imagine them sitting there laughing. Barely able to keep a straight face himself, he stumbled across the divided highway and stuck out his thumb. Traffic was light at this time of day but it took less than ten minutes for a car to pull to the side of the road to pick him up. He climbed in, gratefully, and the car got back into the traffic.

The old man behind the wheel wearing a baseball hat and smelling of alcohol tried to start a conversation, and Mattson turned in the seat as though interested, but intently watched the Ford across the highway as it roared past his abandoned Toyota heading for a break in the highway where it could make a U-turn.

As they neared Warner Road Mattson pointed to the side of the road. "Can you let me off here? I forgot something and I have to go back."

322

"Sure," the driver was surprised, but he pulled over and stopped.

"Thanks a lot, buddy. I appreciate it," said Mattson, getting out of the car.

"No problem," said the man, and then, as he was pulling off, he added, "Better get that face looked at, son."

"Mattson nodded, and then turned to see the cars coming from the direction of Battle Creek. They were about half a mile down the road, coming toward him fast. Mattson turned and began walking. It had occurred to him in the car that if they had lost sight of him, they would probably go back to the Toyota and wait. And they would have lost him if he had stayed in that car. Now, at least, they knew where he was and if another car picked him up, he would be easy to follow. 'You bastards aren't as sharp as you think you are,' thought Mattson, as he put his thumb out for a second time.

None of the oncoming cars slowed to pick him up, and it would have been too obvious for the Ford to stop, so it, too, had to pass him. Neither of the men in the car even glanced at Mattson as they sped by. "They must really be pissed," he thought.

Mattson continued walking. He had plenty of time to kill and it didn't matter if he got a ride. When he got to Burns Avenue he took a right, deciding to walk the quiet neighborhood street to White Bear Avenue. It was the closest place he could think of to find a service station with a tow truck, and there would be plenty of restaurants in the area where he could get something to eat. He didn't bother looking for the Ford anymore. He knew they would be somewhere close watching him, so he just tucked his head into his chest and kept walking.

It was ten minutes after one o'clock when he walked into a service station on White Bear and looked for a mechanic. On his way he had stopped at Burger King and ate a Whopper and three cups of hot coffee. He was already tired and he knew he would need the caffeine for his trip.

"Can I help you?"

Mattson turned to find a man in blue coveralls wiping his hands on an oil soaked rag and looking at him, curiously, obviously wondering about his bruised face.

"Yeah," Mattson managed a small smile. "My car died out on 61. I was hoping someone could go out and take a look at it?"

"Where, on 61?" asked the man.

"Just this side of Battle Creek." said Mattson. "I was on my way to Newport when the damned thing just quit running."

"I'll take a look," said the man, "but I'll probably have to bring it in here. Did you check your gas?"

"The gas is fine." said Mattson.

"Okay," the man nodded. "We'll take that truck over there." He gestured to an old blue and white tow truck sitting at the side of the building. "You can ride along and show me where it is." The mechanic stuck his head into the office window and yelled at a man behind the desk. "I'm going out to get one, Charlie. I'll be right back." He turned and motioned for Mattson to get into the truck.

The bone jarring, bumpy ride back to his Toyota took about ten minutes. Neither man spoke. The mechanic pulled in front of Mattson's car and backed up, getting into position to hook it up for a tow. Mattson smiled slightly getting out of the truck as he saw the Ford pulled over to the side of the road about half a mile behind them. He followed the mechanic who was standing at the front of his car looking at the engine.

The mechanic leaned forward and tugged at a couple of cables. "Get in and try to start it," he said. "I want to hear what happens."

Mattson walked around to the driver's side and sat in the seat. The key was still in the on position. He clicked it off and then turned it back on. One small click met their ears. Mattson got out and walked around to the front again.

"Sounds to me like your battery is dead," said the Mechanic. It could be wires, maybe your starter or alternator. I can check it out back at the station."

"You think it might start with a boost?" asked Mattson.

"It could." The mechanic shrugged. "That won't fix the problem though. You want me to try?"

Mattson nodded. "It would be a big help," said Mattson. "I really have to get down to Newport."

Without speaking the mechanic turned and walked back to his truck. It took him a couple of minutes to start his generator and adjust it. He came back with a cable in each hand. He hooked one cable to each terminal on the battery and then walked back to his truck and revved up the generator. After a couple of minutes he signaled for Mattson to try and start it.

Mattson got back in the car and turned the key. The starter spun over for about ten seconds and the motor suddenly came to life. Before Mattson got out of the car the mechanic had disconnected the cables and had them back in his truck. "You got lucky," said the man, "but you better get that looked at the first chance you get. I think you got a wiring problem."

Mattson nodded, taking out his wallet. "What do I owe you?"

"Twenty-five for bringing the truck out here, ten for the boost."

Mattson pulled out a fifty-dollar bill and offered it to the man, who began searching his own wallet for change.

"Keep it," said Mattson. "I really appreciate your help." Everything so far had gone completely according to plan, and he was anxious to get going before something screwed up. He watched the mechanic get in the truck and drive off, and then walked to the back of the car as though checking the rear end. As he bent down, he pulled up hard on the trunk, but it was secure, and he knew that when he opened it, he would find the briefcase.

He almost laughed as he looked down the road at the Ford still sitting there, waiting.

Sit there, you bastards," he said, half aloud, as he got back into the Toyota and started driving. He was beating them. They didn't know it yet, but he did, and that was enough. He knew he would have to go into hiding, but that would be a small price to pay. He also knew that, somehow, sooner or later, he would find a way to get the Hedgerow report to the public.

He could see them following as he came to Newport and swung the car up the ramp to get onto 494, heading north. It was part of the beltline circling the twin cities and he knew it would take him to I-94, toward St. Cloud. From there he could pick up US highway 75 and have a straight shot across to North Dakota. By this time tomorrow he would be sitting at his uncle's ranch on the other side of Helena. Pulling a pair of sunglasses from the visor to protect his eyes, he lit a cigarette, and settled back for a long ride.

Chapter Twenty-Nine

Carl Jacobs sat glumly in the passenger seat of the Ford. He had been sitting in this seat for hours, and anger darkened his entire face. Art Bruckman was driving, weaving in an out of the traffic, trying to keep the little Toyota in view at half a mile distance.

"How the hell long are we going to keep this up?" he asked Carl.

"Just keep driving," growled Carl,

The sky was darkening in the west as storm clouds began moving in. Soon it would be raining, and the traffic was growing heavier by the minute.

"I'm going to have to close the gap," said Art, stepping down on the gas." He felt his own anger rising. Carl outranked him, but in all of their years working together it had never been an issue. Today for some damned reason he had suddenly gone military on him and he was getting pissed off. He had noticed the snappiness in Carl's tone immediately after Berghoff had called him this morning. Since that time they had been back and forth on the phone constantly, and he had no idea what they were talking about. But he knew that each time they talked Carl's mood became blacker, and he was getting sick of it. Art's anger suddenly transferred from his brain to his foot as he pushed down on the accelerator. The Ford leaped ahead and within seconds they were only a few car lengths behind Mattson in the Toyota.

Interstate 694 began curving to the left, merging back into 494, but Mattson continued straight ahead, following Interstate 94. "Shit," exclaimed Art, "He's heading for St.Cloud!" He swung the car into the right lane, almost hitting another car as he forced himself into the traffic that was also going in that direction.

Carl grabbed the phone that was hanging on the dash and angrily pushed two buttons. Almost immediately Berghoff's voice came on the line. "Yes? What is it?"

"This is Carl, again. Have you gotten any more details?" His voice was anxious.

"Nothing definite," said Berghoff, his voice strangely subdued. "Apparently someone fucked up. I'm waiting to hear from Clifton, but he can't even get any information." He was silent for a minute, and then asked, "where are you now?"

"Were on 94. This asshole is heading toward St. Cloud. How the fuck long are we going to screw with him? He hasn't made a move all day and now he's just daring us to do something!"

"You're sure he had no opportunity to pick up anything?" asked Berghoff

"Nothing." said Carl "The only person he saw was that other reporter, that Benny Morris. After Morris bought him some clothes they went to the motel and Mattson cleaned up. Morris dropped him near his car, and he spent the rest of the time trying to keep that piece of junk running."

"He didn't go near the newspaper?"

"Nah," Carl shook his head. "He knows we've been behind him all day. He hasn't made a move. He's just fucking with us,"

"Okay," decided Berghoff, "break off for now. He probably thinks he can still get his job back. Morris got him the room for a week, so he'll probably go back there tonight. It's the only place he has. We'll get back on him in the morning. He's too damned scared to go near anything right now. Besides, if this is as bad as it looks, I'm going to need you back here. Okay?"

"Okay," agreed Carl. "And maybe tomorrow you can put someone else on him. Someone he doesn't know? Just make sure I'm around when we grab him again."

"Don't worry, Carl." Berghoff promised, "I'll see to it."

Carl nodded, satisfied. He hung up the phone as he spoke to the man driving. "Berghoff says to break it off, Art. That asshole ain't going nowhere."

Art let his foot ease off the gas. He still had time to make the turn onto 494 and he curved the car in that direction. As they turned away, Carl's eyes narrowed and followed the path taken by the little Toyota. He said nothing, but he sat nodding his head as though he had just decided what he was going to do to Mattson the next time they met.

Mattson, looking in his rear-view mirror, saw them break away and breathed a sign of relief. He was surprised that they had turned off. He had spent the past fifteen minutes trying to think of some way to lose them, but he knew that his little Toyota was no match for the car that they were driving. The exhilaration he had felt earlier was gone and he was left with only a dull, barely perceptible, throbbing between his eyes. He would have to see a doctor pretty soon. He wondered if his nose was becoming infected. He put the thought out of his head and tried to enjoy the fact that they were no longer following him. He pulled forward on the steering wheel stretching his back and immediately felt the tension leaving his body. "Hell," he thought, happily, "he could drive all night and by this time tomorrow he would be in Montana." Leaning forward he flicked on the radio, and then sat stunned, as he heard the announcer's voice.

"...bridges and tunnels leading into New York City are closed and all airports in the New York area have been shut down. We have just received word that all domestic flights have been grounded by the U.S. Federal Aviation Department." The radio went silent for a moment and then the announcer continued. "For those listeners just tuning in, let me tell you what we know at this time. At 8:46 this morning, American flight 11 from Boston crashed into the North Tower of the World Trade Center. Flight 11 carried 81 passengers, two pilots and nine flight attendants. The Boeing 767 was hijacked and diverted to New York." The announcer's voice was cracking with emotion. "At 9:03 a.m. United Flight 175, also from Boston, crashed into the South Tower of The World Trade Center. This Boeing 767 was hijacked after takeoff and diverted to New York. A third plane has hit the Pentagon and the White House has been evacuated. ...."

"Shit!" Mattson was gripping the wheel so tightly his knuckles turned white. This was the reason they had turned off. "But, what the hell was happening?"

His mind flashed back to the night in the hotel room. His struggled to remember what it was that Paul had said, and then, suddenly, he remembered.

"It's going to take something big," he had said. "Some colossal tragedy to jumpstart this thing."

Mattson felt a sudden chill as his mind went to the briefcase in the trunk of the car. "My God!" he said to himself. "Is this it?" His foot unconsciously pressed down on the gas

THE END.....

www.ingramcontent.com/pod-product-compliance
Lightning Source LLC
Chambersburg PA
CBHW061325170626
46817CB00001B/319